The Sleep Clinic

Albert Wauquier

Costa Press

Copyright © Albert Wauquier 2013

Albert Wauquier has asserted his right under the Copyright, Designs and Patents Act 1988 to be identified as the author of this work.

Publisher CostaPress

ISBN 978-1482559040
SBN 1482559048

For Katherine Homan

"One of the villagers´ favorite entertainments was trapping birds, painting their feathers, then releasing them to rejoin their flock. As these brightly colored creatures sought the safety of their fellows, the other birds, seeing them as threatening aliens, attacked and tore at the outcasts until they killed them."

Jerzy Kosinski
(The painted Bird, Afterword xiii, 1976)

Any man, who under all conditions insists on making it his business to be good, will surely be destroyed among so many who are not good.

Michael Ennis
(The Malice of Fortune, 2012)

As an aged poet once said, "I do not remember all the details, but what I remember, I do remember perfectly."

Selden Edwards
(The Little Book, Intro by Flora Zimmerman Burden , 2008)

Preface

Sometimes flashes of the past come to the surface of our consciousness like falling stars, sprinkling their sparkling dust upon the sky. As in dreams, our neuronal circuitry in the brain makes connections of memories of people, events and places, as random as the dust explodes into the ethers. These images, whether standstills or moving at varying speeds, elicit elation and sadness and seldom are peaceful scenes of heavenly pastures.

My brain is no different and some of my memories became a story, "The Sleep Clinic." While fictional, this story is based upon images and events from my past and therefore contains autobiographical elements. It is a story in which the physical characteristics of the main characters are altered, but their personalities kept close to what they actually were. Some of the characters are created, existing only in my imagination and added to flavor the story. The story takes place in a hospital and a sleep disorder center, but no St. Elisabeth Hospital and sleep center exists in Plano, Texas.

Although the timeline of my life as described in the story is not accurate, Annie's and my love story is quite real and she is the amazingly fearless and faithful wife of this story. True also is that I am a doctor, board certified in Sleep Medicine. Only part of my training and work as stated in the story is correct; I have been a Professor at several universities including the University of Leiden in the Netherlands, the Medical College of Ohio and Texas Tech University Health Science Center's Department of Neurology.

A sleep disorder education is interwoven throughout the story, with several cases coming from actual patients. For the curious of mind and to not take away from the story, there is a glossary at the end of sleep terminology.

While fiction, this story could start with "Once upon a time," but the fact is the emperor always had his clothes on.

1

Winter in Ohio was on display and the icicles on the gutters would continue to grow for months to come. The sky was as blue as during a bright summer day, but the sun was not melting the ice on the pavement in front of Dr. Robert Vermeer's apartment. The cold cut like a knife, but he walked with his jacket unbuttoned holding a set of folders under his arm. A man of average height, with a well-trained build, clearly someone who spent time in the gym, wore nothing on his head and his auburn hair curled into the back of his neck.

In his younger years Robert's blue eyes had attracted many a girl. They probably fell for his see- through eyes, whose promised dreams they got lost in. But back then, he was too busy as a student, assembling the building blocks of a career. And even now in his late twenties, any relationships were fading into a kind of holding pattern.

Today's cold was clearing his brain of the dust from the library and his tiny student apartment. Just what he needed to celebrate his promotion to Associate Professor in the Department of Psychology at Bowling Green State University. This was the culmination of his work since coming to the US as a post-doctoral student from Belgium. Now he felt rewarded for all his efforts and genuinely in possession of his title as Professor Dr. Robert Vermeer.

During his studies Robert became fascinated with the mysteries of sleep, especially the transition from being fully awake into no-man's land. The mechanisms behind falling asleep were a subject of much speculation. Perhaps, Robert mused, a young researcher working in a small university would one day find the mechanisms behind falling asleep, worth a Nobel Prize.

Robert kept up his keen interest in sleep disorders by practicing in a sleep disorders clinic run by the neurology department at the Medical College of Ohio, a short 25 mile drive from Bowling Green. It was the ideal counterweight to his lectures on the theoretical aspects of the enigmas of sleep and leading discussions examining hypotheses that were stuck in a virtual rut. He also needed the practice to qualify for taking the exams to become a certified clinician in sleep medicine.

While walking this morning to his lecture on the theories surrounding the significance of dreams, Robert thought about his introduction. Although some people doubt they ever dream, the fact is that every night, we dream, but we often do not remember that we did. It's a classical literary subject, as Shakespeare's Hamlet, pondering about committing suicide, says, "To sleep, perchance to dream. Aye, there's the rub." Even in death, Hamlet might be pursued by dreams not bringing peace.

The class Robert intended to give was part of an inventive and challenging course called 'Think Psychology'. But today's was not a time for heavy thoughts. He wanted to entertain the students by discussing art and dreams, asking what is behind the picture, letting reality dissolve into fantasy. It would end in the almost philosophical question whether dreams were real. Yes, today would be fun.

* * *

As Spring Break approached, Robert's life had been rippling merrily along the banks of academic career building. Soon he would recharge his batteries with a vacation to Belgium, visiting family, left behind in their own world, and friends, lost but not forgotten.

He was enjoying the rediscovery of his native country, expecting his time there to pass easily by, without much excitement. This leisurely tempo was cut short the evening he went to a large art gallery party, organized by a painter friend who, along with some friends, created a movement of painters called 'The Wild Ones.' Their topics were wild, their colors were wild, and so were their brush strokes.

Robert dawdled through the gallery, gazing upon painting after painting depicting distorted scenes from everyday life in vivid colors, 'wildly' put on canvas. He also looked around at the colorful spectators as well, some looking as wildly attired as the paintings on the wall. Of course, there were the fancy-dressed ones, who followed the latest fashions, the partygoers and the 'did-you-see-me?' people. Altogether, this motley crowd was like a slowly moving tableau vivant. Robert strolled among them, amused, holding a flute of champagne.

Then, standing before a painting of a wrecked car, the headlights still shining on a wet shimmering street, was a girl Robert thought looked familiar. He studied her figure, the way she tossed her long dark hair and then slowly pulled it back to the side, revealing a cute little pink ear. When she moved to stand next to his painter friend, Robert knew for sure that she was definitely the one. He approached them, and standing slightly behind her, asked in a soft voice, "May I offer you a glass of champagne?"

She turned around, still smiling because of a comment from the painter, and opened her lips to speak. But her mouth remained agape and her inquisitive eyes open wide. Then, closing her mouth she smiled, her lips curling with delight. The years had not changed her. He broke the silence saying, "Hello, Anna, long time, no see." She blushed and whispered "Robert, what are you doing here? I thought you were in the US." His heart skipped a few beats and in a flash, he remembered how ten years earlier they had promised never to leave each other.

They had been close in high school, although he went to an all boys' catholic school and she to an all girls' catholic school. Despite not seeing each other that often during the school year, they vowed to wait for the other as they diverted into separate higher education programs. Robert went on to the university while Anna's stern father sent her to France for further education. He wanted her far away from home, for fear she would become engaged to Robert. At least that is the way Robert interpreted it. Consequently, their lives went into different directions. Anna obtained a degree in communication science and went to work for an agency dealing with producing advertising and information material for businesses.

He looked at her, admiring how she had grown into a smart looking young woman, much more beautiful than he had remembered her when she was just eighteen. Her wide open eyes were a deep blue, with a tiny spot of yellow in the corner of her left eye. She had full lips that played with a smile and made her eyes sparkle.

"Yes, Robert, a glass of champagne," she said looking at Robert who stood staring, having already forgotten that he had offered her a drink.

The painter was just another friend of hers, nothing serious. As Robert's body warmed and his face blushed hot, they strolled around the gallery, her skirt dancing about her legs turning more heads. Once the music started, his painter friend urged people to free up the middle of the room. "Ladies' invitation," he announced, and with that, Anna took Robert by the hand. For that moment, the world stood still and they were at their last dance. Now, ten long years later, they were cheek to cheek again, Robert's right arm around her narrow waist. Their feet promenaded to the passionate tones of the Argentinean tango 'La Cumparcita' and their bodies met, withdrew and came together with the rhythm of the bandoneón. They danced every dance, until he tucked his nose into her hair and murmured "Lost and finally found, Anna. Don't leave me again."

"I never did,' she protested, "My father sent me away."

Robert kissed her and she responded with passion. Later, as he joined her in a ride to her apartment, Robert knew he would no longer be the butterfly touching the petals and moving on to the next. Anna was the one, the only one, and the beginning of their lifelong friendship was sealed that very night.

When Robert traveled back to Bowling Green, Anna was with him. Her pain of leaving everything behind in Belgium became eased by the discoveries of a new land that would be theirs to enjoy exploring together.

They became an inseparable couple and a year later, surrounded by friends and family, they married. Soon a daughter was born. She had her Mother's eyes and her Father's lively disposition. Anna decided to stay at home for a while to take care of their child. Life was good and easy, maybe too easy for Robert.

Through friends at the University, Robert learned about a position in the Department of Neurology at Texas Tech University in Lubbock, Texas. All he knew about Lubbock was that Rock and Roll singer Buddy Holly was born there and his was the only statue in the whole town. Not only were renown sleep researchers working at Texas Tech, but they also planned to establish a sleep disorders center for which they sought a sleep clinician with research experience. Robert applied for the slot.

Over several months, Robert and Anna discussed the merits of this position. Ultimately, Robert convinced Anna that this was a golden opportunity, playing down the fact that Lubbock, Texas was a city where everything centered on cotton and cattle and nothing around art and culture. Besides, Robert said enthusiastically, it was only an hour flight to bustling Dallas, and leaving behind friends and family could only strengthen their personal relationship. Conversely, Anna was encouraged by Robert's endless energy for this promising venture, which came with a few built-in safety nets, among which was that he would get tenure and as such, his job was safe.

*　*　*

Robert and Anna sat in an American Eagle twin-engine plane en route to their new destination. They flew over a desolate landscape, nearly void of trees and water yet completely blanketed by cotton fields. Lubbock appeared to be a perfectly square grid with one long street diagonally connecting the upper left corner with the right bottom corner and a Loop that seemed to keep Lubbock confined to within the Loop's borders.

It was a sunny day, but bitterly cold winds blasted down the streets. Each time the car crossed an intersection, the car rocked and their heads hit the top of the car. Besides the stiff Lubbock winds, they later learned about the flat Lubbock streets and how they would flood when it rained. Everywhere, pickup trucks bobbled their way through town and no one dared walk the rushing waters of the street.

Anna sighed and looked around with a face that wondered, 'Is this to be our promised land?'

From the airport they drove to the north and entered the Tech campus, which covered an enormous expanse. This would become Robert's academic home for many years.

Pessimistic, however, about a future living inside Lubbock, Anna found a realtor who showed them a perfect house in the Lubbock outskirts.

Life settled again, new friends were made and Robert was happy and productive, until, that is, that day when, after years of routine, work became stale, the cotton boring and the cowboy dances annoying.

Then out of the blue, a company in Kansas dazzled Robert with enticements of a booming business, high society life style, private planes to secret meetings and destinations all over the US, and streams of money that would flow in to fund their retirement. Above all, his skills as a sleep clinician would flourish beyond imagination. While Robert's fervor was raised to a level of no return, Anna harbored her reservations but along with the realization that her husband was in need of a new space and a new challenge. She also speculated how his courage in joining this company and leaving the university where he was a Professor reflected the main characteristics of his astrological sign, Aquarius. Surprise decisions were nothing new, but up until then, such decisions mostly concerned matters without major consequences to their lives.

The company's plan was to set up sleep disorders centers throughout the US in collaboration with participating physicians. Physicians were contacted, visited and submitted an overall proposal. Robert's role would be as a liaison between the physicians and the newly established sleep centers. It all sounded pretty good in theory, but the key was getting a physician to sign a contract, which was no less than a rip off. Moreover, the CEO was a control freak who didn't want to hear that the contracts they proposed to the physicians were just not working. During the course of his first year, Robert's optimism waned and he feared for the worst.

2

The week began with news that their nets had caught a big fish. A doctor in the suburbs of Chicago had signed a deal for a six-bed sleep center. By Wednesday, however, the contract had come back unsigned, with a yellow Post-it note saying, "Screw somebody else". The office walls shook as the Somnus company president exploded, spewing forth every four-letter word he knew and slamming his fist so hard into a file cabinet drawer that the next day he came in with a swollen hand heavily swathed.

On Friday, following intense discussions with a doctor about opening a sleep center in Seattle, Robert heavyheartedly returned the phone to its cradle. No deal there, either. According to the good doctor by virtue of his calculations, the Somnus contract was deceptive as his take would be substantially lower than the amount quoted him by Somnus' chief financial officer.

Drained and depleted, Robert leaned back against his leather chair and contemplated giving Anna a call. Just hearing her voice would chase away the cumbrous web slowly engulfing him. He nevertheless took comfort that it was Friday. Anna would be preparing a favorite dish, often Italian, accompanied by a powerful red wine that he would choose from his small not-quite-a-wine-cellar collection in a corner of his basement.

Robert was startled out of this reverie when his phone rang. He lifted the receiver and heard the company president bidding Robert to "Come to my office."

A young chap, tanned from spending time on the golf course, the president's ever-present toothy white smile was conspicuously absent. Dressed in a designer polo shirt on top of black slacks and looking sporty as always, he waved his injured hand toward a chair in front of his desk for Robert to take a seat. The door opened again and, without uttering a word, George, the CFO, came in and sat next to Robert. The president opened by saying that during the past year Robert had been delinquent in his duties. Robert countered that any delinquency was due to Sales' inability to close on potential contracts. George remained mute, staring at the back of the president's computer screen. Robert felt sweat pouring out of his pores, the room becoming too small and words sounding muted.

The president responded, his cold eyes riveted upon Robert: "I'll make it short, Doctor. We have to save. Cost reduction is what we need to do. Your services are no longer required. Your check will be mailed to you for the last week."

Robert thought he had misunderstood. "The last check?"

"Maybe we can hire you back as a consultant."

"You tell me you will not pay me anymore and then you say that maybe you can hire me back as a consultant? I am not believing my ears."

The president rose from his chair, indicating that the conversation was over. "Leave your keys and the company credit card with George."

Robert staggered back toward his office, George trailing behind. As Robert reached his office doorway, he spotted a cardboard carton sitting on his desk. His exit was already in progress.

Speaking in regretful tones, George said, "Please take any and all personal stuff with you, Doctor. And now, if I may have your key and your card. I'm so sorry, really."

Robert looked at George, feeling both sad and cheated, but thinking that this had to be happening to someone else.

Fifteen minutes later, Robert departed his office with the box in both hands. He placed it on the hood of his Mitsubishi in the parking lot of the business that had just discharged him. One thing he no longer wanted to do was call Anna. Instead, he scrolled through his list of cell phone numbers and stopped at Frank, his lawyer. He pressed the number and within seconds heard Frank's deep voice.

"I need to talk to you immediately," Robert said.

"Well, Robert, aren't you lucky. I just happen to be in between clients. Come on by and tell me your hot news." The phone clicked.

"Right," Robert thought. "Soon you'll know how lucky I am." And for the first time he began thinking about how relative luck is. The luck of one person can be disaster for another. In this case, the lucky one was the lawyer who, by picking up the phone, had switched on the clock that, like a piano metronome, would tick away Robert's dollars.

Robert drove to Downtown in a "Why me, God?" daze. After entering the parking garage beneath the high-rise building, he took the elevator to the top floor with its magnificent view, deep plush carpeting, soft muted sounds, and a platinum-blonde receptionist proudly displaying her plastic surgeon's handiwork. Not in the mood for her fake smile and friendliness, Robert cut to the chase. "I'm here for Frank."

"I know Dr. Vermeer, please take a seat. Coffee with cream, isn't it?"

"Why not," he managed to say.

Frank marched into the reception area, his arms open and a wide smile on his face. He greeted Robert as if they were best friends.

"Hi Robert, great to see you. What's going on?" Not waiting for an answer, Frank walked toward his office – a place Robert thought was like entering a private kingdom. Its palatial floor-to-ceiling windows graced a view of the city.

Luxurious Oriental rugs covered the floors and the room furnishings included polished leather chairs, a marble coffee table and a cream-colored couch with silk cushions. A stack of binders perched on the corner of his desk and a few manila folders lay in the middle.

Robert took a seat, blurting out how he had been summarily notified that, as of today, his services were no longer required, he was no longer on salary and his presence was no longer welcome on the premises. "I don't understand, Frank. I just don't understand."

From the moment they sat down, Frank activated the clock on his desk, a practice he observed with every client. Time is money and every minute counted.

"You were fired," Frank said matter-of-factly. "You are out of a job," he repeated, "It's that simple."

"But why?"

"Why is irrelevant now. The bottom line is that your employer can do what he wants."

Frank explained something that Robert had never heard about before. Kansas was an 'employment at will' state where employers could fire an employee unconditionally. It never occurred to him that he would be a victim of the law in the literal sense. Being from Belgium, Robert began the painful realization that job security in the US was not a 'given,' that social benefits hardly existed, and that he might have to empty his savings in order to save his life. And Frank could only help by emptying those savings even further.

"Go home and start looking for a job, Robert," Frank said. "This decision is irreversible."

Then he leaned forward, switched off the clock and said in tones laced with pity, "I cannot charge you for this consultation."

* * *

Robert dreaded driving home to tell Anna his dream had ended before ever getting started. He walked zombie-like into the house, stammered "I'm out of a job, Anna," and collapsed into her arms. She had feared this happening, aware of all the ongoing tensions within the business. So many times Robert came home fatigued, disappointed and despondent because the president controlled everything, would not allow any initiative and then complained that everyone stuck to the sidelines, doing nothing.

To add insult to Robert's injury, the president's lack of planning or consistency, while nevertheless maintaining that one had to stay open for change, had somehow now become Robert's fault. To make matters worse, Robert could not stop wracking himself over how he had given up his tenured university position for an adventure that could end so abruptly.

When he left behind that comfortable university life in exchange for the potential of becoming wealthy, his friends saw it as a sign of an early mid-life crisis. It was like leaving his wife for the excitement of a younger one, the unknown, and a world of new possibilities. He tried to convince his friends this was not a mid-life crisis, but they nevertheless believed he had temporarily lost his mind.

In effect, Robert was like the protagonist in Andrew Davidson's novel 'The Gargoyle' - a porn actor who not only suffered severe burns from being locked inside his crashed car, but also lost his primary working tool, his penis. Shriveled into a bundle of pain, he needed his entire concentration just to push a ball up the groove of a wooden plank. Yet, this was the beginning of his recovery, without hope of ever returning to being the person he once was. Robert identified closely with the Gargoyle, burned, crushed and without hope of ever recovering.

3

The day after being at home as an officially unemployed person, Robert made an office out of one of the upstairs bedrooms. To keep despair at bay, he decided to work eight-hour days, with a short pause for lunch. His job now was to find a job.

The centerpiece of his desk was his laptop. Robert opened his personal folder and clicked on 'Biography'. He scanned through the files 'Curriculum Vitae' and 'Brief Resume'. He read these again and then added a line about his most recent job, hating how he only had just a little over one year's duration to show for it.

Then he did a computer search on addresses, looking for the directories of sleep centers and adding those to his email list. He generated a short cover letter and emailed it with his resume. Having to search – no beg - for a job was such an obscenity. He had never been out of work before.

After e-mailing a few hundred letters and receiving at the most an acknowledgment of 'received,' Robert turned melancholic and ceased any further such attempts at finding new employment.

Over the next week, he scoured magazines and journals, looking for job offers. Finding nothing remotely close to his specialty area, he began entertaining the possibility he might have to find something else to do.

Nevertheless, Robert went about visiting every single sleep center in town. Colleagues who greeted him warmly as soon as he entered the door turned cool once he mentioned he was searching for a job. Typically, they told him he had missed an opportunity that had just become filled, but invariably, his formerly friendly associates were now beating hasty retreats and turning him one cold shoulder after another.

If the centers in the surrounding areas did not want him, he reflected, perhaps he should create his own. But setting up a sleep center was cost prohibitive and would take too much time to build referral sources. Thinking about interacting with business people, however, prompted Robert to consider focusing his attention on those very members of the sleepless society.

He registered for a convention of people working in the communications field. More than 200 participants strolled throughout the conference hall of the Sheraton Hotel. They visited small company booths exhibiting their various forms of communication services, while awaiting the keynote lecture of some famous motivational speaker unknown to Robert.

He stopped by booths where crowds of people clustered. He introduced himself as a sleep expert. That usually elicited the attention of those looking for a quick gratis fix to their own sleep issues. Robert avoided those questions by describing how fascinating sleep is. Before they ran off, he cautioned them that, if they suspected they had a problem, they should consult with a sleep specialist. He freely distributed his business cards, which, of course, got buried among all the others gathered at the meeting.

At one of the booths, a self-assured looking woman asked Robert about his profession. He told her that he was consulting for companies interested in helping their executives improve the quantity and quality of their sleep in order to increase their work efficiency.

"Tough sale," she said in a matter of fact tone.

He shrugged his shoulders, but at the same time, it hit him. For years, he had seen executives walking into the Sleep

Clinic to seek help for sleep problems. In actuality, many of these people came to see a doctor because they could barely keep their eyes open during the day. Their problem was one of staying awake.

Executives did not want to hear about sleeping more. They wanted to sleep less, so their workday could be longer. He needed a different approach from the one he took when dealing with patients. Instead, he had to convince business executives to maximize their time asleep and at all cost avoid sleep deprivation. Yet, ultimately, Robert knew that there was no getting around the fundamental fact that in order to feel good and function at prime efficiency, one would still need eight hours of sleep each night.

After the communications convention, he started work on a concept he called "Sleep Fitness" and prepared a series of lectures. He assembled colorful folders containing all the power point presentations he planned to give. For the cover, Robert selected the Vincent Van Gogh painting of a farm couple taking a nap against a haystack, under the burning afternoon sun, a colorful display of tranquility and peace during siesta time. The text explained how a short fifteen-minute nap could rejuvenate a person and charge their life batteries back up to full power.

There was just one small problem, which Robert, playing the ostrich, opted to ignore. He lacked a marketing plan putting him on the field from which to make his sales pitch to company executives. Actually, there was the larger and more critical problem that Robert was no Dr. Phil, whose size alone made an impact on an audience and who via his launching site on the Oprah Show was able to pilot himself straight to success. While Dr. Phil could no doubt make an unannounced sales visit, come across as a successful person, ready and able to convince a company that they needed him, cold calling and making a quick sale simply was nowhere in Robert 's repertoire.

In any case, he worked tirelessly on his concept, developing presentations and making a list of potential companies to contact. All along, though, he agonized over going on the road and soliciting business for his project, which truth-be-told had an unproven track record, much less future.

Not surprisingly, Robert, who was neither a sales person nor a marketing man, failed miserably. After all, clinical work was his specialty, not selling himself nor helping business people fight off sleep so they have more time to make more of the almighty dollar.

* * *

As time went by, so did Robert's financial resources. He had to sell one of his retirement savings plans to cover his daily expenses. Escaping to his upstairs home office did not improve his mood, but rather made him wonder what he was doing there, wasting himself on employment efforts that were getting him nowhere. He quarreled with Anna. At times, he became obnoxious, only to come back to his senses and feel ashamed. More and more he sat in the living room, staring at nothing, and then, when cabin fever set in, make aimless trips into town.

One day Robert sat alone in a Corner Bakery restaurant. He felt consumed with self-loathing over spending his precious time and money just sitting there. Depression crawled inside his head, like a snake piercing and penetrating him with her venom of despair. He looked around at the people enjoying their food, laughing and in lively conversations with one another. He lowered his head, pushed his food aside and sat with his head between his hands, until he resolved to quit denying reality and begin owning up to it.

He drove home feeling like a pupil coming with a bad report card. Although Anna had steadfastly supported him throughout this ordeal, he felt guilty for having made such a bad decision in the first place. But how could he have known the crazy control freak boss he would become saddled with?

Even though Anna could rightly blame him for his poor judgment in leaving his tenured university position, she wouldn't. She knew well how much he wanted and worked to solve the problems that he had in a way created.

Driving home used to be a pleasure. He would listen to the public radio program 'All things considered', ethnic music, excellent interviews and background information of the news of the day, as time and distance disappeared beneath the wheels of his car delivering him to his modern styled home. He would enter it from the garage via a small hallway to the kitchen where Anna deftly wielded a chef's knife cutting vegetables and preparing the evening dinner. After kissing and chitchatting, Robert would relax on the dark brown leather couch and take pleasure admiring the contemporary art they had accumulated over the years. He savored being home among these surroundings. Sometimes he focused on a watercolor displaying a town, by the Russian born Andrei Rabodzeenko living in Chicago. Other times he studied the 'Russian Poets' by the Belgian painter and poet Jan Van Riet or, another favorite, the Belgian-born world renown painter, Pierre Alechinsky, all of which had created a striking contrast to what had been his dull university environment. Normally, this was his time for an evening of reading a book, perusing through magazines and watching the news. Today's scenario would be a far cry.

    When he found Anna in the kitchen, he asked her to sit down and talk with him. "I'll make some tea first," she said, knowing that tea would help lift away the stress she saw lying so heavily upon his face.

    She chose mint leaves, fresh and 'wet like fine earth newly swept by rain' as she'd learned from Luwuh, a Chinese poet from the eight century. She boiled source water and added the leaves when air bubbles surfaced. During the third boil, before taking the kettle from the gas stove, she added a drip of cold water, as Luwuh would say, to revive the youth of water.

Anna served the tea in cups she inherited from an old aunt. The cups aged with the aunt and aged even further, sitting in a curio cabinet of theirs displaying different object d'art. There was a watch, a powder box, a Roman oil lamp and a vase, all inherited from some family member, all worth memories of no value to others.

For Robert and Anna, drinking tea always broke any tension that disturbed their togetherness. This time, though, the tension held fast.

Robert had trouble even finding the words, but Anna allowed the silence to wait for them. Downcast and demoralized, he ventured forth saying, "It's so ridiculous. I am a psychologist. I should know what to do, but I don't." He shook his head and grinned, "You've said before that I cannot be a good psychologist for myself and you are right. Here I am, at my wits' end, unable to stop feeling so hopeless and helpless and headed for a mental break down."

Anna took him in her arms, sensing that what he needed was someone to understand his frustration. He had worked feverishly hard but in spite of his unrelenting efforts, nothing was working out. Yet, Anna had faith that they would come out of this. Until then, they would just stare together into the abyss.

* * *

Two more weeks went by with nothing happening. Robert's despair and disappointment returned. He resumed sitting in the living room but this time entertained the possibility of writing a book on sleep problems for the public at large. Years ago, he had published a short book, which had been well received by the medical community. A book club had even listed his book. He knew that becoming wealthy from writing a book was reserved for an elite few, the Olympic champions of literature. Nevertheless, a book could help him get involved with a speaking tour and there was no telling what other opportunities that could lead to. Yet, for that, Robert would need to find an agent. Did he really want another chapter of his career life influenced and controlled by an outside power?

By the third week, Robert sat, leafing through a few professional magazines, when he came across several advertisements in the journal 'Sleep' announcing job opportunities. Immediately he sent them each a short resume along with his extensive curriculum vitae.

Receiving a favorable response from three of them, Robert was beyond elated. Surely, the tide was finally turning in his favor. Of particular interest was a position in Plano, north of Dallas, Texas. It seemed to be a very large sleep center affiliated with St. Elisabeth Hospital. Robert called and spoke with Dr. James Stone, the director of the Sleep Disorders Center, who suggested scheduling an overnight stay. During the day Robert could observe the facility, in the evening he could meet the entire medical group and the next morning speak with the administrator of the medical group about contractual matters.

* * *

A few weeks later, finally feeling upbeat about himself, Robert was on his way to Dallas Forth Worth Airport. Details from the advertisement were few about the sleep center, other than it was a sizeable one. Googling it did not provide any more information beyond the name and address of the Sleep Disorders Center at the St. Elisabeth Hospital. The Membership Directory of the American Academy of Sleep Medicine offered the same information.

When he placed a second phone call to the sleep center's Medical Director, Dr. James Stone, he got a woman on the line who represented herself as a sleep technician and someone who knew Dr. Stone's demands exactly. She said her name was Lisa and that none of the candidates who had applied for the job fit the profile. All were physicians with too high demands. Rejecting them all, the group adjusted the job profile such that 'Board certified in Sleep Medicine' doctors and non-physicians were now viable candidates for the position.

From what Lisa was saying, Robert began believing his chances were good. They became even better when she said they had not yet received one single application for this position and pressure was rising to get it filled. Robert had to fight not to get his hopes up too high.

4

Robert sat crammed into the middle seat of American Airlines flight 1119 on its way to DFW Airport. The cranberry juice jiggled in his cup, as did the wild imaginings inside his head. Although euphoric at this opportunity to interview for a position as a sleep clinician in a large sleep disorders center, Robert also had sobering flash backs of his recent months of grinding idleness and unemployment.

Confident and self-assured was the attitude Robert told himself he needed to project. This was his chance to get back into clinical work as a sleep specialist, using his skills to care for and treat patients, just like before at all the clinics and universities where he had made his international mark. This was the dream job he absolutely had to make come true. Everything depended on the coming interview with Dr. Stone.

The plane landed in sunshiny Dallas, basking in a mild breeze from the south. Robert regarded this as a sign of welcome to the city where everything was possible. He took a taxi to the South Fork Hotel, an old-fashioned establishment reminiscent of the South Fork Ranch on the 'Dallas' TV series. Many people in his Belgium homeland were fans of that show, but Robert had little use for the soaps and the love-hate struggles of their sterile characters.

On its way from the airport, the cab took I-635 Lyndon B. Johnson Freeway, for the locals 'the 'LBJ' as the cabdriver explained. They exited at I-75 and went north for a short stretch, before turning on the access road leading up to the hotel.

After checking in, Robert headed to his room to freshen up and change clothes. He looked into the mirror and thought, not bad. He was a man of average height, with a well-trained build, clearly someone who spent time in the gym. His face was clean-shaven and tanned from being outside all those long months of not working inside his old office at Somnus.

Heeding Anna's advice, Robert had his hair trimmed, short business style, the 'Ascot cut', the hairdresser had said. Similarly, he had changed his casual attire for a dark blue suit, which had been hanging for years in his closet, and for which Anna had bought him a white shirt and bright blue tie. The face in the mirror reflected a man on a mission.

Fifteen minutes later, he emerged ready to charm and impress his potential employers. The first one to meet was Dr. Liborio Salvo, a young doctor who conducted clinical consults at the sleep center. After lunch with Dr. Salvo, Robert was to visit the center and meet the director, Dr. James Stone.

It was close to noontime. Robert was downstairs in the hotel reception area looking for Dr. Salvo among the few people there. When the main door swung open, a man of medium height, dark eyes, oval face, sharp chin and black shiny hair combed backward, entered and started scanning the room. He was dressed in a white shirt with yellow tie, light brown sports jacket, black trousers and shoes. Italian slick, that had to be him, thought Robert, as he walked toward him.

"Dr. Liborio Salvo?" he asked.

"Robert Vermeer?"

"Yes," Robert said, a bit taken aback, but without flinching that he had not likewise been addressed as Doctor. Robert was going to mention that his name came from the Middle Ages when persons living near a lake were named 'van der meer', later shortened to Vermeer, a name made famous by the Dutch painter of light. But Robert restrained himself from making such small talk to the grave looking Dr. Salvo.

"Follow me to my car. We'll go straight to the restaurant. I hope you like Italian food?" he said talking over his shoulder.

"Sure. Italian is one of my favorites," Robert replied to the back of Salvo's head. Robert made a mental note that Salvo not only had an Italian flair, but also a need to be in charge, topped off with a touch of arrogance. Robert envisioned a mirror image of the infamous Berlusconi.

Exiting the hotel they walked to a shiny black coupe parked by the side of the front door.

"An Audi," Robert noted as he let himself into the passenger seat.

"One of the latest, a 2000 TT" Salvo replied, throwing the car into gear. As he hit the gas pedal, Robert was slammed back up against his seat and pinned there while Salvo drove South on I-75 to W. Northwest Highway and the entrance into the vast parking lot of North Park Mall. Ahead, at one of the mall entrances, was 'Maggiano's Little Italy' restaurant.

The décor reflected a traditional upscale restaurant with cherry wood paneling, sturdy tables and comfortable chairs. White china on burgundy tablecloths and crystal glasses adorned the tables. Large black and white photographs of cities in Italy and movie stars of the Fifties finished out the room. Waiters in white shirts, bow ties and black aprons bustled between the tables and sounds of Frank Sinatra singing 'That's life' filled the room along with the aromas of pasta, garlic and parmesan cheese.

The restaurant was packed and people waiting to be seated hovered about the entrance. Not so with Salvo. Headwaiter Ernesto guided them to an outside covered terrace and their reserved table at the far end, facing the entrance with an all-encompassing view of the terrace. Robert smiled to himself, picturing Salvo in the role of a capo in position to look out for spraying bullets.

Still smiling to himself, Robert inquired, "You are Italian, Dr. Salvo? Your name certainly is."

"My grandfather was. I was not raised Italian."

Before any plates arrived and dispensing with any small talk, Salvo commenced firing off questions. "How did you find out about the position?"

Salvo probably knew, but Robert nevertheless explained that he had seen their ad in the journal 'Sleep' and had even briefly spoken with Dr. Stone, the contact person mentioned in the ad.

"The Medical Director of the Center. Yes?" Robert asked, seeking confirmation.

Salvo nodded. Robert did not mention the second conversation he had with Lisa.

"As you will see, Robert, we have one of the largest centers in the nation. We are swamped with work. It goes without saying that we expect a lot from the person we hire. To begin with, that person will be responsible for the sleep study interpretations as well as for consultations with, let's call them, 'difficult patients', people with insomnia, nightmares, depression-related sleep problems and what have you. We don't want to waste time on them because the internal medicine clinic in the hospital is where the doctors are needed to work, far more than over at the sleep center."

Major mental note: This hospital's internal medicine doctors only want to treat straight forward sleep apnea patients, not any so-called 'difficult patients' requiring extra time and consideration. Time is money and these doctors are not wasting any of it on patients.

Salvo then proceeded to explain that Robert was the last of many applicants the group had already evaluated and, if this visit went well, he would be the last one they would consider. Again, Robert did not mention his second conversation with Lisa and inquired instead about 'the group'.

"Imcare, Inc. is a physicians' group, organized as a partnership in a similar way as lawyers' groups. Most of us are internal medicine doctors, which explains the 'Im' of

Imcare. Over 20 physicians are in the group and almost all of them are partners. Dr. Stone and I also practice in the sleep center, while Dr. Gary Cohen is the group's businessperson. For nearly 20 years, St. Elisabeth's hospital administration has appreciated and respected him as a physician and decision-maker. He is the one who keeps an eye on all clinical activities, both inside the Hospital and over at the Sleep Disorders Center."

Wondering what Salvo's dark and darting eyes were seeing as they scanned and inspected Robert, Robert made another mental note. Make a positive impression on Dr. Cohen.

After lunch, they got back into Salvo's Audi and took the Dallas Tollway north to the Plano Parkway exit. A few minutes later, they were on the grounds of the St. Elisabeth Hospital campus. Via a small side street, they passed the massive brown brick institutional-style hospital building. If the intention was to be impressive with its size, it instantly succeeded.

A bit further down on the left side and away from the street stood an inconspicuous two-story brick building, with a large paved side parking lot. Robert admired the manicured lawns in front of both buildings and the trimmed green bushes, bordering the pathways to the buildings. This wide stretch of land had formerly been cotton fields, probably accounting for the absence of any trees.

Salvo parked at one of the 'Doctors Only' sign. As Robert emerged from the car, he stretched and studied the building with a slightly slanted wooden shingle roof that housed the Sleep Disorders Center. This was the place where Robert hoped his next dream job would come true.

No one was posted at the entrance hall counter next to the staircase leading to the upper floor. Ahead were double doors, above which hung a large 'Sleep Disorders Center' sign. Another sign to the side of the double doors asked that visitors enter quietly as people might be sleeping.

"Empty for now," Salvo said, waving at the staircase and the upper floor.

Robert followed him through a short and wide hallway leading to the reception area, where three African American women sat behind the reception counter. A middle-aged Caucasian woman sat at a small desk facing the wall in a tiny side room. From one of the back rooms came a man dressed in blue scrubs. He turned and shook hands with the heavyset woman waddling behind him with the gait of a duck, lurching her weight from one foot to another, all the while panting heavily. A three-hundred-pound mass of health issues, Robert thought.

"I'll see you back here a few weeks from now. Julie will schedule your next appointment," he said.

An African American woman with a round, happy face and dark wide sparkling eyes, Julie, arranged for the patient's next appointment. While doing so, she stole a glance at the potential newcomer to their ranks.

When the man dressed in blue scrubs turned towards Salvo, Robert was introduced, "This is Dr. James Stone, the medical director," Salvo said and then excused himself saying, "I have to leave now to go over to the hospital. I'll return at five o'clock to pick you up and take you back to the hotel."

After watching Salvo disappearing through the double doors, Robert faced the man, who might become a colleague. Under his scrubs Stone wore a disheveled white T-shirt and on his feet sneakers, presumably to not make any noise walking. Peering over glasses perched on the tip of his nose, Stone surveyed Robert as if evaluating a new patient. Then, without a word, Stone turned away and walked over to the side counter where he signed off on a chart and dropped it on Julie's desk.

Between Lisa's assertion that Robert was the only viable candidate and both doctor's 'Iceman Cometh' demeanors, Robert couldn't help wondering just who and what to believe about his chances at the Sleep Disorders Clinic of Plano.

5

That very same Monday morning Dr. James Stone had left the intensive care unit in a black mood from having been on call over the weekend. During that time he had ample opportunity to dwell on the impending visit of a sleep center candidate, forced upon him by his fellow internists. Still dressed in his green scrubs, he walked briskly from St. Elisabeth Hospital to the Sleep Disorders Center across the street. The scrubs felt sticky, but he couldn't care. This was his uniform, not the suit, white shirt and tie that all the Imcare doctors wore.

Chiseled like a rock, Stone's facial features were sharp, the lines on his creased forehead prominently revealing his disappointment with the world around him. His graying dark hair and black eyes made him look fierce. The stride of his slender frame resembled that of a stalker.

During the week, none of the patients required urgent attention,but Saturday or Sunday night they always got worse. His beeper had gone off five times on both nights because the new nurse could neither understand nor follow his instructions. Instead of her doing her job, he had to keeping running over to the hospital to do it for her. His car didn't even have time in between calls to cool off. He probably should have just slept at the hospital, but then that would have required him to work even harder.

"Forget about sleep when you're on call, especially with a new nurse around," he said to the head nurse, up herself for 36 hours and falling asleep as he spoke to her.

The patients in the intensive care unit were the ones warranting full attention. Most were on respirators needing lung suction, requiring open wound care, adjustment of life support medication and continuous oversight attention. All but the believers in the will of the Almighty were subject to the laws of natural consequences, the end result of nature and nurture.

The blinking and beeping monitors for an older man suffering from advanced lung cancer showed major swings in blood pressure, heart irregularities and out-of-line blood gas counts. The one line electroencephalogram of the frontal cortex showed erratic waves and pauses, as if his brain had started to disconnect.

It could not have been worse. During the middle of the night, the monitors went into full alert. The newly hired nurse dissolved into panic mode as too many things went off at the same time, something James absolutely detested. Pushing her aside, he checked the monitors and issued commands, but no intervention on the lung cancer patient would work. Stone made the decision not to resuscitate and to let the patient go. He had made this decision many times before, but he still disliked doing it.

So, in the early morning hours, Dr. Stone had to bring this sorrowful news to the family members, causing him to stay even longer at the hospital. Only the wife came. He put on his mourning face to tell her, but she, having expected this to happen for a long time, retained a sad resignation as well as a kind of relief that the misery was finally over. Dr. Stone took her hand into both of his, looked gravely into her eyes and assured her that hospital administration would gently prepare her husband for "the next step of his way into heaven. We were blessed to grant 'The Spirit of Care' emblazoned on our hospital's banner."

Hours before, nurse assistants, in a hurry, had shoved her husband's body into the morgue down in the hospital basement. Another body waited nearby on a bench against the sidewall. The nurse assistants would come back to put that body in the fridge, but for now, it was one body too many and would only hurt the hospital's statistics.

James arrived late for the seven a.m. doctors' meeting. One of his colleagues was discussing the impact of allergens on lung disease and the methodology for treating. For this boring speaker, James set his brain on automatic pilot and stared at the podium with eyes at half-mast.

James awakened to the sound of shifting chairs and people leaving. He slipped back over to the intensive care unit and made a quick routine check before a colleague took over for the day shift. Now the coast was clear for him to retreat to the sleep center.

As the Medical Director of the Sleep Disorders Center, James had escaped the hospital, making a virtual sport of being at both places while being at neither. When they needed him in the hospital, he waited before returning the call, telling his colleague that he had been in consultation with a patient in the sleep center. When he was in the hospital, he was not available for the sleep center, due to patient demands in the internal medicine unit or at the doctor's office building where consults were conducted. Sometimes he played God and completely left the hospital campus grounds. As with the catholic school answer to the "Where is God?" question, "God is everywhere, in heaven, on earth and in all places," James could be anywhere and nowhere.

For James, the goal was to satisfy his don't-bug-me credo. Although his colleagues were on to his game, they still shook their heads in dismay when they needed him and he wasn't there. At meetings, they regularly told him he was unreliable and needing to change his lousy laissez-faire attitude, which was exacting a terrible toll on each of them. For a short while after such complaints, James would shape up, but only to once again resume the hide and seek game playing. As long as he could stay at the sleep center, James could be his own boss and spend his least stressful hours of the day.

* * *

At 9:15 a.m. Stone's arrival at the Sleep Disorders Center was met in the Reception Area by an in-unison greeting from the four women staff. He grumbled, "For me it's already been morning for too many hours." After stroking through his graying black hair, he brought out his Nasonex and sprayed heavily into each nostril, completely ignoring the once-a-day one spray in each nostril dictum that he gave to his patients.

"I've been on call," he said, nodding and then slouching away, sniffing. The women knew to avoid speaking to him any further and freed him to go and hide out in his office.

He sank into his leather reclining chair and called his wife. "Hi Hon, sorry I woke you last night. It was one of those horrid nights again when I couldn't come home. I'm at the Center now and I'll be here for the rest of the day."

She also knew he was in no mood to hear about their youngest grandchild, who was with her for the day, too sick with the flu to be in school and the cracked water pipe that had flooded the kitchen. Good morning, Vietnam! All this could wait for the evening when he returned from the hospital and would be in a better mood.

They chatted briefly, after which he told her that, unless something came up at the hospital, he would be home by five for a short while. Dr. Robert Vermeer, a candidate the group was considering hiring for a position in the sleep center, was arriving, but James assured his wife that "I've no intention of hanging around for someone who could be coming to take over my program inside the Center that I built. I'll go ahead and attend the dinner tonight, but only to get a closer look-see at him."

He dozed and mulled about the patient they had lost the previous night and the new guy coming to interview. From what he had seen in the resume, the guy's ambition seemed bigger than their plans for the entire Sleep Disorder Center. Also, considering how working was not James' forte but apparently was the new guy's, what future could they possibly have together?

Before meeting Vermeer, James overheard the group ecstatic about Vermeer, who on paper looked to be their best candidate ever. This did not sit well with James who prided himself not only in founding the sleep center five years ago, but also on building an additional source of income for the group. 'Business was going well,' he thought. 'Why was he being_expected to share his domain with some unknown doctor? Was this some kind of takeover attempt?

:"Whatever," James concluded, "I'm not putting any cushion under this guy to make him feel welcome."

He opened his desk drawer, sifted through the mess and pulled out his bottle of Maalox.

6

It was already four o'clock in the afternoon when Stone took Robert to tour back of the Sleep Center. Behind the double doors there was a large rectangular space with multiple rooms off to the side. The light colored walls were eye pleasing, much in contrast to the outside view of the building. In the middle of the space was a circular set of cabinets containing screens and computers, in the center of which sat the technicians, a group of young women dressed in street clothes.

All stole glances at Robert while pretending to be absorbed in their work. One of them smiled at him. Robert guessed that she was Lisa, the one he had spoken with when he had called the center for the second time. He nodded slightly in her direction. Dr. Stone pointed at a large open cabinet against a wall on the other side of the tech area. It was stacked high with patient charts and binders.

"This is what awaits for the person who joins our group, sleep recordings to be analyzed and for which we need a diagnosis and suggested treatment," he said, looking inquisitively at Robert. "You've studied patients at a university clinic, haven't you?" posing a fact rather than a question. Robert answered affirmatively and waited for the next comment.

"We've met with a lot of candidates and are in the process of evaluating them. I've forgotten how many, but you're the last one of the series."

Remembering Lisa's message, Robert thought, how this one lies too.

While walking around the technicians' area, Dr. Stone said, "Tonight you will meet some members of our group. We'll discuss the operation of our center and what we expect from the person selected to join us." He paused as if he expected a question.

Robert said "A lot, for sure."

Stone turned around. "My office is back in this section too, because I want to be close to the sleep technicians. I don't want to run all the way up to the front to get a chart. Dr. Salvo likes to be in the front, which is fine with me since there's no space back here anyhow."

Robert was awe-struck by the wide-open spaces and multiple rooms. Stone explained that the rooms were all clinical study bedrooms, ten in total, each with their own bathroom and shower. He walked into the circular technician area and motioned for Robert to follow. "All our sleep recordings are computerized and stored on CD's. We also videotape every patient during the time of preparation with the different electrodes for monitoring and of course during the sleep recording. I assume you are familiar with these techniques?"

Robert nodded; how could he not know? Again he noted that the display of the recording of brain waves (electroencephalography or EEG) was far more distinct on a computerized system, each line representing a particular region of the brain. The view could be altered, enlarged, reduced, widened, narrowed, something that helped pattern recognition but was impossible to do with a traditional paper recording. Robert remembered having to handled the heaps of paper stacked in a large room, each stack representing 1440 folded pages each 20 or 30 second of recording, all that all for a single night's sleep recording.

His neurologist mentor in the Netherlands had taught him to see the meaning and clinical significance behind those scribbles. He learned that looking at brain waves, eye movements and the tension of the chin muscles allowed one to distinguish different stages of wakefulness and sleep. Recognizing abnormalities in the wave patterns became an art form and helped to detect epileptic activity, deterioration of mental activity and neurological brain disorders. It had all required years of training and many pages to turn. Nowadays the results were the same and the information to know the same, but the computer made reading easier and the storage of recordings a space saver.

Identifying each page of 20 or 30 seconds long awake, light sleep, deep sleep or REM sleep became a task for the techs supervised by the sleep specialist. They also noted the events that occurred during sleep, such as diminished breathing or total arrest of chest movements, heart rhythm events or periodic movement of the legs and so forth.

Stone took Robert back to the reception area. They passed the patient waiting room where the door stood open. An obese person was snoring with his mouth wide open, saliva dripping from his chin. The others patients stared ahead with the typically complacent expressions of persons waiting their turn to see the doctor. Robert did not like the musty, stuffy, sweaty smell of the waiting area, although he had to concede that rarely did he encounter smelly persons. Americans are known for their excessive hygienic care, taking more showers than any other population. The few exceptions were often the very obese people, who could not take care of bathing themselves. The smell in their rooms sometimes even made Robert queasy, so he felt for the techs having to be so close to such patients while putting electrodes on their body.

Stone continued his tour.

"The majority of the patients at the center have sleep apnea and need a sleep study to prove our assumption and assess the level of severity. The rest of the patients are a mixture of people with insomnia, leg movements during sleep, nightmares etc. We don't like to send patients away to other centers," he said, "but sometimes we have to, because we don't have time for lengthy consultations. For us, that's a waste. The newcomer will have to deal with those types of patients."

Stone suddenly asked, "Do you have experience with insomnia patients?".

Robert was startled, for he had already become habituated to just listening to Stone's monologue.

"Yes I do. I know about behavioral treatment for insomnia patients and indeed it needs to be a lengthy process in order to be successful," Robert replied remembering Salvo literally making exact the same comment.

"Good," Stone said and took a chart from the counter.

"I understand that Dr. Salvo does consultations for the sleep center. I presume that he is also boarded in sleep medicine?"

"Not yet, he is preparing to take the first part of the exams shortly."

"Hmm," Robert said furrowing his brow.

Then Stone said, "I have to continue with my patients. See you this evening." and vanished behind the counter into a consultation room.

Robert was left alone. He nodded at the reception people and got a big smile from Julie. He decided to walk back to the front of the building and stroll around outside. What he had seen up to now pleased him immensely. It really was the largest sleep center he had ever visited and far and away the best furnished and equipped. However, his encounter with Salvo and Stone were remarkably lacking in cordiality. Was this purely coincidence, was it premeditated, or was something so fundamentally amiss that Robert's visit was exacerbating it?

7

Salvo drove Robert back to the hotel, where he had an hour to rest and refresh before the dinner meeting with the major players of the Imcare doctor's group, in particular Dr. Gary Cohen, Chief of the group. Robert filled the sink with hot water, washed his face and decided to shave again. He needed to look his best for those deciding his destiny.

Soon he was entertaining thoughts about how to present himself, what to say or not say and what he could do to convince the group that he should be their first choice. Maybe he wasn't the only candidate, maybe they had not been lying. Yet what could he change? They already had his life story and his extensive career in the field of sleep medicine as a teacher, lecturer and clinician. Let them do the talking, he thought and observe instead the various players, to get a feeling for who was who.

The Imcare group met in a private room of 'Pete's Kitchen', a high-end restaurant in service and décor. But not in the kitchen, Robert told Anna that night. As frequently happens in American restaurants. The vegetables were overcooked to the point of being mushy and sticking together like paste and a thick creamy cheese sauce obliterated any taste the overcooked chicken breast might have had. Chewing the chicken was like gnawing on rubber, but of course Robert ate it out of politeness. The highlight was the wine served at the sommelier's suggestion, a California

Charles Krug Merlot, a rich wine soft to the pallet with a wealth of black cherry and black currant. Robert and Dr. Cohen were the only ones savouring red wine; the others preferred a $21 Chardonnay, available at Kroger's for six and a half dollars.

Dr. Cohen took the lead in the conversation. He was dressed boutique style, like he had just walked out of one. A light blue shiny tie contrasted with his dark blue suit and his white shirt. He had a round spectacled face, behind which peered his dark intense eyes. His black thinning hair was oily and slicked back and his bronze skin was the remainder of a trip to the Caribbean or some other exotic place. His relaxed demeanor fit a man doing well financially and having nothing to prove. Sparse gesturing with his hands appeared to follow the cadence of his words addressing the silence of his listeners.

"We are in need of a person who could help the two sleep center doctors reduce the workload and more importantly, simultaneously devise a strategy to grow the center. Ms. Priscilla Jackson, our newly appointed Imcare Office Administrator, may give you more precise information, but I am told that the eight-bed center is only operating at a 50% level. There is thus much room for growth. Up to now, the growth of the center has depended entirely on word of mouth. We have never used any specific marketing tools, because the quality of our work has spoken for itself. The new person will have to be both creative and sparse on expenses."

Robert nodded, for there was nothing to add. Stone sat with his head bent forward, seemingly inside another world of thoughts. He was also being totally overlooked by Cohen, which put a new spin on the group's dynamics. Stone's eyes flitted around the room to find Robert, who forced a smile.

Maybe, as the director of the sleep center, Stone not only liked the status quo, but also regarded any newcomer as an adversary, rather than a colleague. Insufficiently versed in office politics, Robert opted to go along with whomever was calling the shots. Right now that was Cohen.

Obviously lodged deeply into 'Chief' Cohen's back pocket, Salvo sat looking around nodding his agreement with Cohen's every second sentence.

"Tomorrow you will visit our business center and our administrator Ms. Jackson will inform you on the great benefits our company offers. You understand that in the event you are offered a contract, you will not be a partner in our group, but we'll nevertheless extend most benefits to you. We are looking forward to a long-lasting relationship," he said looking around at the table for nodding confirmation. In Germany, the doctors would now be knocking heavily on the table demonstrating their approval. Here everyone nodded a courteous affirmation to foregone conclusion.

After savoring their validating muteness, Cohen continued, "Ms. Jackson will also inform you about the next steps of our hiring process, although our group still needs to complete evaluating the remaining candidates as well." Was Cohen one more liar Robert would have to listen too?

With an elegant gesture Dr. Cohen took his glass of wine, lifted it as a salute to his audience, drank and put his glass back on the table. For a second, Robert thought that perhaps Cohen would continue the theatrics and throw his glass over his shoulder. Instead, Cohen shoved his chair back, stood up and as if on command, everyone else followed suit. The sign had been issued that the audition was over.

Salvo kept his quiet during the drive back to the hotel. As he entered the circular roadway leading up to the hotel entrance, Salvo broke his silence to say that tomorrow at 8 a.m. Ms. Jackson would be coming to pick up Robert for their meeting.

* * *

Back in his room, Robert called Anna and gushed about the day's proceedings. "The talks went well. I had to answer some questions, mainly about my background, but they already knew it from my CV. They talked more than I did, in particular Dr. Gary Cohen, a doc who looks like he stepped straight out of an Armani boutique. He is the guy they all listen to."

Pausing for a moment, Robert resumed enthusiastically. "I have a strong impression they want me, Anna. They said over and over again that they had more candidates, but I know they were just trying to sell me on wanting the job."

Anna asked, "How did the medical director come across?"

Although that perked Robert's attention and concern, he wasn't dampening the elation and joy that he wanted to share with Anna. She needed more convincing than he did, but there was no doubt with Robert that this job had to be and was his.

He told Anna that Stone had kept to the sidelines. "Well," Anna responded, "maybe he is more a listener than a talker."

Robert said he did not have such an impression, only that Dr. Stone was holding his cards tight to his chest. "He is a difficult person to judge." Robert continued, "All in all though, I'm feeling positive and think it could be such a fantastic job. Tomorrow, I'll be talking to the administrator and probably hearing more about salary and benefits and stuff like that."

From listening to this upbeat Robert, Anna knew that her husband had finally found and reclaimed his innate energy and optimism. She also knew that she would have to wait before she could understand the situation better. Robert sounded tired now and she did not want to hold him any longer. She wished him goodnight.

"Talk to you tomorrow, Anna. Love you." Robert had no trouble falling asleep.

8

Ms. Priscilla Jackson walked towards Robert who was waiting by the Hotel reception desk. From a distance, he saw a slender blond woman, dressed in a skintight dress and walking catwalk style in stiletto high heels. Her smile made tiny cracks in her rather heavy maquillage. He returned her smile and they shook hands.

"Dr. Vermeer, nice to meet you."

"Pleasure is mine, Ms. Jackson."

"Priscilla," she smiled again. "Dr. Cohen told me that your meeting went well."

"Yes, it did."

"They were impressed by you. Let's go to my office."

They drove to a corporate office building on S. Custer Road, just North of Legacy Drive in the North of Plano, entered the building and went straight to the elevator. She pressed the button for the third floor. He followed her to a corner office, which had a wide view overlooking Twin Creek Golf Club.

"Nice view," he said.

"Corner offices usually do," she confirmed.

Robert sat in a leather seat facing the window. She leaned back into hers, crossed her legs. He glanced at her and waited.

She seemed to be studying him until she said, "Our doctors form a powerful group and they have an excellent rapport with the hospital. Dr. Cohen, our business liaison, has worked with them for almost twenty years. His connections with the hospital administration are of direct benefit to us. As I am sure you heard, the Sleep Disorders Center is hospital based and the technicians are their employees," she paused, maintaining her inquisitive look.

"The hospital administrator for the center is Dave Jacobs. I don't want to hide that he is a rather weak person. Someone we would like to see replaced. For the moment, we have to deal with him. In the future, we may take control. However, for now, it is good to remember that administration of the Sleep Center belongs to the hospital."

She paused and kept her gaze fixed upon Robert. He took note of her legs and from there of her face. In her late thirties, well preserved, he thought. She smiled a lot and looked at him from beneath her eyelashes.

"Doctors Stone and Salvo run the clinic and we file the insurance companies for their consultations and interpretations of the sleep studies. Because our doctors work mainly in the hospital, we are accumulating too many sleep studies, which remain uninterpreted for weeks. That is where you might come in. The position requires a person who can help with cleaning up the backlog, assist in patient consultation and increase our patient volume. I trust Dr. Vermeer that you understand the importance of the position you applied for."

"I'm well informed and it would be a pleasure to join the group in that capacity."

"Good. I'll bring you to our accountant who can explain to you what we would need in case we offer you a contract. After that, I'll bring you to the airport. Sorry that we cannot
take you out for lunch, but we all have a lot of work to do this afternoon."

Robert met briefly with the accountant who basically told him to wait for a potential offer. All he needed was Robert's social security number, his address and a copy of his passport.

***

A week later, Priscilla called sounding enthusiastic. The group wanted to extend an offer to him and therefore, could he return for a second visit.

Robert booked a flight back to Dallas. Gone were the spider webs of depression, the bad temper and the feelings of failure. Robert was sure his upbeat attitude had no doubt convinced the doctors' group that he was the chosen one, even though there was no other candidate.

He took a cab to the Imcare corporate office where he was to meet with the accountant and Ms. Jackson. Her secretary Milton greeted him with a faint smile. He offered Robert a seat and let Ms. Jackson know of his arrival. Before he entered the office, Milton mentioned -discreetly that another person was waiting for him as well, a Mr. Greg Forman from Schwaber Investments, the investment brokerage company. "It's looking pretty good," he whispered and Robert thought that Milton had even winked.

Priscilla came out from behind her desk, one big smile. She shook his hand firmly and turned to Mr. Greg Forman whom she introduced as the investment broker. She emphasized that Greg was the moneymaker for the doctors. While they slept, he made their money grow. She pointed at him like she was presenting a trophy, a tall middle-aged man, who looked like a well-groomed former football player. His tailor-made suit, his shirt with golden cuff links and a clearly visible Rolex broadcast that he was well off. Greg's handshake made the bones in Robert's hand shift.

Greg had no time to lose. "The doctors of Imcare know by experience that I invest their money wisely. I hope Dr. Vermeer that in the event you join, you will rely on my service. Of course, you retain the freedom of choosing another company for your investments, but I assure you that I will not disappoint you." He sat relaxed in the chair, marketing his services to a potential client.

"I am prepared to show you, - what I achieved last year with a portfolio that I will randomly select from my list of clients."

Robert felt his skin almost percolate, utterly exhilarated that on top of his salary and retirement contribution, there was also a handsome profit sharing. If the question came up about when he wanted to start, he would have to restrain himself from jumping up and down, yelling "Right now!"

Back in Priscilla's office, she told him she would get in touch with him after a final discussion with the doctors and then send a contract proposal for him to evaluate. Out of time she summoned Milton and told him that she would be going out of the office.

"On business," added Milton with a nod to her.

She fluttered her eye lashes and silently mouthed "Yes, on business."

"And could you please drive Dr. Vermeer to the airport?" she redirected Milton, who immediately took his coat and motioned Robert to follow him out to the parking lot.

Milton was another one who wasn't a big talker and Robert saw him occasionally checking the rearview mirror. Robert sank, dreamy eyed into the backseat, deep into reverie.

Surmising that Milton might be an excellent source of information, Robert inquired, "Have you been Ms. Jackson's right arm for long?"

Milton replied in the affirmative.

"Then you must know everyone I have met very well, yes?"

With a meaningful undertone, Milton replied "Aw, yeah."

Once home, Robert opened his front door, attempting to appear downcast and -tendered a sullen hello to Anna.

"Is it that bad, Robert?" she asked, trying to feign pouting, for he could not hide his happiness from her. He fell into her arms and kissed her a long time. The days of suffering and uncertainty were finally behind them.

Within a week, Robert received a contract proposal and took it to his attorney for examination. Frank said he did not see any issues, as long as Robert complied with the contract terms. Frank also pointed out there was a non-compete clause, which stipulated that in the event Robert left Imcare, he could not work as a sleep clinician within a 30 mile radius of the Sleep Disorders Center. Since Robert was expecting to stay for a long time in this new position, he did not consider this clause to have any bearing or importance.

Robert FedEx-ed the signed contract back. Two days later Priscilla called to tell Robert that he could start in three weeks on November 10. Anna and Robert were overjoyed to not only get the type of job he always wanted, but also to recover rapidly from the financial burdens of the past year. Robert would rent an apartment in Plano while Anna arranged for the physical move there.

Robert's first day blessedly approached quickly, eager as he was to jump feet first into this remarkable job opportunity. Whatever office politics there were at the Sleep Disorder Center, Robert's intention was to steer clear of them by focusing strictly on his work.

9

A few days before leaving on the trip to Plano, Robert phoned Dr. Stone to let him know that he would be arriving by car. Stone's clipped reply was, "You're expected on Monday the tenth." End of conversation, plus a reminder of the special handling Stone was going to require. No matter, thought Robert, a problem to deal with later. Right now, concentrate on the drive to Plano and making the first day on the job a good one.

Tense, tired and hungry from the trip, Robert arrived in Plano just after noontime. The D&A's American Bistro on West Park Boulevard appeared as the first decent place for a quick lunch. Dressed in a suit, white shirt and tie, the dress code for doctors, he did not fit in with the casual dress code of the D&A clientele. Robert ordered a burger, fries and a coke, a true American lunch but not one he ever ate at home. Taking quick bites, Robert wondered why he was eating a burger. Whatever, today he'd need all those calories.

As he ate, he reflected on the past he had left behind and tried to imagine what lay ahead. So physically close to his dream job, Robert felt an odd stirring inside him. Although the center was the biggest and best one he had ever worked, Robert knew deep down that the material furnishings of the workplace weren't what really mattered. The people were who mattered and so far, those at St. Elisabeth's were not showing much promise. Then again, maybe Stone was anxious about the new situation as well. Robert refused to worry. He was glad for this brief respite, to pause and breathe deeply before embarking upon the grand opportunity that awaited him.

After paying for lunch, he took another deep breath, smiled and reminded himself that this was the opportunity of his lifetime and to attack it head on. "Here I come!" he shouted aloud as he drove up to the hospital building.

Along the side of the building, there was a stretch of parking spots reserved for doctors. For a moment Robert hesitated, conflicted between being democratic or being privileged, and then parked at a reserved spot, relishing the feeling of belonging to an elite club again. He entered the building through the double doors with the sign 'Sleep Disorders Center' overhead. The hallway led straight to a reception area where one of the African American women greeted him with a smile saying, "I'm Julie, Doctor. Dr. Stone is in the back waiting for you." She stressed the word 'waiting'.

Robert walked over to the large midsection of the room where four technicians sat at their workstations. At the first workstation, a young blond heavyset woman smiled at him and whispered, "I'm Lisa. Before you came for a visit, I spoke to you on the phone, remember?"

"Yes, I do."

"You better go over to the kitchen area, Doctor; the director is anxiously waiting for you there."

Robert raised his eyebrows and walked hastily into the direction she pointed. He found Dr. Stone standing in the kitchen with a coke in his hand, looking vexed.

"We did not know when to expect you."

"Well, I believe I told you that I would be driving here today. I got up at four this morning, hoping to make it before noon. It didn't work out, though, because I did not realize the heaviness of Dallas traffic. Maybe I did not express myself clearly enough?" Robert shrugged his shoulders, feeling stupid that he was already defending himself.

Dr. Stone flipped on his mobile phone.

"He just arrived. Yes, he's here with me. Yes. Yes. Hmm." he said. He turned his back to Robert and listened some more. "Bye." Closing his phone, Dr. Stone turned back around saying,

"Well, I need to get to work."

Bewildered that Stone was just going to leave him standing there, Robert asked, "Can you tell me, Dr. Stone, where my office is?"

"I don't know." Stone replied, glaring at Robert, and then added, "You can use this space here."

"You mean the kitchen?"

"Yeah." He lifted his can of coke and slowly took a sip.

"There is no other space?"

"Not that I know of."

Looking around at the littered Formica table and four non-matching chairs, Robert's cheeks flushed. There was a fridge, a toaster, a crummy coffee machine and a small greasy microwave oven. This was a place where one wanted to spend the least time possible, not a whole day in the office.

"Do I have access to a computer?"

"We don't have one for you. As you may remember, the computers in the tech area are the property of the hospital."

"Weren't the clinical reports of the studies generated by a computer?"

"Well, the technical report by the techs."

Stone waved at the cabinet with the hundreds of patient folders.

"I thought I showed you this."

"You did, Dr. Stone."

"You take one of the files and review the sleep recording of that patient on a computer. Maybe you can ask one of the techs to show you how it works and then use one of their computers, if they don't need it for their analysis and, they do not object."

Robert was stunned by this icy reception. He fought the urge to walk out. Perhaps he should call Priscilla; at least she would know what was going on.

Continuing with his cold stare, Stone said, "For the clinical reports, we dictate the results using a phone. A few days later, we get the typed report back and add it to the patient's file."

"Perhaps you could show me how this works, Dr. Stone?"

A personal ID allowed access to the dictation system. They had to give the patient specifics and then dictate the report. He gave a sample of his own standard format to the dictation personnel, which made it easier for them to follow. "I presume that you have your own template for dictating a clinical report," he ended.

"I do."

Talking to Robert's shoulder, Stone said "OK, but you will have to tweak it to fit our requirements. If you need further help, you can always ask the techs."

Robert nodded, stung by the realization that Stone did not want him around, that Robert was on his own and that he would be working in such a hostile environment. He was determined, however, not to let Stone deter him. Robert would prove himself by plunging in and churning out dictations on the hundreds of accumulated patient folders. Stone could decide for himself when to change his mind about Robert.

"I have to go," Stone said. "Priscilla will be around later to pick you up."

Forcing a smile, Robert went over to the tech area. A woman in her thirties with a full face and ruddy cheeks that looked like they had weathered a farm's sun and wind welcomed him. Seemingly fed with junk food and wrapped in the clothes of a Russian nesting doll, she was as round as she was high, with no discernible female figure, and far from Robert's taste.

"I'm Sarah Fetters. I am the head sleep technician and I report to Dave Jacobs, the hospital administrator in charge of the sleep center operation."

Robert said "Glad to meet you. I'm Dr. Robert Vermeer."

"I know who you are, Sir." she replied, both indignant and offended.

Suddenly, Robert became aware that the - staff consisted entirely of women. He had never dealt with a completely female staff before. This would involve vigilance in making no remarks that might be perceived as sexist and of avoiding at all cost the slightest physical contact. A friendly hug could rapidly turn into sexual harassment, should one desire to interpret it that way.

Sarah Fetters confirmed that, besides the doctors, there were 22 women on staff, four in the front, one of whom was Susan, an Imcare employee, taking care of insurance billing for the patients coming in for a consultation. Eighteen of the sleep techs worked in the back. Of course, the night techs he would not see regularly, because they worked three consecutive nights of 12 hours starting at 7 o'clock in the evening. The daytime techs worked five eight-hour days. Most worked either nights or days; there were hardly any times that a tech had to switch to another shift. Sleep studies ran every night with the exception of Saturday.

Fetters said that they had a capacity of running eight patients every night. Robert made a quick calculation. "With such a schedule, you could have 48 patients per week."

"Could be over 200 a month, Sir, but we aren't getting there."

Robert acted as though he did not hear what she said. "These are big numbers and the potential monthly revenue for the hospital is high, because they collect the technical component for running the sleep studies. Correct?"

"Yes, but the clinical interpretation of the sleep studies is what brings nice money to the pockets of the doc's," responded Fetters.

Depending on the reimbursement from the insurance companies, an average of $250 could be reached. That would mount up to $50,000 a month. Whoa! However, she reiterated that they were not achieving such numbers. "How many studies do you actually have in a week?"

She responded with "Not enough, but even with the ones we have, the doctors cannot follow them up. They are way far behind."

Robert walked, with Fetters following in his footsteps, the blind leading the dog. He looked inside the rooms, opened the bathroom doors and checked the sleep tech kit with the electrodes, patches, paste glue, bandage and tape and other equipment and material on a rolling cabinet. It contained material they needed to attach electrodes to the body of a patient, so that they could measure sleep-wake patterns and different physiological measures needed to study events during sleep. It was the task of the technicians to prepare the patients for an overnight study.

"Nice spacious rooms, delicate colors and tasteful bed linen. Looks comfortable for the patients. Impressive, Sarah." To himself he thought of her as Fetters, but he addressed her by her first name.

She nodded with satisfaction.

"The hospital spent a lot of money to make this an upscale top sleep center."

"I can see that." Robert looked around with pleasure. Nice working environment for the techs, he thought.

He shot a glimpse into Stone's windowless office. Dark green and mauve color dominated the walls and only a single light bulb illuminated the depressing décor. A poster from a previous national sleep association meeting was the only wall hanging. The office was as vapid as the man who inhabited it. Robert could not imagine that Stone did not know that bright lights could cheer and raise moods and even help stave off depression, probably something he never discussed with his patients.

Robert strolled back to the technicians' area "Can you show me a sleep recording of one of the patients on one of your computers?" he asked Fetters.

She searched through a box of CD's, pulled one out and put it in the slot. She pressed play and the recording of a sleep recording came on to the screen. He looked at the signals of the brain waves, the respiration pattern recorded from the nostrils, the respiratory movement of the chest and belly, oxygen saturation in blood measured via a finger probe, heart rhythm, leg movements and a few measures more. In the top right corner of the screen, he saw a video of the patient. He almost looked like a Christmas tree, with all the electrodes attached to his skin and the leads tangling around, coming together into a bundle at the back of the patient's head, leading to the recording system.

"You pulled out the best recording that you have, I presume?"

"No, Doctor. I randomly picked out a study and showed you one of our typical recordings."

"If that is the case, congratulations. That is the way I like it, an excellent recording. In the coming days you will have to show me how I can pull up a study and how you generate your technical report. Maybe we can sit together and look at a few patients."

"Sounds fine by me. You tell me when, Doctor."

He noticed that she did not use his name. The generic 'doctor' seemed good enough to her.

At that moment, Priscilla Jackson made her grand entrance, walking in her high heels with her chin held high. Robert had to admit that he found her most attractive. Her surprise visit made him wonder about her intentions. Was this just a courtesy call or did she possibly care for him?

10

"Hello Dr. Vermeer, are we getting accustomed?"
"Just a start, Ms. Jackson."
"It's Priscilla, Doctor."
"Okay, Priscilla."
"Did you meet James Stone?"
"I met him only momentarily, because he had to get back to somewhere."
"Did he show you around?"
"Kind of. He said that he needed to be at the hospital." With tongue in cheek, Robert added, "I still have to find a place to sit and a computer to work with. He told me that I could office from the kitchen."
"You'll get used to him. That's James. He likes to run away. He doesn't like problems and commitment," she said shrugging her shoulders.
Robert wanted to ask whether his presence was a problem for Stone, but instead he inquired, "Have you found a place for me to stay tonight? I remember you told me you'd look for a temporary place, for a month or so."
"Sure. Let's get out of here."
Outside the building by the driveway stood a silver grey four-door Lexus Sedan ES.
"Nice. Company car?"
"As the administrator for Imcare, I have a lot of driving to do for the doc's so they treat me well. It's reciprocal," she said nodding affirmatively.

After slipping behind the steering wheel, she pulled her skirt up to above her knees. Robert could not avoid noticing that move. She turned to Robert. "Your résumé speaks volumes and the group has a high opinion of you. You will enjoy being a member of the group, but you will have to learn to deal with James Stone. Sometimes he is a pain in the butt. He always has excuses for not being where he needs to be, but I am sure, Doctor, that you will find a way to manage."

"I am learning, Priscilla."

She nodded and started the car. "I found you a place, but don't expect too much. It's a tough market for apartments right now. Here's hoping it will at least suit your immediate needs."

They drove North on I-75 and exited before reaching the new town of Frisco. On Willow Lane, they drove west for a few miles until they reached an area with apartment complexes. On the side of the first large building, a sign indicated that these were the 'Springwood Apartments'. Behind it was another building of dark wood construction with grey and black siding. The entrance door opened into a small dark hallway with two elevators. They took one to the second floor and walked down to unit number 212. Upon entering the place, Robert stopped dead in his tracks, repulsed by what his eyes beheld.

The tired, smelly and dusty apartment had brown wall-to-wall carpeting and contained shoddy furniture that must have come from a second hand store selling it for the fourth time. The place consisted of a small dining area with a square wood table and four mismatched stools. On the other side were couches dressed in a fabric with large vividly colored flowers, a coffee table, and a varnished wood table with a small screen TV on top. At one end was a kitchen area with rough wood panel cabinets and a rusted cooking plate. The bedroom contained two single beds and a comforter from the same flowery fabric as the sofa slipcovers.

"This will do for now," he said, his face no doubt expressing disgust at the decor. The window faced a badly treated lawn and another group of apartment buildings. The other side faced a large parking lot. The last rays of sun did not brighten the place. They simply highlighted how shabby it was.

"I'm sure you will not be staying here for long, Robert. Imcare has paid for three months of rent," she said, placing her hand on his arm and holding it there for a few seconds.

He tried to smile, noting that she was addressing him by his first name. He let that familiarity pass without comment but nevertheless felt uncomfortable, still accustomed to the formal manners of Belgium. While he had abandoned that degree of formality upon moving to the States, in the place he came from, one only used the first name after becoming friends or when asked to drop the family name. In a way, it protected the individual from being too cordial from the very beginning and it avoided any tendency to become too personal too fast. In hospital settings, though, the personnel usually address the doctors by their family name, whereas the doctors use the first name of anyone they address. Priscilla seemed to be on a first name base with the doctors or was it just with him, he did not know which.

"Are you getting hungry?" Again, she touched his arm.

"I got my share of calories at noontime, but yes, I am kind of hungry."

"What if I take you to a restaurant not far away from the hospital? 'Pappadeaux Seafood Kitchen'. They serve excellent salmon. Afterwards, I'll drive you to the sleep center parking lot where you can pick up your car and move into your place. How does that sound?"

"Sounds like a good plan to me, Priscilla."

They got in her car and drove south on I-75, exited at Campbell Road, turned to the left going under the highway and continued back north along the access road. She drove into the parking lot of Pappadeaux's Seafood restaurant. It was 6:30 in the evening and the place was already packed

"Would you like a margarita to start with, Robert?"

"Not now. My day began very early this morning and tomorrow will be a busy day. I'd like to open tomorrow with a clear head."

"Maybe a glass of Chardonnay with the fish?"

"Fine, thanks," thinking he better not ask for a better wine than the cheap chardonnay served days before.

They ordered and looked around.

"This is a place I like. The food is good and one can always meet interesting guys. For a single like me, there are opportunities. Don't get me wrong, I am very selective in choosing my friends."

For a second, Robert sensed that she had winked at him again.

"You are married, I see." She glanced at the ring at his finger. "Yes, for quite a number of years," he said, annoyed that she was fishing for information about him. It was much too early in the game to become so familiar.

Priscilla appeared to be an attractive, well-maintained woman, slender and dressing with style. Robert knew that she knew her strengths in drawing attention to herself. He had to keep himself from falling into this woman's clutches, charming and alluring as she was.

When dinner was finished, he refused any dessert and made it clear he was ready to leave for the hovel of an apartment that the group had rented for him. Robert hoped and expected to be out of there within the month.

Robert shook hands with Priscilla, wished her a good night and drove to his apartment. It felt cold when he entered so he switched on the heat, and for a brief period stared out a window. Tomorrow, he would air the place out and of its stifling odors. His mind tossing and turning, he did not feel like going to bed right away;. He went into the bedroom and pulled the blankets away. The sheets did not look fresh so he went to a closet where he found a set that appeared to be clean. In the coming days, he promised himself to give the whole apartment a good long looking over.

He grabbed the telephone and called Anna to tell her that everything had gone very well and that he was ready for a good start in the morning. He was especially careful not to tell her about the attractive woman capable of diverting his attentions.

"Sleep well and love you, Anna."

Robert crawled into bed, weary from the day and Dr. Stone's stony attitude, thinking, "I need to make it clear to him that I have no intention of taking over his position. Better yet, I won't say anything, just do my job and that way he will see for himself that I have no designs on his job. I'll keep my cool and let him warm up to me."

11

Robert spent the first week holed up in the kitchen reading patient charts and sleep study reports. Often he couldn't use a tech area computer until after 5 p.m. when the daytime techs were gone. He designed a template for a standard dictation report, which contained a summary of patient data, a brief technical description, a description of the sleep-wake patterns and events observed, such as arrest in breathing (apnea), leg movements and abnormalities in the EEG such as seizure activity. The report ended with a section on possible diagnoses and a suggested treatment plan. These reports were inserted into the patient's charts and a copy was sent to the referring physician. Thereafter, the patient saw the referring physician or came in for further consultation with the sleep doctors.

This standard form went via interoffice mail to the dictation department. They gave him his four-digit code number to access the system. He called from a phone in his kitchen office. It was far from an ideal arrangement, but he put that out of his mind and worked diligently to reduce the mountain of charts awaiting interpretation.

Dr. Stone routinely passed the kitchen on his way to his office, pretending to not notice Robert's presence. A few times, Stone went into the kitchen for a coke, stood looking aimlessly around and then left without saying a word. Once he managed to ask how things were going. Although Robert disdained his kitchen office as much as his dumpy apartment, he answered matter-of-factly that everything was fine. While the smells of the kitchen and the techs nuking their frozen meals in the microwave made Robert gag, even worse were the techs eating that crap nearby him.

With limited access to a computer, Robert had diminished capabilities for putting the data he acquired into a file. He scribbled his sleep study notes into a notebook and started a log for the studies that he had analyzed, adding specifics about diagnoses and treatments. Hardly anyone could read his notes, though, the result of a fine motor skill deficit that he was born with.

When he was a kid, teachers beat on his knuckles with a ruler to get him to improve his handwriting. They failed to understand that he could not help his congenital handicap and he failed to perform to their satisfaction. At the university, however, his quasi legible writing was deemed that of a doctor and fit his image perfectly. Subsequent secretaries learned to read his writing, which to some looked more like cuneiform characters and to others as a series of open o's, d's and p's looking like u's. At the end, they learned to decipher his writing and became proud members of the select club who could read and understand his penmanship.

When Robert asked the head tech Sarah Fetters if a computer could become available, she told him she would have to forward a request to Dave Jacobs, the administrator. However, because he was a member of Imcare, she doubted that he would comply with such a request and so never filed one.

Two days a week, Salvo came to see the patients assigned to him. He always came impeccably dressed, Italian style, much in line with Dr. Cohen and much in contrast to Dr. Stone. Salvo made no effort to converse with Robert and as soon as he saw his last patient, he would rush back to the hospital.

Knowing how difficult the Sleep Medicine Board exams were, Robert considered asking Salvo how his preparations were doing. Stirring that pot might reveal more about who Dr. Salvo really was. However, not having the luxury of a moment off task, Robert stuck to his strategy of doing a good job despite his wretched working conditions.

During the second week, hospital administrator Dave Jacobs came to the center for his monthly meeting with the techs. Up until this point, Robert had only heard about him and hadn't yet had an opportunity to meet him. A tall man in his thirties, dressed in brown, from his sweater to his shoes, entered the Center toting a thick folder and projecting an image of wisdom and modesty.

Jacobs headed for Fetters' tiny office, closing the door for a private pre-meeting chitchat. Meanwhile, all the technicians were sitting like chickens on a stick around a large oval conference table placed diagonally inside a bedroom not used for sleep studies. When Jacobs entered, he took his seat at the far end of the table away from Robert.

Fetters, waving in Robert's direction, announced "This is the new doctor."

"Dr. Robert Vermeer is the name," Robert said as he walked up to shake Jacob's hand.

Jacobs nodded with a faint smile, offered a limp paw, and said "Hi."

As soon as Robert took his seat, Jacobs began speaking about the work of the sleep center organization and then shifted to reviewing budget planning for the last quarter. As Robert listened he also couldn't help noticing the into-outer-space expressions on the technicians' faces. This was seriously dry stuff, to which no one objected, questioned or added.

The techs roused from their lethargic states, however, when Jacobs mentioned that the hospital wanted all employees to attend a seminar on the significance of 'the spirit of care'. Even though attendance was voluntary and the topic was related to primary patient care, Jacobs was pressuring them to attend by making a list certifying those to be in attendance. Who could dare risk being noted in the nun's secret accounting books?

"Do not forget," Dave said in a soft preacher's voice, "that the spirit of care is at the core of what we do. This is a catholic hospital and we need to follow the guide of our Lord and through Him, the nuns who are leading this hospital to serve people."

Jacob's message and methodology was not much different from Robert's catholic education, where guilt was used by the teacher priests to indoctrinate the catechism, a catholic document everyone from primary school onwards learned to know by heart.

Catechism Rule # 2 asked, "Does God see everything?" The answer was "Yes, God sees everything, even our deepest thoughts." Any questioning or thinking of 'sinful thoughts' took you straight to hell.

At the end of high school, a priest summoned Robert to the office. A summons to such a 'Private 'audience' could lead to anything. The priest opened with a speech about every student being an example. Then the priest shifted to reprimanding Robert for consistently not attending the Wednesday morning mass, which although not obligatory, implied a moral duty. Robert agreed, "You are right that I have not been going to mass on Wednesdays, but you should know that I am not planning to in the future either. I prefer to be a good humanist instead of a catholic hypocrite."

The priest opened his mouth and then closed it. After contemplating a while, he closed the conversation with, "You may go now, Robert. I hope that being a humanist does not exclude your being a good catholic as well." Despite the priest's attempt at mediation, Robert would from then on practice his humanistic faith, not that of his Catholic upbringing.

After the meeting, Robert went to Jacobs asking him about a workspace and computer. He said he was not sure and that Priscilla from Imcare would have those answers. After all, Imcare employed him. As such, Robert fell outside the jurisdiction of the hospital, even if they benefited from the services he provided. For anything else, Dave said that

Robert could rely on his assistance. Yet, Jacob's body language and facial expression indicated otherwise. Yes, he held the administrative reigns and drove the workhorses for the hospital, but Robert' horse was of a different color.

The next day after meeting with Dave Jacobs, Lisa ambled into the kitchen, took a coke and a chair facing Robert. When he looked up, it was as if he was seeing her for the first time. She had smooth skin, a face surrounded by dark, almost black hair and light brown eyes radiating an appealing intelligence. She wasn't slender, but she had a certain grace that would not fit a thin girl.

"Hi," she said with a bemused smile, "the kitchen doesn't like someone like you."

"You're telling me?" he smiled, leaning back into his chair. "Any suggestions?"

"I think I can help you. But, we need to involve Sarah; she's in charge here."

Robert couldn't imagine what was coming. "I'm all ears, Lisa."

"Meetings are held in a room where we all sit jammed together, while right out there in the rear of the tech area, there is so much more room."

Lisa raised her finger - and told him to sit tight. A few minutes later she dragged in Fetters and continued with her brainstorm. "How about we move the conference table to the back of our center? It will fit better there, and we won't all have to be stuffed into that tiny space where we usually meet. Since that room isn't used for sleep studies, Dr. Vermeer could use it for his office. See?" Lisa went over to one side of the table and said, "C'mon, let's do it."

Along with another technician Jennifer joining in, the table was out of the small room in no time and into the large space at the side of the technician's area.

"I don't know what Dave will say about this. After all, this is hospital space," said Sarah.

"As far as I know, Imcare rents this space," responded Lisa who was coming across as full of action and initiative rather than bent on just following bureaucratic rules.

"Right, but I still..." Sarah went quiet and then retreated to her office, offended over their disregard for her authority. Robert relished being a spectator at this struggle between being a leader or a follower and imagined Fetters going straight for her phone to report the new unauthorized furniture arrangements. Nevertheless, he was impressed with how two problems got solved by one logical solution.

Not before long, Lisa has fashioned a little kingdom for Robert. She located a high-back vinyl chair, and with Jennifer, pulled in a three-seat couch which they set up against the wall in front of the desk. Additional office furnishings streamed in from elsewhere in the building. "Don't ask questions," was Lisa's mantra as she conspired to complete the reorganization of the office space.

Over time, the couch would become a favorite spot for the techs visiting Robert. If that piece of furniture could talk, what a life-altering role it would have been able to play.

"Every room has a phone jack," Lisa said, "and I think I know where I can find you a telephone."

Within a few minutes, Lisa was back and ready to wrap this project up. "Imcare will have to find you a computer, Doctor, but here's a phone for you to use. Now you're almost all set. And don't you go worrying about Dave; remember that you're the doctor!"

Robert gladly occupied his new office, which - like any other bedroom in the center -had its own separate shower and toilet.

Stone walked by just as Robert was settling in. He stood at the door, looking amused.

"Taking a bedroom as your office, Robert?"

It was the first time that Stone had used his first name. Although taken aback, Robert smiled. Was this the beginning of Stone's acceptance, or was he having fun seeing

Jacobs be countered? Then again, Stone himself had converted a bedroom into his office.

Robert told Stone all about Lisa's suggestion to put the conference table out in the center where there was ample space for it. Everyone in the whole center could comfortably meet there, and eight of the ten bedrooms were still reserved for patient studies. "I just hope that Dave won't object," said Robert.

"He's a nuisance. Forget him," answered Stone. "As long as we have sufficient bedrooms, this arrangement is fine by me," and walked off. Robert wanted to say thank you, but he just smiled his appreciation to Stone's back and thought, 'Bingo, I finally scored a point with the man'.

A few days later, two men in overalls brought a desktop and a large computer screen to Robert's office. They installed it and said "From Imcare, Doc. Sign here for a receipt."

Half an hour later, Priscilla arrived at the center, all sweet and smiling a wide victory smile. She was elegantly dressed in a white blouse, a burgundy skirt to just under her knees and her signature black pantyhose and high heel shoes. Robert's eyes could not keep from taking her all in.

"Don't you worry about Jacobs, I've already worked this little problem out with him. We pay rent for this space so, like I told you, we're working on an arrangement where we won't have to deal with him in the future. Be patient, Doc, just a little while longer," said Priscilla who winked her eye at him, touched his arm and left. He watched her departure closely, while weighing all the different dynamics going on. He was still in the dark about much of the operation and especially the relationship between the doctors, the hospital, and the center. Robert's instincts nevertheless cautioned him that he was smack in the middle of some high-stakes game.

During the coming weeks, Robert interpreted all the records and completed all the charts. Imcare filed the insurance companies at $360 per reading. If they received full payment, Robert would have generated over $50,000 in a little less than a month, not bad for starters. His goal, however, was to make the center more efficient and to fill more beds a night. It was time to think hard and make plans, with or without Stone.

12

On Friday evening, Robert drove to DFW airport in a joyous mood. Anna was coming to spend the week with him, and American Airlines was on time for a change. The half-circular AA terminal was brimming with people -toting bags, strollers and briefcases, a traffic stream of travelers hurrying in orderly chaos. Robert had learned years ago to weave between bodies, without touching any, in vast contrast to bustling European places where everyone bumped into each other without even realizing, much less apologizing. The terminal reeked of fast food and sweaty people and kerosene from airplanes arriving and leaving the gates, while the announcements of departures and arrivals blended in with the steady hum of voices.

    Robert entered baggage claim area number 16, full of expectation in a way he had not felt in a long time. Silly, he thought, I'm like some adolescent waiting for his love to appear. He had so much to tell her and he could hardly wait.

    She entered the room in the midst of the many people pushing their way toward the luggage carousel. At once he recognized her soft, serene face where a gentle smile lingered about her lips. Hiding behind a man, waiting to pick up his bag, Robert longingly at her searching the crowd. Once she spotted him, her face lit up and her smile beamed. He saw her lips form 'Robert' and ran to her. Clutching her tightly, he murmured into her ear "Welcome to Dallas, love." As they kept holding each other and he buried his nose into her shoulder length auburn hair.

The traffic on 635 was rush hour brisk, but it moved. They exited at Preston Road and went north. He kept stealing glances at Anna, making sure she was really with him. Meanwhile, she was taking in all the sights, the gleaming lights of the upscale and dramatic office building architecture. Robert's chest tightened as they closed in on the apartment. He was bracing himself for what he knew was coming.

The moment he opened the apartment door, Anna's mouth dropped. Covering it with her hand, she said horrified. "Oh, my goodness. You have to get out of here, the sooner the better."

To break the tension, Robert went to the fridge for a bottle of Champenoise, a sparkling wine made from grapes outside the Champagne region in the northeast of France. Real champagne would not have suited their present budget very well.

"Wait, Robert, let me get comfortable first. Where is the bathroom?"

He went ahead of her and again predicted how she would look around, run her finger on the sink and the glass doors of the shower. "Needs cleaning," she said.

She went into the bedroom and pulled down the covers from the bed. Robert had made sure that there were fresh sheets on the bed. At least that would please her. She opened her suitcase and placed her light cream-colored pajama's on the bed. After showering, she dressed and before sipping the second glass of sparkling wine, they held each other tight, kissing and caressing one another. The night was long with more than enough time to make love. Without saying much, they took pleasure in their togetherness.

* * *

On Sunday, Robert took Anna to see the sleep center. The space and the luxury impressed her. She had never seen a sleep center so large and nicely appointed. Once inside his office, she looked around. "You need some pictures on the walls, and your certificates too. I'll do some shopping next week."

As they were leaving the center, Anna declared, "Today is not your working day, Robert. Are there any good movie theaters we could go to?"

"There's a good cinema in Plano called Tinseltown. Before you came, I checked the schedule on the Internet. There's a movie playing that I'm sure you'll like. It's 'The Merchant of Venice,' Shakespeare's play about the rich Jew Shylock with Al Pacino in the leading role."

He recalled when they saw it performed in a small theater in Bruges, what a brilliant play of judgment it was, the lamb and the scapegoat, with a defeated Shylock and a triumphant conclusion. Anna was delighted with Robert's recommendation, but Robert had his reservations about a movie version.

"Let's go for lunch first. I'm hungry and don't want to eat in that junkyard place of yours. Imcare couldn't do any better?" Anna asked while they walked to the car.

"It's only short term, a few months," he replied apologetically, knowing that he could be dead wrong. It all depended on the sale of their house. However, since he was spending more time in the clinic than in the apartment, what did it matter, at least for now?

Robert took Anna to 'La Madeleine,' a restaurant designed as a French bistro, modified 'a la mode Américaine'. They stood in line all the way from the entrance door to the counter. Once they reached the counter, they placed their order, moved down to the end and paid at the register. There they received a square wooden block with a number on it, which they took and positioned on their table. Servers wearing aprons and black berets lent an additional French flair and served the plates of ordered food in exchange for the numbered wood block. Anna enjoyed a quiche and Robert a Portobello mushroom sandwich, dark flat mushrooms sprinkled with balsamic on toasted bread, a pure delight. There was self-service for 'French' coffee, which tasted better than that in most other restaurants, and so both loaded up on their caffeine quota for the day.

After lunch, they walked across the street to Borders and perused the latest books. Anna chose one of the James Patterson page-turners and an atypical work of John Grisham, 'A Painted House', as described, 'a moving story of one boy's journey from innocence to experience', a book she had heard about but never read. They walked out with their purchases, in time for the movie.

Al Pacino's Shylock was exceptional. Although they knew the story, the movie was still a rediscovery. The play ends with an unexpected judgment in favor of Shylock, who insists that repayment of a loan be made, as agreed by a signed contract, with a pound of flesh from the man who received the money. Shylock insists on fulfillment of the contract, regardless of the inherent consequences.

Believing he was victorious, Shylock was ecstatic, but Portia, a young woman disguised as a lawyer, was not yet finished. 'He' employed a quibble, stating that Shylock could remove that pound of flesh only without spilling a single drop of blood. If he did, he would, according Venetian law, lose all his land and goods and be punished for taking a man's life.

Shylock then switched from being a flamboyant, demanding and unreasonable moneylender to a crawling, miserable and vanquished creature, all masterfully portrayed by Al Pacino.

This gave Robert pause about how invaluable contracts were when drawn in one's favor, but what a disaster when not. Still at the start of his contractual arrangements, he believed that his were fine. Should he have paid more attention to the details? What could one know, though, with renewable contracts, like the one that he had? It simply suggested that he would be evaluated year after year and that performance counted.

   Robert and Anna departed the movie theater in good spirits, ready for a relaxing evening. Both felt cheered, being back to normal, with fewer financial worries than from the past year.

13

On Monday morning, Anna dropped Robert off at the sleep center. Their plan was for him to stay for lunch at the clinic and call her in the evening when he was ready to come home. Having the car and the whole day to herself, Anna searched the grocery store advertisements and made phone calls to real estate companies. By noontime she had finished shopping in plenty of time for her Century 21 real estate appointment for three o'clock that afternoon.

At the Century 21 office, the receptionist introduced Anna to a middle-aged man of average height, with wavy white hair and moustache, which partly covered his upper lip. He was dressed in a blue sport jacket with a square design fabric, dark pants and a light gray shirt with open collar. His blue eyes smiled pleasantly as he looked at Anna with curiosity and intelligence.

"I'm Charlie, nice to meet you," he said with a firm handshake. Anna immediately felt comfortable with him. He presented a mixture of casualness with a touch of refinement and dignity, not your typical salesman.

"You called the office a while ago and said you were looking for a house. The secretary wrote your name down as Anna van de Water. Correct?"

"Yes," she said, noticing right away that he pronounced her family name almost perfectly. He speaks fluent American English, but, she thought, there's also a faint hint of a European language. Anna was good at detecting languages and often identified the right country of a non-native speaking English person. She could not tell exactly what she heard in Charlie's speech, but that wasn't relevant now. She did not want to divert attention to that subject. She would find out later.

He invited her to a conference room and asked her what kind of house she was looking for. Anna told him a modern home, with abundant wall space to display her paintings and a small discrete backyard. She also indicated that she wanted to move as soon as possible. Charlie said he would select a number of houses for them to see during the coming days and pointed out that in Texas, most houses had a swimming pool, in contrast to those in northern states. Anna was already seeing herself sitting poolside.

During the following days, Charlie picked Anna up at the apartment in the morning and showed her houses he thought might fit the profile. They looked at houses until early evening. This scenario repeated day after day.

Being together those days provided opportunities for them to know each other better. Anna readily volunteered about their hectic life, but nothing about their months of desperation and despondency. Charlie in turn told her a mini version of his life.

Originally, he had come from the Netherlands, which Anna did not expect to hear since Charlie lacked the typical Dutch accent. She suspected Danish or Swedish, because they speak British English with a bare hint of a foreign accent. Only if you have lived and worked a long time in the US, could your English sound American, never like a native one.

His father had been a university professor, he told Anna, but his family relations were troubled so he left home when he was 18 years old. He moved to the US, became an American citizen and joined the army. Thereafter, he started a construction business and led a life of continuous challenges.

* * *

Towards the end of the week, they found a modern house that might be 'the one.' Anna characterized the house as 'not bad,' her euphemism for 'I like it enough to buy if there are absolutely no alternatives.'

Late Friday afternoon, Robert joined both of them to see the chosen house. They had to drive way north to Frisco, an area under development surrounded by cleared fields. After second consideration, Anna thought much less of the house. Also, Robert expressed disinterest in living around construction that would be ongoing for years to come. He preferred seeing a better house in a better locale, preferably closer to the hospital.

By the time they had returned to the real estate office, Robert understood why Anna had been speaking so enthusiastically about Charlie. Robert had particularly noted and appreciated Charlie's cautious reserve. To Robert, it reflected keeping a respectful distance, which over the years had unfortunately become an old-fashioned social custom. Charlie's approach allowed time for a relationship to develop, rather than rushing into it.

Reluctantly, Anna prepared to return to Kansas City and Robert regretted their being unable to find a house right away. They agreed to give it more time and trust in Charlie's skills to come up with what they wanted. Robert and Anna said their good byes to one another, each feeling as sad as the other about resuming their bachelorhood lives.

Two weeks later, Charlie called Robert with news that he had found a house. It was slightly above the planned budget, but one fulfilling all the criteria put forward by Anna. At lunchtime Robert and Charlie made a quick visit out to the house. Yes, that was it. He called Anna and told her Charlie had found them the house that fulfilled their wishes exactly. Anna scheduled the next Friday flight back to Dallas.

After picking her up at DFW Airport, Robert headed straight for Century 21 where Charlie took them to a house on Sandy Trail Lane in Plano. It was love at first site. The two-story house facing a quiet street had an impressive entrance with a staircase leading to the second floor. The living area had a large arched bay window, covered with elegant curtains and draperies on the side. There was a separate dining room and small family room that led to the swimming pool and terraces. The large crème colored kitchen had cherry wood cabinets and windows to the floor that overlooked the swimming pool, surrounded by manicured bushes and a fenced terrace. Each room was painted in a different color, as if designed to fit the purpose of that room. The house was turnkey ready for occupancy.

The price of the house was indeed higher than their budget, but Robert and Anna did not hesitate putting an offer on it. After some haggling, the sellers accepted. The obligatory house inspection was still needed to expose any faults, but they did not expect anything major. They celebrated this find by having dinner with Charlie.

Not long after, the house inspection cleared and the house closing took place. Anna arranged for the physical move, instructing United Van Lines to bill Imcare, Inc., a perk that Robert had managed to arrange when he negotiated his contract. The day of the move, Anna marveled at the speed by which everything was wrapped and boxed. Before sunset, the truck was ready to roll and Anna spent the night at a hotel before flying to Dallas and her new home.

* * *

Anna and Robert had promised Charlie that he would be the first guest in their new home, and so it happened. Charlie brought his wife, Maureen, a native Texan with big blond hair, blood red lips, bright sparkling eyes and a smile that conquered hearts. Robert took to Charlie's personality and his manners. He spoke quietly, was slightly formal and above all, he not only knew a lot, he was a good listener too. His white wavy hair and moustache added to his distinguished appearance. Maureen contrasted with vivid colors both on her face and in her clothing. She was the flamboyant one, although without a doubt admiring of Charlie and deeply in love with him.

Robert served them 'Kir', a dry white Pinot Grigio, with a generous splash of Crème de Cassis made from black juniper berries. Robert told them that they would be having dinner in the European way. Not like Americans who go to a restaurant thinking that the faster the service, the better it is. "They run into a restaurant around 6 p.m. and hope to be out an hour later. 'Fridays', a fast food restaurant chain, even advertised that if your food was not served within five minutes after your arrival, dinner was on the house. How could good food be prepared fresh and from scratch in five minutes?"

Robert elaborated that when Belgians go to a restaurant, they go to meet friends and enjoy the food along with companionship and conversation. They take their time. Europeans also lingered over coffee and cognac. Before dinner they would take care to determine who would be 'the Bob of the night' to bring the imbibing guests home safely.

"Anna has been in the kitchen preparing us a nice dinner. So let's enjoy the evening without rushing." Maureen and Charlie were quite surprised to be served dessert at 11 p.m. but they never complained about it getting too late. When Charlie and Maureen left, they thanked Robert and Anna profusely, promising to invite them back. With Americans, however, one could never be sure if a return invitation would actually materialize.

Shortly thereafter, Charlie, true to his word, invited them for a cozy dinner in their modest Dallas house, off Greenville Avenue, south of Mockingbird Lane. Being from European decent and a good cook, Charlie knew how to make an exquisite dinner and keep up a lively conversation. Robert and Charlie's casual acquaintance soon developed into a deep friendship.

14

At the clinic, Robert started seeing patients, three days a week, starting at 9 a.m. The rest of the time, he concentrated on getting the overnight study reports analyzed and dictated. When writing these reports, Robert kept his door closed, which signaled the techs to leave him alone. An open door was an invitation to visit and ask him anything they wanted. This system worked like a charm.

What did not work like a charm was running the clinic together with James. The front office scheduled patients for both doctors at the same time and at half-hour intervals. When James stopped by to make his perfunctory peek at Robert's patients, he would often start the consult all over again, as if to check whether Robert had done a good enough job, or perhaps simply to annoy him. While this involved no impact on the patient, it threw off the timing of the consultations so much that they were constantly running behind. It also made James mad that he had to stay longer.

One time, Robert was done with a patient but James was nowhere to be found. Meanwhile, another patient was waiting in another consultation room. Half an hour later, James made a leisurely entrance into the consultation room. When Julie, the scheduler, remarked that he was running behind, James told her "Dr. Vermeer could have continued with the next patient." Of course, then the delays would snowball, but that did not seem to be of concern to Dr. Stone. Robert kept his outward cool, but not his blood pressure from rising.

Eventually, James decided that Robert's consults and reports were excellent. Thereafter, he skipped the details and readily signed off on Robert's reports. James even became friendly toward Robert, discussing cases with him and asking for his opinion. Any patients suffering from insomnia, nightmares or simply poor sleep, James gladly passed over to Robert. "A waste of time for me," he would say.

Robert cared about such patients who seemed so helpless, having already suffered for such a long time, and not even remembering anymore when their sleeplessness all started. Often, they were tough patients to deal with and the ones who had a problem in changing their behavior. Once helped, though, they were grateful and Robert felt rewarded that he had been able to ferry them through the ordeal.

One of Robert's first insomnia patients Donna L. complained about not being able to fall asleep. According to her it took over an hour, sometimes more. Robert asked her a series of questions related to her sleep habits, the timing of going to bed and waking up and the situation around going to bed, her activities half an hour before going to bed and whether she had a TV in her bedroom. This was all to determine whether he could find a reason for the reported sleep onset insomnia. With Donna he focused on what the insiders called 'sleep hygiene', anything related to going to bed. It was evident that Donna remained active till bedtime and watched TV in her bedroom. Also her timing of going to bed and waking up varied widely.

Robert planned to work on changing her behavior and to be sure of her varying schedule he gave her a wrist monitor, a watch-like device that measured movements on a continuous base for repeated 24 hour periods. After a week, he wanted to see her back, make a print out of her day night activities and consult further on sleep hygienic measures.

Robert was not keen on hypnotic drugs, but eventually he would put her on a mild hypnotic drug to specifically help for sleep onset insomnia, for a few weeks, while also continuing with behavioral measures. A few months later, he had a happy Donna in his consult. She had a far more regular sleep-wake schedule and could do it without medication.

Although Robert saw a fair share of insomnia patients, an overwhelming majority suffered from sleep apnea. Those patients frequently quit breathing in their sleep for seconds up to a minute long, and then had to gasp to get air. It could happen from five times an hour to up to 40 times an hour or more, each time with negative impacts upon both heart and brain. Untreated sleep apnea shortens life span and becomes a deadly disease, for sleep apnea patients could even die in their sleep.

The problem is a mechanical one, the airway closes off and then opens when the patient gasps for air. The traditional treatment is also mechanical. The patients wear a mask over the nose and mouth and air under pressure blows into the nose and mouth, so that the airway remains open. CPAP (continuous positive airway pressure) is the name for this machine. It is ugly to see and uncomfortable for the patient, but it is 100% effective. Commonly, the sleep specialist advises the patients to lose weight for many apnea patients are obese.

One of the first apnea patients was a hospital employee, Suzy Dickinson from the personnel department. She was a young, but morbidly obese woman who had that typical duck walk. She smiled a lot during the consult, wiping the sweat from her face and panting to breathe. A sleep study was scheduled and she scored on average of 31 apneas per hour and the oxygen saturation in her blood dropped to below 50%.

There wasn't a moment to waste. Suzy was fit for a mask and given CPAP. At the end of the night, she reported that she had not slept so well in years. This was a typical reaction to a first night on CPAP. She was asked to continue with the treatment and return to the center for a checkup and assessment of her compliance with the machine. She became one of the regulars at the sleep center for checkups with Dr. Salvo.

* * *

Mondays and Thursdays were the days that Salvo consulted with his patients. As always, he was impeccably dressed under a bright white lab coat, his chest adorned with a doctor's signature, the latest in silver and black stethoscopes.. Yet, to Robert, Salvo' eyes did not project those of a kindly and helpful doctor.

Working solo, Salvo sped through the consult schedule, always finishing first. Since payment of patients and reimbursement differed depending on the length of the consultation, Salvo adhered strictly to the allotted time and not a minute more. In his estimation, any time over the scheduled allotment was a financial loss. He rarely spoke to Robert. Once his consults were done, he would go to the tech area, look around and select a solo patient chart to interpret, leaving all the rest for Robert.

At five in the afternoon Salvo' routine departure phrase was "I'm off to the hospital." Robert doubted that Salvo actually went back to the hospital, since several times when Robert crossed the street to the hospital after five in the afternoon, Salvo' Audi 2000 was no longer in the parking lot.

One day Robert was waiting at the reception desk to get a chart from Julie. When Salvo came out of his office, Julie told him that there was a patient waiting. However, there was a slight hitch; the patient did not have any insurance coverage.

Salvo turned to her as if bitten by a snake and hissed, "Then send him away. I'm not seeing any one who cannot pay. You should know that. We do not offer free medical services here."

Julie pressed him saying, "Sir, this man is really sick and needs to be seen by a doctor."

"Then let him go to emergency. I don't care."

"Doctor, I…"

"Enough and don't argue with me." He jerked his head back, slammed the chart on the desk and marched away.

Robert could only shake his head and return to his office. He dare not defend Julie and the patient for fear of getting in trouble with the group.

When it happened again, Robert brought the issue up with Priscilla. Her curt response was: "No insurance, no pay, no service. Imcare is not a charity corporation. End of story."

Occasionally, if a patient were in especially dire need, the front office would ask Robert to briefly see the patient for advice on what to do. He would jot some notes on the chart, but did not make a report and so the patient went without being billed. When he had worked at the university clinic, he saw non-paying patients all the time, but the university received an annual payment from the city to take care of those indigent patients.

Robert knew he had to be careful. Imcare paid for his time and he did not want to risk being fired for seeing patients without billing.

15

Priscilla entered the Center unannounced during a morning when there was no clinic. A few minutes later, Salvo came in, almost colliding with Robert who was standing at the reception area chatting with Julie. Priscilla and Salvo said "Hi," to Robert as they headed for Salvo' office.

Then Salvo stuck his head out and said, "Julie, don't disturb us for any reason. Got that?"

"Yes, Doctor," she replied meekly. Robert went to his office with the stack of patient charts that he had gotten from Julie. He switched on his computer, pulled up the sleep recording of a patient and opened the chart on his desk. He started to review the sleep recording as well as the notes written by the technicians who performed the recording. What an interesting case, he thought. He called Lisa and asked her to pull the video recording of that patient.

She put the video in the slot and they both looked at the screen. While asleep, the patient jumped out of bed and swung his arms around wildly. This went on for a few minutes, after which the patient lay down quietly and continued sleeping. The technician went into the bedroom, reattached a few leads, and all the while the patient did not wake up. Robert fast-forwarded the recording and during the next rapid eye movement sleep or REM sleep episode (the period during which dreams usually occur), a similar thrashing occurred, but now the patient was kicking violently with his legs and jerking his head, pulling off the electrodes.

Towards the end of the night, during the fourth REM sleep period, the same thing happened. The whole event was highly unusual, since during REM sleep, a person is actively paralyzed, a measure taken by nature so we cannot act out a dream.

This patient had somehow broken through the paralysis, while continuing in REM sleep. Robert thought this was such a powerful illustration of a 'REM sleep behavior disorder' that he would have to present it to Stone and then during an upcoming lecture that he was making at UT Southwestern Medical School.

So intent was Robert on watching the monitor screen that he jumped when Priscilla tapped him on his shoulder. "Hi, Dr. Vermeer, I didn't know you were that scared of me." She flashed him a big smile.

"Sorry, I didn't see you coming."

"You have a minute? Let's go to your office."

Robert asked Lisa to mark the tape and place it together with the others that he was accumulating of different sleep disorders. Lisa smiled and said "Sure, Doc." He could count on her.

Priscilla closed the door and dropped on the couch in front of his desk.

"Comfy," she said, crossing her legs. He got an eyeful of her black stockings and high heels and swallowed hard. Sexier than I imagined, he thought, feeling a tingle of attraction creeping in again. The next thing he noticed was a patient chart in her hands.

"You know we earn money by charging patients," she stated flatly. Her smile had been replaced by a glacially cold stare.

"Of course, what else?" Robert's attention was drawn to the chart.

"Susan in the front office is an employee of ours and paid to file insurance claims."

Robert thought that he knew the routine and had followed the procedure. Once posted in the chart, Robert's reports went to Susan, who handled billing the insurance companies. Her 5' x 5' closet of an office was so crammed with folders and binders that there was limited range of motion. If she wasn't sitting at her desk facing a wall on which her computer screen was mounted, she could only swivel her chair and step around the stacks of charts covering the floor.

Susan was a middle-aged woman with brown curly hair surrounding her serious face. She did her job quietly and often went home, long after others in the front office had left for the day. Her husband had passed away the year before, so no one was expecting her at home, which was one of the reasons she gave for staying late. Robert thought that more than one person was required to do this crucial job, but Priscilla wouldn't hear of it.

"I think Susan is a hardworking and overworked person," Robert said, right away regretting his comment and preparing for some reprisal.

"I have been running some checks and finding things missing in the charts. I have also found some notes in there on a number of patients, whom we did not bill for services rendered. Could this be an oversight, Robert, because I have to assume that you charge for every consult, right?"

Robert's mind began racing. What does she know? Did one of the women at the front desk tell her? Was it Susan? That he could not believe.

Not waiting for an answer, Priscilla said, "Can you call the front office and ask Susan to join us?"

He did so, and a few minutes later, Susan knocked at the door.

Priscilla, shifting to the far end of the couch said, "Sit down, Susan. I asked you to come here, because I need Dr. Vermeer as a witness to assure that everything is done according to employment regulations. I have asked you repeatedly to give me updates on the insurance claims and have often had to wait for more than a week before getting these reports. I have also checked 100-plus charts and missed finding billing in nine of them. That's nine percent, which is only for the charts that I checked. We have thus lost nine percent of our income due to your inadequate performance."

Robert wondered, "What is going on here and why in my office?" Susan sat at the edge of the couch, her hands clasped in her lap and her head bent forward. She ventured to explain that she might be behind on billing, considering that, with the addition of Dr. Vermeer, the number of patients now being seen in consultation had increased substantially.

Priscilla seemed not to have heard. Instead, raising her voice just a notch, Priscilla said, "I have your written dismissal with me." She opened her purse and gave a letter to Susan. "You are hereby fired."

Robert watched the scene totally astounded.

Susan raised her head and whispered "Fired?"

"Yes."

"The month is only halfway over, Ms. Jackson."

"We will pay you an extra week."

"Couldn't I continue working until the end of the month?"

"No, you can go to your office and pack your stuff. We will mail you your final check."

Tears ran down Susan's cheeks. "I need this job. As you know my husband passed away a few months ago."

"Sorry for your husband. The point is that we are not satisfied with your performance and we are losing money. I gave you a warning, but it did no good."

Susan looked at Robert who was incredulous what he was witnessing.

"You can go, Susan. Now."

Priscilla waited until Susan was out of the office and leaned back into her seat.

"Robert, we need loyal and efficient employees, not sloppy ones like Susan. I have been watching her for a while. Not charging patients for services provided and forgetting to bill others. Come on." She shook her head.

Robert asked about the possibility of a second chance. Maybe these were the only mistakes she made or maybe she was just behind with the billing. After all, she is alone, and the number of patient billings had indeed been steadily increasing.

"Robert, don't make me tired."

Then suddenly Priscilla asked, "Want to go out for lunch?"

"Priscilla, I would love to, but I have my meeting with Dr. Cohen today."

"Well, another time then. Have a great meeting, Robert," she said. As she turned, she looked over her shoulder and smiled broadly.

The door clicked shut, leaving Robert to contemplate whether Priscilla was one tough taskmaster or just a bitch? Poor Susan didn't deserve such treatment. I hope I'm not one of the reasons for her being fired. She had nothing to do with my notes, which did not indicate a consult.

As Robert left his office and was walking in the direction of the front office, he glimpsed Priscilla, waiting for Susan to pack up her stuff. Robert pulled a U-turn and went to the tech area to talk to Lisa and divert his attention. He still worried how much he might have been part of the reason for Susan's dismissal. Apprehension started creeping in, so he decided to give her a call, maybe to see how he could help her find another position. Then he decided not to. He would help those patients who could not afford to be seen by Salvo. That was what mattered. What happened to Susan may have nothing to do with him. It was just some pretext that Priscilla needed to fire her. She wanted to come across as a tough manager and show off to Robert. Maybe he'd call Susan anyhow.

* * *

A few days before, Imcare had held its meeting at their headquarters. They did not invite Robert to attend.

They never planned to invite him in the future either, because there were issues they did not want Robert to know about and there was the all-important factor that Robert was not really a partner.

At this meeting, Priscilla gave a general report on the billing and then a separate one on the sleep center. Dr. Cohen said he had heard that, despite the addition of Robert, revenues had not increased as much as expected, there were some billing irregularities discovered by one of Priscilla's assistants, and there were patients who did not have to pay.

Cohen asked, "Is this all just a rumor, Priscilla? There's always a bit of a truth even in the wildest rumors. What's going on?"

"Sir, the issue is not number of patients, but billing. I have been checking on this for several months now and I can assure you that we will solve the problem. Jeanne, my assistant, will be taking over, for she has experience in this area and she can take on the sleep center as an additional task. We will also save on personnel, because I am letting the one from the sleep center go."

That was all Cohen wanted to hear, another problem solved.

He kept looking at Priscilla. "And how is the new guy doing?"

Without waiting for a reply, he continued, "I scheduled a luncheon with him and we plan to have monthly meetings. I figure this way I'll get to hear more than I'll ever get to hear from you, James." He stared at James, waiting for an answer.

"I would love to hear your voice, James. Is the new guy as good as he appeared to be when we hired him?"

James decided that since the bottom dollar line was all that counted, any other talk was just hot air.

"He's running the clinic with me and I must say that he is a thorough professional. I am giving him all the oddball cases and those we don't want to spend much time on. He does the majority of the sleep center charts and makes good reports. I think we're filling his time well, Gary."

That was all they wanted to hear. Moreover, Cohen had just gotten some information for a move to play in his next power game.

16

Robert stood, waiting outside 'Scarpa", an Italian restaurant close to the hospital that Gary had chosen. Gary entered the parking lot driving the latest model Jaguar and took a parking slot on the side. He exited smiling, admired his masterpiece by patting the hood and locked the doors with the remote. Strutting like a peacock up to the entrance, Gary was a walking advertisement for Armani and the Bahamas and reveling in the envious looks he was receiving. He brushed a virtual piece of dust from his jacket and smiled a greeting at Robert.

"Nice machine you have there, Gary."

"Just got it. I have a sweet deal with a car dealer. I change cars a few times a year and the dealer selects the latest for me. Say, if you need another car, just let me know. I'll introduce you to him."

"My Mitsubishi still does a great job, but thanks for the offer anyhow. Who knows, maybe in the future," Robert replied, all the while thinking that he could barely afford just the maintenance on the Mitsubishi.

As soon as they entered the restaurant, Gary was surrounded by a sea of smiling faces. Some came up to whisper into his ear and others to take him by the arm. Gary accepted their attentions as if he were a king. In a sense he was like a king, a man of respect with charm and style who knew all the right people and who could make quick decisions on consequential matters.

Robert followed discretely behind and no one noticed him. When they took their seats, Gary looked around, nodded to a few guests, and in no time a waiter approached the table.

"The usual, Doctor Cohen?"

He served a white martini with a small cube of ice and one green olive.

"What would you like for a drink, Robert?"

"Hot tea would do it for me. Thank you."

The waiter came with a wooden box of teabags. Robert chose a mint tea and few minutes later the waiter was back to take their lunch orders.

"You are adjusting well to the new situation?"

"Sure. It's a great center with lots of possibilities."

"Good to hear, that's what I think too. And how is the clinic going?"

"I have clinical consults three days a week together with James."

"How is it to work with James?"

Robert shrugged his shoulders, reluctant to say much. He volunteered that James was a good doctor, but that respecting a time schedule was not one of his strengths.

"You've got that right, Robert. We hope you'll help to straighten that out. James tends to be lazy, wanting to do everything his way. You'll have to work with him on that. By filling your position, we've given him the help he needed. Now he knows he has to work harder to make the Center a more efficient place and spend more time in our intensive care unit in the clinic."

Although James was the medical director, Robert was the clinical director who would move the center forward, a title he had proposed for himself. While titles are not needed to do a good job, they serve the purpose of delineating realms of responsibilities.

It was as if Gary read his mind. "You're our investment in the Center, Robert. You realize that, don't you?"

"Yes, Sir."

Gary told Robert that they had big plans for him so that his role would become more significant. Dr. Stone would keep his medical responsibility over the Center, but he was needed more in the hospital where the number of the internal medicine beds were going to be increased.

Gary kept talking as he ate, as well as an eye on Robert, whose ego was growing exponentially over the possibility of becoming a VIP at the center.

"Robert, listen. We can't complain too much because we are dependent upon the hospital for the physical location of the Center and for keeping their rent low. But there is underutilized space there that we need to expand and to grow into. What is needed for you to show is how we can take this Center to the next level and that is more than just space."

Gary said that he would be arranging a meeting with the hospital Executive Vice President, Mrs. Elisabeth Bitterman, VP Ms. Maria Frost, the sleep center being one of the services she supervised, and administrative director, Dave Jacobs. Robert needed to create and present a convincing business plan on how to bring the Center to the next level.

Gary summoned the waiter, paid the bill and said to Robert "The meeting will be next Thursday, probably over lunch. Priscilla will give you further details. I'm counting on you, Robert." After they shook hands, Robert watched Gary go off to his Jaguar.

His head erect, Gary moved like a well-toned athlete. Robert heard that Cohen spent an early morning hour in the gym four times a week. Afterwards, he indulged in a quick massage from his preferred Thai girl, with the fitting name of Tukata, a baby doll. Paid well, Tukata wanted to keep her job, but she earned every penny, providing him with exactly what pleased him the most.

* * *

The first thing Robert did back at the office was make a note in his planner about the upcoming meeting, an unnecessary act because how could he forget about it? He made another note, 'Develop a concept for the hospital meeting'. Robert's mind had begun planning it, without him even being consciously aware.

He went over to the tech area to look at a recording of a patient who the techs thought had a nocturnal seizure. Since they were not sure, they asked Robert to look at the recording. Studying the brain waves while simultaneously looking at the corner of the screen displaying a video recording of the patient was a great technological advancement. Robert noticed many artifacts in the brain wave recording due to the patient moving, but there were no spikes or spike-wave complexes indicative of a seizure in brain. Concentrating so intently, Robert did not notice the time, just the quietness of the Center.

He cherished those moments when no one disturbed him. All day long he was surrounded by the female techs, chatting continuously, with the highlight of their daily discussion starting at 10 in the morning about the luncheon options. No wonder most of them were overweight. When they whispered, Robert knew their topic, hospital gossip about the doctors and their love affairs. Not caring to listen, Robert was nevertheless no stranger to the existence of the organizational 'grapevine'.

After techs Jennifer and Lisa left for the day, Robert called Susan, who answered her phone after the first ring. He told her how sorry he was that Imcare had fired her. Then he added: "I'm a bit afraid that I am part of the reason Priscilla reacted so strongly. I should have talked to patients and made notes in the charts for which you could bill."

Susan insisted that he had nothing to do with her being fired. "Priscilla was hounding me with unreasonable demands and then completely disregarded any of my requests for help. Anyone can see that my job is for more than one person. I even suggested my joining up with the administrators in the main office, who are doing the billing for the other physicians. No, Doctor, she just doesn't like me. That is why I am being fired."

Robert could hear her choking up. "Is there anything I can do?"

"Not right now," she'd responded, "but if I may, I'd like to call you when I need a reference." Robert said that she could call him anytime and felt some solace from having done the right thing by calling her.

17

At five thirty, James walked into the Center, grabbed a few charts and took them into his office. He appeared not to notice Robert. Priscilla followed in his footsteps. The door to his office was half-open so Robert could not avoid hearing their conversation.

"James, now that you have additional support for the Center, the group wants you to spend more time in the hospital. I know that you know that, but some of the colleagues are telling me that you always tell them that you need to spend more time in the Center. I am a bit confused."

"Priscilla, I am still the doctor who decides which patients I need to see."

"In no way would I doubt that, Doctor."

"Well then, we are talking about the same old complaint. They just cannot let me do my job. They always need me more in the hospital, but I need to spend time here with Robert. He is still new and I need to guide him in the way we operate. My time here is a valuable investment, wouldn't you say?"

"Sure, but I thought that we hired a fully trained and experienced person who is, according to your own admission during the last Imcare meeting, already proficient and productive. I do not understand why you are telling me now that he needs your help."

"Priscilla, this is my Center and as long as I am the Medical Director here, I will decide what is needed and what is not. I do not need your interference."

"I am just giving you feedback from the group, Doctor Stone, which is that you are needed more in the hospital clinic."

"Consider your mission accomplished. Please, I still have a bunch of work to do."

"Think about what I told you," she said and walked out. She glanced at Robert who acted as if he had not heard anything. He smiled at her. She gave him a short one in return and hurried off.

Two minutes later, James came out and stood next to Robert.

"Routine analyses or is there anything interesting I should see?" he asked in a voice that sounded blasé, but Robert could sense it coming.

Robert pointed at the screen "Well, the techs thought that this patient had a seizure, but I did not see any spikes or spike-wave complexes in the EEG that would allow me to draw that conclusion. What I see is movement in sleep and artifacts in the EEG related to the movement, that's all."

As if James had not heard what Robert was saying, James blurted out,

"You saw Priscilla coming out of my office. It's always the same. They want me to be in the hospital more but I have so much work to do here. You've helped to clear up our backlog, but even with you working here full time, there is still a lot of work to do. I also won't appreciate that they overlook the fact that I was the one who started this Center and for six years, nursed it along almost single handedly."

Robert assured James that he has done a wonderful job and that they had a great Center. Robert was there to make it even better. At least that's what he hoped. He even suggested that they could be a great team.

93

Stone shared that Salvo still had to get his board certification in sleep medicine. After that, he might want to continue doing sleep clinic and reading part of the charts. He also shared that he thought Salvo was young and that they needed to let him find his own way. Then, pulling a reversal, James asked whether Robert had any problem with Salvo.

"No, but we really do not get to see him much before and after clinics. He comes, does his job and leaves."

"That's exactly what I want him to do, Robert." Then, slapping his hand on the computer top, James pronounced, "It's you and me, Robert, we are in charge here."

He walked back to his office. "Time for me to go home, Robert. I need to take the grandkids to the hockey game tonight. See you."

Inside his office, Robert reveled that he and James were finally on a first name basis, that James was really opening up to Robert, and that James had even gone so far as to declare them as the team 'in charge' of the sleep center.

* * *

Robert went to his car anticipating a relaxing dinner and evening with Anna. He had been on the job six months and everything was moving in the right direction. Anna was feeling comfortable in their new home, the neighbors were helping her find her way around, and Charlie was always on call whenever Anna needed him.

On his way home he stopped by 'Liquor One' and selected a Reserva Tuscan wine, that he was sure Anna would like. Friday evening was always a good start for the weekend. He had been spending quite a bit of time in the center on Saturdays, but now the time to catch up on reading the charts was over. He had made it a goal to finish with all his readings by Friday evening, knowing that Monday mornings would be busy with recordings from Friday and Sunday night.

It all felt good, but preparing a presentation for the hospital administration weighed like a stone inside his stomach. He understood so little about the organizational structure- just that the sleep center property and its technician employees were under control of the hospital. Robert still needed to understand Imcare vis-à-vis the hospital, beyond the fact that Cohen was held in high esteem by the hospital administration.

The challenge to make a solid presentation to the hospital next week could make or break Robert's career and future with Imcare. He wanted to show how he could 'bring the center to the next level', a statement made by Cohen upon hiring him. To be honest though, while Robert feared that his ambitious plan could fail, he feared even more whether he could convince the hospital just to go along with that plan.

Robert set about creating a fancy power point presentation and developing the content that would convince everyone that they could achieve the goal of making the center one of excellence. For a while, he forgot that he wasn't acting alone, that Drs. Stone and Salvo and the Imcare administration all had to endorse his plan, as well as the hospital administration, which held authority over the physical plant and the technicians. That weekend would be a tightrope, balancing time to work on this plan without neglecting Anna and a visit from Charlie and Maureen.

* * *

With the onset of longer summer evenings, Anna and Robert could enjoy sitting out on the terrace by the pool, each with a book and one another's company, soaking up the sunshine. The shade of the fence spreading midway across the pool was the sign for them to sink inside the cool, refreshing water.

As it swirled over Robert's skin, the waters ferried away the day's stress and irritations. Holding his head below the heated water of the whirlpool spa and snapping his head up to gasp for air drained Robert's brain of troublesome thoughts.

Anna, however, swam her laps slowly with elegant breaststrokes, holding her head above the water, perusing her surroundings. She seemed to have nothing to clear away from her mind. Robert hoped that her days went as smoothly as how she passed with quiet tranquility her moments with Robert.

Charlie and his wife Maureen became regular visitors to their home. Robert called them habitués, a French word that he fancied to connote their special status. Charlie and Maureen's presence at the house became such a routine that it felt as if they belonged there. Yet, they did not come too often, for each visit brought a fresh new vibe. There was never any question about what to do or what to talk about; their friendship just flowed naturally and automatically. Robert developed a deep sympathy for Charlie and it seemed reciprocal.

Charlie was someone with whom Robert could not only speak freely on any subject but also obtain some needed perspective and feedback about what was going on at the sleep center. Theirs was a friendship continually nourished by their sensitivity and caring for one another.

At the end of August when Charlie and Maureen were visiting, Robert was eager to tell Charlie about the presentation he had made at the hospital. As they sat on the lazy chairs out by the pool, Robert opened a bottle of Leffe blond beer and poured two glasses, bully in the middle and opening at the top.

"Before we get down to business, let me explain what we are having here for drinks," Robert declared. "This is a well-known Belgian abbey beer, its name derived from 'Our Lady of Leffe' abbey founded during the middle of the 12th century. The monks brewed the ale for centuries, but by the middle of the 20th century, businesses had taken it over.

While it is sad that today this excellent ale is no longer brewed inside the abbey, its velvety taste can still be savored as before, just like wine."

"Gezondheid," said Robert, "To your health". .

18

The morning of the hospital meeting opened with an arctic front threatening to invade Dallas. Robert hoped that the atmosphere of the meeting would be balmier. He crossed the street to the hospital building, hands in his pockets and a folder tucked under his arm. From the corner of his eye he caught a glimpse of James in the alley. Robert didn't wait for him, headed instead for the elevator and took it to the third floor. Upon exiting the elevator, he almost ran directly into a set of double glass doors. He pushed the doors open and walked the plush carpeting leading up to the reception desk. The receptionist directed him to a conference room where a projector and a screen were installed at the end of an oval table. A young woman entered the room and said "Dr. Vermeer, I can help you set up for your power presentation. Do you have a handout?"

"Thank you and no. I assume that someone will be taking notes," he smiled nervously and then yawned. Robert always yawned before giving a talk, no matter how familiar he was with the subject. This symptom of being nervous appeared to be uniquely Robert's, as he didn't know anyone else who did that.

He had compiled both format and content into an attractive marketing presentation along with a strategy to 'bring the center to the next level.' But he did not personally know the players, just some names and titles, and consequently felt he was being thrown to the lions, with his brain for their fodder.

The door opened and two women accompanied Dr. Cohen. He presented them as Mrs. Elisabeth Bitterman, Executive Vice President and Ms. Maria Frost, VP with responsibility over the sleep center. They shook hands, lips tight together and heads nodding slightly forward. Mrs. Bitterman had climbed from the ranks of a nurse all the way to the top. She was a big woman with curly blond hair surrounding a puffy face. She appeared, Robert thought, to be literally and figuratively carrying a lot of weight. Why is it, he wondered, that so many nurses are overweight, poor advertising for a member of the health providers profession. Ms. Frost, on the other hand, appeared to waste away into the background, skinny, with dull brown hair in a bun and dressed as a nun, the color of her dress blending in with that of the walls.

Dave Jacobs, the hospital administrator for the sleep center, entered behind the two women and made a beeline for the far end of the table. Stone and Salvo completed the panel of judges.

Once everyone was seated, Dr. Cohen said, "You can start, Dr. Vermeer, we are all curious to hear your plans for the sleep center."

Chafed by the lack of any welcoming introduction, Robert skipped his own flattering remarks and started in right away with his first slide, which showed a three-legged stool each with a different color, one standing on a G, the other one on a P and the third one on an R. He paused, looked at the perplexed-looking faces and explained, "Dr. Cohen asked me to give a presentation on how I see ways to bring the St Elisabeth Sleep Disorders Center to the next level. In my mind there are three legs to the plan. He switched to the next slide showing a graph, with years on the horizontal axis and numbers on the vertical axis. One of the points was highlighted. "This point in the curve shows the number of the sleep studies done at the center in the past year. The curve must continue to go up. We do not want to see a flat line." He used a laser pointer to indicate that.

"The first leg of bringing the center to the next level stands on G for Growth." From what I gather, the growth of the center up until now has been solely based on word of mouth from physician to physician and from patient to physician. It is commendable that growth has been achieved that way, but we can and have to do better."

Robert observed that he was getting their attention. Stone looked stern-faced, but he always did.

"Because the Center depends on referrals, we may consider talking to groups of physicians, letting them know that we offer a speedy and efficient service, with good feedback on patient referrals through our reports and personal calls. Talks to physician groups would involve my giving a presentation about sleep disorders and treatment. We could even request sponsorships from companies like *Respironics* or *ResMed*, which deliver equipment for our sleep apnea patients."

Robert knew that would get the doctors' attention. "We should also speak to our own group, for we see relatively few referrals from Imcare doctors. This is a task that I think could be performed by our medical director and Dr. Salvo."

Upon mentioning Stone and Salvo, Cohen turned his palms up, as if indicating what can we do about them? Robert continued talking about marketing, but to avoid losing their attention, he moved to the next slide.

"Up to now, we have only been treating adults, but there is a huge need for a pediatric service. The second leg of bringing the center to the next level stands on P for Pediatrics becoming a way of expanding our service. There are many children who have a sleep disorder and there is a wide variety of sleep disorder types."

He started to list some and illustrated each with pictures and citations that Robert had received from pleased parents in his previous positions. "If we build a pediatric unit, it will also enhance the image of the hospital."

"You seem to have experience with kids, but none of us have experience in pediatrics," interrupted Salvo. Robert wondered whether this was an indication that Salvo did not like the idea.

Mrs. Bitterman inquired, "What would it take to build a pediatric unit? We have a good pediatric department and pediatricians with whom the sleep center could work. I would like to see a detailed description on the needs of such a unit, including what your role would be in it."

Robert was encouraged that he had hit a point of interest to the hospital. Conversely, Salvo had pointed out that none of the sleep docs were ready and no one in the center, including any of the technicians, was qualified to handle such cases.

"Well," Robert volunteered, "I am sure we can find a pediatric tech and as suggested by Mrs. Bitterman, there might be pediatricians who are interested in addressing sleep problems.

He looked around at the silent faces and continued, "I am ready to create such a pediatric center, if given the opportunity. No doubt it will enhance the reputation of the sleep center, which in turn will be of benefit to the hospital." He could almost hear James grinding his teeth over the extra work, additional responsibilities and, worst of all, dealing with kids and parents.

"Well," said Mrs. Bitterman, "such a service would fit into our expansion plans for the pediatric unit."

Robert smiled to himself. He had scored a point and shut down potential arguments from Salvo against the pediatric unit.

"The final leg of the upgraded Center stands for R, running clinical research studies." As soon as he said those words, Mrs. Bitterman sat up straight and asked, "How would the hospital benefit, Doctor, from conducting clinical research in the sleep center?"

Robert pointed out that research was nothing new for the hospital, considering how the cardiology group in the hospital was currently involved in research on inserting metal wire tubing, called stent's, into an artery to keep the blood flowing unhindered. Mrs. Bitterman nodded in agreement and said, "I still do not understand, though, how the hospital would profit. The cardiologists get access to newer technologies and often get these techniques for free."

"Similarly, clinical research in sleep medicine would help us in getting to work with the latest techniques and newest discoveries in the field, all of which would no doubt increase our reputation and widen the patient range we could serve."

Finally, Mrs. Frost opened her mouth for the first time. She wanted to know how much a research study center would cost the hospital, to which Robert replied, "Nothing." He paused looking at the skeptical faces. "As I see it, the research will be funded by drug companies and manufacturers of equipment used in the sleep disorders centers. Furthermore, any costs would be offset by the profit generated by such studies."

Everyone was silent, waiting for further word from Mrs. Bitterman. "Well, thank you for your presentation. The implementation of your ideas and programs will require additional thinking. I would like to emphasize that the hospital needs to be involved in all aspects of the process and that you have to keep in mind that we are not a charity organization."

Robert's face reddened. '...not a charity organization'? So much for Jacobs telling the techs that the spirit of care was at the core of the mission.

She pushed herself up on the surface of the table and walked away, followed by Mrs. Frost and Dave Jacobs. Cohen went over to Robert and said, "Well done, Robert. I appreciate your enthusiasm, but remember that you are part of a group with James and Liborio. Remember also what Mrs. Bitterman said about the sleep center being theirs. She will be watching the budgets closely and so will Imcare."

With those parting words, Cohen left, Stone and Salvo close behind. Robert lingered a while in the conference center, recalling what he had said and how each had reacted. There was much work ahead,` just providing Bitterman with a plan for developing a pediatric sleep center unit. One complication that had escaped him was the hospital owning both the Center and the techs, and he sitting smack in the middle of the hospital and the doctors' group.

* * *

Several meetings later, the hospital administration approved the plan for a pediatric sleep center, but with reservations about the research plan. Robert and Lisa visited sites in the hospital where they could install the pediatric sleep center, and, fortuitously, there was a suitable one right on the hospital's pediatric floor. While Robert drafted an operational plan and engaged an architect to design a two-bed center, Lisa developed a schedule for the technicians, taking into account that studying babies and children was far more labor intensive than that with adults. One of the reasons was that two technicians were needed during the initial hookup of a child. With some inventive scheduling, three technicians could handle two children for an overnight study.

Robert was sitting on top of the world with this project and making plans to announce the new service to the public. Naturally, James was going along with it as long as he did not have to do anything. James even confessed to not knowing anything about sleep disorders in children, but agreed on a weekly meeting to discuss the studies in children. This sounded to Robert like a major victory. Wonder of wonders, James admitting he had something to learn, anticipating doing so, and ready and willing to give up some of his control.

19

Word spread and within a few months, Robert was consulting with the first children in the pediatric clinic. Simultaneously, the personnel department was searching for a technician with experience in pediatrics.

Candidacies were arriving to the desk of Ms. Suzy Dickson, a newly appointed employee. For a number of years she had worked at the hospital as an aide in different services. She had not been fitting into any of those services when, quite by accident, she found an application for work in the personnel department. One of her friends worked there and recommended Ms. Dickson to the personnel director who was anxiously trying to fill that open position. If he failed to do so, he would lose the money allocated for that position in the new budget.

Suzy Dickson made quite an impression on the director, being a young woman of 5 feet 4 inches, weighing an impressive 220 pounds. Her small eyes almost disappeared into the deep flesh of her cheeks. Her other impressive feature was a long list of experience in different departments. The director attached no significance to the fact that most of these positions had lasted only a few days to a few weeks because they nevertheless counted as 'experience'. Thus, Dickson 'knew' the hospital and the associates working there, which appeared sufficient for Ms. Dickson to qualify for this managerial position.

Her first day in the office, Dickson put her pens and pencils into a McDonald's cup on her desk. A frequenter of fast food restaurants, she evidently placed MacDonald's at the top of her favorite dining list. Another favorite of hers was the color pink. Her planner had a pink cloth cover and her ballpoint pen was topped with a pink plume.

She put a stack of job applications on the corner of her desk and gazed upon them with singular admiration. All set to function, wedged into her fake leather seat, she used her pink plumed pen to punch in her Mom's phone number.

"Hi Mom. I just became an associate in the Personnel Department and guess what, I have my own desk and I can close the door to my own office! Aren't you proud of me?"

After chatting a while with her Mom, Dickson hung up and called Robert's office.

"Dr. Vermeer, Suzy Dickson calling from the personnel department. Could you please come to my office? I have a stack of applications for you to look at," she said with a sense of triumph in her voice.

"Who is calling?" Robert asked.

"Miss Suzy Dickson from the personnel department over at the hospital," emphasizing the word Miss, "I'm calling you regarding the applicants for the pediatric sleep technician position. There is a stack of applications waiting for you on my desk."

"Okay, Ms. Dickson, where is your office?"

A few hours later, Robert went by her office, wondering why she did not go to his. Maybe there were some papers to complete. Then he thought that the name Suzy Dickson rang a bell. Wasn't she one of the first heavy-set women he saw as a patient in the sleep center. He had diagnosed her with sleep apnea. In the follow up consults, she became a patient of Dr. Salvo. Now she was returning to the scene in a totally different capacity.

The sun was shining and he enjoyed the walk outside over to the basement where the personnel department was located.

He greeted Dickson and mentally confirmed the connection. There was no doubt; she was one of Salvo' patients. He decided not to make any mention of her sleep study, knowing that would engage him in an unwanted lengthy discussion and on top of that, she was not his patient anymore. Although she had not ranked high in his 'first impression' department Robert subscribed to the 'actions-speak-louder than words' school of thought. He would wait and watch before passing final judgment.

Robert culled through the stack of applications. There not being, as yet, any formal training or education available to become a sleep technician, most sleep techs learned on the job and subsequently took courses to become registered. As a result, several applicants had neither experience nor training. Others had worked in sleep centers before, but then lacked pediatric experience.

Only two candidates appeared to be promising, but Dickson advised Robert to consider a few more applications. In order to comply with the 'Equal Employment Opportunity' laws, they needed to demonstrate that they had interviewed a sufficient number and diverse types of candidates for the position. She selected three more for him to interview.

Dickson told him that she would make the calls and let him know when they could come for interviews. She counseled Robert on questions he could not ask and she also reiterated that any and all African American applicants had to be scheduled for an interview..

Once Robert had selected the final ones, she would do a background check of the references provided by the candidates. Dickson did not mention, however, that she had never before done a background check, did not know how to do one properly, and planned to just rely on the honesty of the applicants. An additional unwritten demand of the

Hospital was to assure that any potential candidates were good Christians who would become dedicated 'associates'. Dickson was feeling empowered and eager to continue reveling in her new exalted employment status.

* * *

Over the next week, Robert interviewed with the three 'Dickson candidates,' but they were nowhere near capable of functioning in the center. One had not finished high school, but pledged to do so if hired. Another had completed a year of college years ago and was presently a cashier at Wal-Mart. The third one was a technician at an electrical store and in his mind, a technician was a technician. He was sure that he could easily learn how to apply electrodes to a kid's body. "But it's a kid," Robert told himself, "not some transistor."

What a disastrous applicant pool he had from which to select, and what a colossal waste of his time this had turned out to be. Robert wondered whether Dickson had spoken to any of them or checked anything on their applications. He pinned his hopes on one of the two candidates he had identified as having some experience in order to get a jump-start on the pediatric sleep center.

The next candidate was a young man Robert had singled out because of his ample experience at a competitor sleep center in town. He described his previous positions in great detail, and during Robert's testing with a few tricky questions, Robert thought the candidate handled them well. In addition, the young man said he was familiar with computerized recording systems. Robert took him to the technician's area and allowed him to pull up a record. Once again the candidate handled matters quite satisfactorily. In addition, Robert liked his personality and wanted to interview him again. The only downside with him was he had no experience with children.

The last candidate was a young woman in her thirties. When she walked through the door, he saw a slender African American woman dressed in black and white and wearing a faint smile on her lips. Robert extended his hand to her.

"Michelle Alba," she said and with some hesitation, extended a slack palm.

He asked her to take a seat on the couch in front of his desk. She did so, sitting with her legs next to each other, angled to the side, like something she might have seen in an instruction book on 'How to put your best foot forward.' During the course of the interview, she looked down and spoke in a barely audible voice.

Her primary strength was that she had 12 years experience in pediatrics at another hospital in town. This was an easy enough claim to check, which Robert left up to Dickson to verify.

Robert really needed a candidate who could, so to speak, hit the ground running. Considering Ms. Alba's longtime experience in pediatrics, she could probably learn the technology quickly enough from Lisa. Both candidates were able to start soon, as they only needed to give two weeks notice. Not ready to make an immediate decision, Robert told Dickson that while he was deliberating over the two most viable candidates, he trusted that she would be checking out their references.

Robert also sought the opinions from the techs, having had an opportunity to observe both candidates. Everyone sat around the conference table eating lunch, compliments of *Respironics*, a company selling medical equipment, including the CPAP (Continuous Positive Airway Pressure) machine for the treatment of sleep apnea. In the past, Robert explained to his students that a CPAP machine works somewhat like an inverted vacuum cleaner: it blew air into the air passages rather than sucking it out. Doing so avoids the occurrence of any obstruction and thus keeps the airway passage open, preventing airway collapse or sleep apnea.

The techs devoured a feast consisting of a green salad with tomatoes, toasted bread, potato salad, salami and ham. Large bottles of coke and ice tea sat in an ice bucket on the table. There was enough food for a whole army, Robert thought. The techs loved these free luncheons compliment of the sales reps and even the doctors snatched quick bites in between their consultations.

Seated at the head of the conference table Robert asked, "What do you think about the two candidates who were here today?"

"Both are good, I think," said Lisa, "but Michelle has so much experience in pediatrics. I could work with her so that she could learn the sleep technology."

"But" said Jennifer, "the guy is a registered tech, so he already knows what to do. Another plus is his extensive computer experience. He is a man, though, and we don't have any male techs."

Robert got the message loud and clear to pick the woman over the man, regardless of all his sleep study experience and computer knowledge.

"Thanks everyone. I will give it further thought. Lisa will take a lead in helping the new tech come on board because of her experience with kids. I need to make a decision soon, for we want to get our pediatric unit up and running." Robert paused, looking around for any reaction, but there was none. He continued, "If there is one thing I have learned is that you have to make a decision pronto and then stick with it, even if it doesn't turn out as well as you thought. At least that's what I learned back in Europe." As soon as he'd said that, he realized it could be misconstrued and indeed right away got a comeback.

"Ah, Europe," Fetters sighed. "I've never even traveled out of state. I'm proud to be from Dallas. I don't need to travel."

Then Robert made the capital mistake of saying that traveling broadens one's horizons. Fetters responded that her horizon was wide enough and that she could learn everything else from TV. Her chubby face shined and she folded her arms across her broad bosom. Another one, Robert thought, who probably prefers fast food to fresh cooked.

"What about vacation time in Europe, Doctor? I hear they have much more vacation time over there than we do. Do they?" one of the techs asked.

Robert told them that Belgium was a vacation paradise for workers. They had several weeks of vacation a year, everything was closed during the Christmas season, they were often on spring break even during the summer months, and, additionally, there were another ten days of national holidays and religious celebrations.

"They sure don't work much over there," said Fetters, as if the girl who never crossed the Texas border, let alone left Dallas, knew what she was talking about.

Through clenched teeth, Robert replied, "Recently, I read an article in *Business Week*, where they discussed the issue of productivity. The essence of the article was that in spite of having much more vacation, the productivity in Europe was as high as in the US, if not higher. Therefore, more vacation is not necessarily bad. Maybe it serves to replenish one's batteries and then people work harder after a vacation."

As Robert went on speaking about the cultural differences in businesses, he noticed their attention slipping away.

"So," said one of the techs, "are you telling we're lazy?"

"Of course not, that is not at all what I am saying. I mean that the number of hours spent on the job does not necessarily indicate that a person is working. In my mind, it is better to work eight hours intensely, than to be on the job for ten hours while spending several of those hours chatting away on non-job related matters."

Soon, the techs were muttering among themselves, ignoring Robert completely. He withdrew to his office and began pondering the seemingly different worlds that he and the techs inhabited. He also reflected on how words could be twisted, statements intended to educate turned negative and his opinions taken not as an interesting point of view.

Their horizons are so limited, Robert thought, remembering the time he considered leaving for the States. At an international meeting a Mexican friend, not only with an the impressive name but also with an impressive scientific record, René Raúl Drucker Colin, plainly asked him "Why are you so interested in joining the gringo's?" Robert could only smile, asking "Who is the gringo here, René?" They both had a laugh and went for a beer, talking about the gringo's from either side.

Robert resolved to be more careful and less spontaneous in his future conversations with the techs.

At the end of the day, James asked Robert to join him in his office. Their collegiality had been deepening and Robert wondered whether they would be discussing a patient or treatment modalities. He walked into James office wearing a broad smile.

"Robert," he started hesitantly, "I heard from the techs that you told them Americans are lazy." Robert's smile vanished and blood flushed into his cheeks.

"Well, that is not what I said, James. I simply responded to their questions related to cultural differences in lengths of vacation time."

"They say otherwise."

"The techs gossip and gab all day long, and now they are twisting my words."

"I know, they do talk a lot."

"It is worse than that," Robert lashed back. "They have taken to watching soaps over the TV monitoring station when they are supposed to be paying attention to the patient's sleep patterns. And since they are hospital employees, I cannot instruct these so-called 'associates' to do otherwise."

James shrugged his shoulders did not react and then shifted gears, inquiring, "How did the interviews go?"

Robert told him about the various candidates, the two he wanted to bring back for second interviews and the urgency to get someone in place. Word about the pediatric sleep clinic had spread so rapidly that they already had a waiting list. The candidates would be back at the end of the week, so by Monday, Robert planned to have decided which one would get the job.

Surprisingly, James concurred, "I really hope this works out, because this project intrigues me. By the way, Salvo won't be joining us in the ped's clinic. Since you are our expert, you can do those consults."

"With pleasure," Robert said, flashing his broad smile again.

Yet, after James left, Robert stewed over what James said he had heard from the techs. Why were they so intent on stirring the pot and creating controversy? Robert would definitely have to avoid talking to them about anything that wasn't strictly business.

20

That afternoon they had clinic and, as usual, James arrived late. It was a busy time over at the hospital, he'd said for the umpteenth time. Because the rest of the afternoon went well and because routine was settling in, Robert did not care anymore about what James was or was not doing.

Robert and Salvo met briefly at the counter in between patients. As usual, Salvo smiled and as usual Salvo said nothing. Robert wondered whether he harbored any interest in the growth and development of the sleep center. At the meeting with the administrators, he belonged to the ranks of the silent majority. Robert speculated that Salvo was saving any qualms and questions to present directly to Chief Cohen.

Then, to Robert's amazement, Salvo not only didn't run off, he spoke.

"How did the interviews go for the ped's center?"

Robert offered him a brief synopsis, after which Salvo nodded his approval and left saying "See you."

Was Salvo actually doing a one-eighty and showing an interest in the ped's center?

* * *

Entering the hospital through a side door, Salvo walked over and took the staircase leading down to the basement where Priscilla was waiting for him in their secret place. Upon kissing her, he mentioned that he was in a hurry. His wife was visiting her mother, so he had to get home before the kids' nanny left. There was time enough, though, for him to gripe about the new pediatric sleep center.

"Vermeer is deep into developing that ped's center. I'm not involved and don't want to be, but those pediatric consults are so labor intensive that they are eating into how many adult consults we can do. In the time it takes to study one kid, the techs could study two adults." He shook his head and continued "Now, Vermeer is hiring another tech. That one better not be used primarily for kids."

Priscilla listened with one ear; she'd been looking forward to the sex. His wife being gone for the greater part of the day would have allowed them more quality time together. Damn kids.

"And then there's James and Vermeer who seem to be getting pretty chummy. If James loosens or let's go of the short leash he's got Vermeer on, Vermeer will no doubt move in and assume more control. Today though, he really spoiled it for himself with the techs. He said Americans are lazy compared to Europeans. Can you believe it? He drops a few more insults like that and he'll have made himself into a veritable pariah. I love it. Pretty soon James and Vermeer will be easy pickings and we will be able to become more move in and take them down."

Grinning from ear to ear, Salvo grabbed Priscilla and pulled her sweater above her head. She slid her skirt down and pulled her panties to the side. He penetrated her rapidly, biting her in the shoulders. His hand hoisted her up and she swung her legs around him. He pressed her against the wall, groaning and kneading her buttocks. She felt him coming and before she could get full satisfaction, he let her back down. He pulled his pants up, stroked his hand through his hair and panting, said he had to run off. He gave her a peck on the cheek and was gone.

Priscilla locked the door, sank into the couch and finished what they had started. Furious with Salvo for being so self-absorbed and leaving without considering her, she remained in the room trying to compose herself. She opened the cabinet, took out a glass and filled it to the top with wine from the bottle they had opened a few days ago.

* * *

The two candidates for the pediatric center returned on Friday afternoon to respond to questions such as "Why should I hire you and not another candidate? What would you do if you thought a child was having a seizure? Will you allow the mother or the caretaker in the room during the entire procedure? What do you think about having the mother or father sleeping in the same room while we study the child? Does it matter or do you have any preference as to whether you have to work during the night? What will you do when a child cries through the whole night?" All the while Robert was listening to their answers, he was also studying carefully at what their body language was saying.

The young man was amenable to critique and countered it efficiently. He also looked directly at Robert. She answered more prudently in a tone of voice that revealed little emotion. With some questions, she went so silent that Robert had to come up with prompts to get her to respond. That could be interpreted as her being in control, not panicking or being overwhelmed by the questioning.

After interviewing both candidates, Robert still could not decide, even though, he was supposed to call Dickson by Monday to tell her which candidate should be offered the position.

Robert had to take the techs' opinion into account, since they did after all have to work together. The registered tech knew more about sleep, had a lot of experience, but he was a man. All the other techs were women and a man working with them could prompt jealousies and elicit even more gossiping than they already had. Bringing in a woman would not prevent gossip, but they might all feel more comfortable and at ease together. She had also worked for 12 years with children, giving her a much greater edge over the man.

On Monday morning, Robert called Suzy Dickson and told her to extend an offer to Michelle Alba. When Dickson asked about the salary, he explained that according to the personnel department there were three categories. Alba fell into category two, for she was not a novice, but she was not a registered sleep technician.

"We should not deviate from the ranges of the categories. Ms. Alba should start at the bottom of the second category."

Dickson was to take over from there and Robert expected to hear shortly how soon Ms. Alba could start.

Robert felt some satisfaction over his decision; he just hoped she turned out to be who she said she was. His plan was for Lisa and Michelle Alba to work together, until such time as Michelle would be able to take over the lead, leaving Lisa on standby. That was particularly pertinent when a child was being prepared for the recording. Many electrodes and sensors had to be fixed on their small bodies, and there was always discomfort involved. This could not be explained to a baby or a toddler and so involved more than having their favorite teddy bear. That's when a professional technician could do wonders in calming and reassuring the child.

On the practical side, Lisa could start later in the morning and stay later in the evening, when the pediatric service started, to help Michelle prepare the little patients for their sleep study.

Until the pediatric center at the hospital was ready, they used one of the bedrooms not being used for adults. The adult bedroom was furnished with a baby crib and a child's bed with protective side panels.

Robert's first consultation was with a four-year-old boy, the son of one of the hospital employees   He wanted to do his very best in order to begin generating referrals from within the hospital.

The most common complaint was that a child did not want to go to bed or, got up and went to the parent's bedroom. In the field of pediatric sleep medicine, this phenomenon is known as separation anxiety.

Solving this problem requires behavior modification involving both the parents and the child. This process incurs anxious moments of persisting with a given change, but after weeks of training, the goals are achieved, resulting in peaceful bedtimes and sleep for all.

The pediatric unit was taking shape and Robert was eager for his monthly meeting with Gary to tell him about its progress. It was also near the end of October, when Robert should be hearing about his contract renewal. He assured himself that everything would be addressed at that meeting.

On the 31st of October, the day before his meeting with Gary, an envelope arrived from Imcare, Inc. It sat unopened at the corner of the white lacquered cabinet in the living room, the first place he looked when coming home from work. As always, he took Anna in his arms for a homecoming kiss. Before reaching for the mail, Anna said, sounding a bit anxious, that a certified letter from Imcare had arrived.

Nervously he ripped open the envelope and pulled out a ten page document with accompanying letter entitled 'Contract renewal." His heart skipping a beat, Robert shouted, "I got it, Anna. We are renewed with a nice raise." He welcomed a 5 % salary increase and, as he had requested months ago, an additional week of vacation. No doubt Imcare was showing its appreciation for his having cleared up all their accumulated sleep studies, his being caught up by Friday evening every week with his interpretations, the strong growth of the sleep center, and that of the slowly burgeoning pediatric center. His ambitious goals were taking shape and coming into fruition. In truth, however, Robert's deepest source of success and satisfaction was with his patients. He loved interacting with them and caring for them, something that ultimately helped him in his own personal development. Now more than ever, Robert was looking forward to his meeting with Chief Cohen.

21

That same morning the Imcare docs had met briefly to discuss Gary's negotiation with Elisabeth Bitterman about the sleep center. Gary told them that Bitterman was aware of Imcare's desire to take over administration of the Sleep Disorders Center. While she did not object, she warned Imcare to keep an eye on Vermeer, who should be crystal clear about reporting to VP Maria Frost. Mrs. Bitterman also mentioned that although Maria was new in her function as VP, she was coming with good experience from being in charge of several independent units. Mrs. Bitterman did not mention that she believed Maria would develop into another one of her unconditionally devoted and loyal employees.

The greater part of the negotiation concerned how much money the hospital was willing to pay Imcare for the sleep center's administration. "I went for the highest, though reasonable amount," Gary had said, "Remember, for us, it offsets a great part of Vermeer's salary and he is already in operation and eager to get into that position."

James then injected that he wanted to make sure those new profits would not be shared with Vermeer.

"Of course not," answered Gary. "We are paying him a high enough salary to assume this added responsibility." Salvo added that no doubt Vermeer would work his butt off, but more important for them was that they now had direct control over Vermeer. It was almost too beautiful, he told himself.

The group did not have to vote, this was a no-brainer of a move and their getting an effortless $95,000 bonus wasn't an everyday occurrence. Gary had done a great job. They thanked him and hastened off to their respective clinical duties.

* * *

As Robert closed down his computer and readied to drive to Scarpa's for his monthly lunch meeting with Gary, Priscilla appeared in his doorway. One arm was seductively leaning up against the doorframe and light shone behind her slender silhouette. Approaching her, Robert smelled her delicate perfume and felt his heart start pounding. He smiled at her and her eyes returned more than a casual look. Their locked eyes held as they shook hands and before he could express surprise at seeing her she said, "Your contract was renewed and I hope you are happy with what you read."

"Yes. Thank you, Priscilla, it was good news."

"Well Robert, we have an important change to discuss, something that will make you even happier,."

"Really?" His surprise grew.

"I'll take you in my car to Scarpa's."

"Great," wondering where that idea came from.

They all arrived at the restaurant at about the same time. Gary led the way to a table on the far left, against the wall. It was a quieter place, he'd said.

Gary got his martini, Priscilla took iced tea and Robert chose a hot green tea. Priscilla and Gary chatted about the clinic, billing issues for hospital patients, the ever-changing rules of reimbursement by the insurance companies and structural changes in Blue Cross-Blue Shield. Eventually, Robert began feeling they had forgotten he was even there. On and on they went, talking like water flowing from a faucet, just streaming water filling buckets of time.

Robert attended to his tasty lasagna. Scarpa knew how to make it right; not some slushy mixture where the pasta was lost in a tasteless mass covered by a slab of cheese of unknown origin. In Scarpa's the pasta was al dente, bite right. As Robert continued to listen, he began pondering why Priscilla was even there and what news they had for him.

Their talking stopped abruptly, as if cut short by a knife. Turning to Robert, Gary said, "I guess all this stuff is not of much concern to you?"

"In fact no. Or, should I just confess that I do not understand much of these insurance policies?"

"Well, Robert, let me cut to the chase. We told you a while ago that the hospital administrator, Dave Jacobs is more a hindrance than a help to us and we needed to get control of the Center's operation and oversight of the staff. Mind you, though, the technicians will still always be hospital employees. We do not want to carry their cost and the hospital does not want to lose their income."

Robert looked at Priscilla who nodded approvingly, alternating between him and Gary.

After pausing a few seconds, Gary said, "We want you to be the Director, Robert"

"Aren't I already the Clinical Director?"

"Yes, you are, Robert, but we want you to be the Administrative Director of the center as well, in charge of the techs and the Center's operation and budget."

Robert did not respond immediately.

Priscilla inserted, "I assumed that you would be happy not to have to deal with Dave Jacobs. Am I not correct?"

"I guess so."

Robert's mind raced, trying to figure out how he could run the whole center as well as continue his clinical work. This was a proposition of enormous magnitude. Could he pull it off?

Gary resumed speaking again, saying that Imcare would nominate the center's director and the hospital would pay Imcare for its professional service. Robert would be the nominee, of course. Gary mentioned that Imcare had already 'posted a flyer' with Executive VP Mrs. Bitterman.

Whether he lied or was just schmoozing, Robert wasn't sure. Gary said, "She was most favorably impressed with your presentation."

From what Robert could tell, Mrs. Bitterman behaved like a queen mother, expecting everyone to bow and scrape before her. She reigned supreme in the hospital and cunningly parroted the words of the nuns. Robert's impression was that Mrs. Bitterman was more 'concerned about' rather than 'favorably impressed with' his presentation. Her attitude couldn't have been any more straightforward and lacking in any compliments. Yet, if Gary said she was favorably impressed, then it had to be true.

"What would this directorship mean for me, Gary?" Robert wasn't fishing as to whether they would pay him more, he had already gotten a generous salary increase with the renewal of his contract. What he wanted to know were the motives behind this move. For sure, James wouldn't care, although with Robert in Jacobs' place, James would get better control over the techs and that was certainly better than having to accept whatever Jacobs decided. Any gain for Salvo was not so obvious.

"What do you mean, Robert? You will be the Administrative Director in charge of the center. You will report to Maria Frost, the VP, who, besides other services, has responsibility over the sleep center."

"Imcare will be paid for that service?"

"Yes, but if your question is whether your salary will change, the answer is no. In fact, we planned this for you when you were hired; we already incorporated that part into the contractual arrangements, although it is not explicitly stated. Remember when we talked about this before?" Robert looked at Gary and both knew that they were talking at cross- purposes.

Priscilla added hastily, "Also, this new arrangement will be taken into account with the bonus distribution at year's end."

Peering at her from below his eyelashes, Robert thought he was now hearing a different story, as if she were promising him a raise. Before he could confirm anything, Gary continued.

"The $ 95,000 we requested from the hospital for the administrator's function is reasonable, because the hospital saves on Dave's salary, which is quite a bit less than yours. Think of what an opportunity this will be for you, Robert, being in charge of the largest center in town and one of the largest in the country. This is really a high honor proving our trust in your capabilities." Priscilla nodded to add conviction to Gary's statement.

Despite all the extra work this additional position would entail, Robert knew that, in all probability, the deal had already been done. They were simply seeking his rubberstamp approval. Nevertheless, life was looking better and better. By being in charge, he'd have the authority to instruct the technicians in the ways he wanted them to do things, and if he got a year-end bonus, so much the better.

Gary had to get back to the hospital, but since Robert did not have clinic that afternoon, Priscilla told him not to hurry off, just take his time. He thought back to their eye contact in his office. Was Priscilla perhaps entertaining plans for them?

22

As Robert rode in Priscilla's car, the movie 'Les liasons dangereuses' occurred to him. Translated during the late Eighties from a French novel, this film was about Viconte Malkovich seducing a prudish Michelle Pfeifer. But there was nothing prudish about Priscilla saying, "Relax, Robert. This afternoon is free time for you," and then corrected herself with a mischievous smile, "For us."

"I don't think so; there are charts waiting for me."

Priscilla purred, "They will be there later tonight and tomorrow. Take it easy, Robert. Enjoy the moment. You've just been given a tremendous opportunity."

Attempting to deflect her advances, Robert replied, "And a much higher responsibility as well."

Priscilla suggested going elsewhere for a dessert. She knew a cozy place where they served European pastries. "After all, you are dependent on me for a ride back," she smiled naughtily. Robert sighed and thought about the work he still had to do and even more about what possible plotting and planning she might be up to. He persuaded himself that a few hours off couldn't hurt.

As they slipped into her Lexus, Robert noticed Priscilla pulling her skirt up above her knees, remembering the move before. They left the parking lot, turned onto Parker Road and drove east to I-75 entering the highway going Southbound. She sped up, while now and then looking to her side at him. He looked ahead, wondering where they were going and simultaneously watching for any cops lurking around, ready to catch such a speeding car.

"I presume that you love driving fast, Robert? Don't all Europeans? I heard that the Italians in particular do. Great lovers too it seems."

He disregarded the lover comment. "Yeah, I used to like to drive fast," he admitted, remembering his driving at 130 miles an hour on the German Autobahn. Passing under a bridge in a fraction of a second sounded like 'djuuffff,' gone, and 'woe woe woe...' from zooming past the roadside bushes. He loved the sweaty hands and the adrenaline rush, speeding on the left lane, the one for the fast cars.

But then there was the incident on the German Autobahn of Anna screaming when a mobile home switched over into their left lane, forcing Robert to brake hard, laying rubber on the concrete a few inches from the damn mobile home. As Robert cursed under his breath, Anna sobbed and shouted, "If you plan to continue driving this fast, you can let me out right now."

Since then, Robert had become a more cautious driver, aware that he held in his hands the lives of people he cared about. However, alone as a driver, he loved to speed, listening to the sound of the danger he thought he controlled. As with everything else in life, Robert liked to be in control and this new position offered just that.

Priscilla continued driving carelessly, paying scarce attention to the road ahead. Maybe she enjoyed danger and leading a defiant life.

"I guess the risky days of my life are behind me now," he said, coming back to reality.

"Do you have any Italian blood in you, Robert?"

"Not that I know of," Robert said, at the same time thinking about Salvo denying his Italian roots.

She sped up some more. Robert fully expected to see a police car with its flashing lights pulling them over. It didn't happen. "Do you accumulate speeding tickets, Priscilla?"

"I'm expert in finding reasons to dissuade police officers," she said, tugging her skirt up another notch and shooting Robert an enticing glance.

They drove all the way to downtown Dallas and the underground parking garage of the Schwaber Investments building.

Walking from the car to the elevators, she mentioned needing to visit with Gerry, Imcare's investor and someone who Robert had probably met during his interview when they were discussing Imcare's profit sharing system.

"Care to join me?" she asked without expecting an answer.

They took the elevator and she pressed for the 15th floor. Robert smelled Priscilla's perfume perilously close.

He saw her looking flirtatiously at him. Turning to the elevator control panel, she teasingly put her finger against the stop button.

"What if we make it stop now, Robert?" she said, brushing up against his shoulder.

He made a small step backward, dumbfounded. A scene from Al Pacino's 'The Devil's Advocate" crossed Robert's mind, the twirling bodies of seductive women and the faces that became distorted into devilish creatures. At that moment, the elevator stopped and the doors slid open.

"Too bad, Robert, we are already at our floor."

The game was on, but Robert did not know how to play.

They went through swinging doors and entered a spacious hall.

"Welcome back, Priscilla," the receptionist said.

"Have you met Dr. Vermeer? He joined us a year ago."

"I don't think so. Nice to meet you, Sir."
Robert nodded.

"I'll call Gerry to tell him you are here."

While they waited, Priscilla stared at Robert with a Mona Lisa smile and Robert felt the mysteriousness of this day's encounter welling up.

A few minutes later Gerry came and shook hands with both of them.

"Sorry to be so rude, Doctor, but we have some private matters to discuss. I will take you to the conference room and make sure you get some coffee. Milk? Sugar?"

Robert was displeased with this development and had a nagging feeling that he was being used.

"It won't take long," Priscilla assured him, but it still took her half an hour before she showed up grumbling, "Gerry can be such a pain. Sorry, let's get out of here."

They took the elevator down. She blew a few strands of hair out of her face. When they exited at the first floor, she stopped and said, "I hope you don't mind joining me in my retreat?'

Red lights flashed inside Robert's head. Joining her in her retreat? Is she talking about an apartment? They started walking. Although it was November, the sky was clear and the temperature an agreeable 70 degrees. She walked briskly, now and then taking Robert's arm as if to make sure that he was still with her.

They entered the Adolphus Hotel, one of the most luxurious in downtown Dallas, which *The New York Times* had described as "...a Louis XV fantasy on the prairie." Although not Robert's style, the hotel reeked of luxury, baroque style splendor and money, lots of it.

They headed straight for the 'French Room Bar', appointed with cozy alcoves for enjoying intimate company. It was a windowless room paneled in rich American walnut with dimmed lights and a side counter offering a large selection of pastries. Priscilla chose an alcove and settled into a large leather chair. "Go look at the counter and make your choice of pastry. I know what I want," she said.

A waiter appeared and took their orders. There was one other couple sitting very close in a corner alcove, she looking markedly younger than he. Priscilla was no doubt seeking likewise for herself and Robert. This was becoming more and more a kind of a date to Robert, who was having trouble sorting through all his mixed feelings.

The pastry chef baked Robert's meringue cake just the way he liked it, fluffy, crisp at first bite, then melting with the creamy flavorful filling inside. The coffee was not watery thin, but strong, freshly brewed and topped with a dollop of whipped cream. A wrapped piece of Ghirardelli dark chocolate, with mint filling sat on the white porcelain dish next to his cup. Priscilla nibbled on a small cinnamon cake; her legs crossed showing her knees and some thigh in shiny nylons. She gazed at Robert half-smiling and half inquisitively; he could not help feeling Jim-dandy fine.

"Tell me more about yourself, Robert. I know of course about your career life from your curriculum vitae, but there is little I know about you as a person."

"My education, training and a big chunk of my life I spent in Belgium and the Netherlands. I'm a converted American with strong European roots, which sometime show too much."

"That does not tell me much about the person. Who are you, Robert?"

Silence. He really did not want to say anything more, knowing he should not even be sitting there with her. More silence and her surveying him with anticipation.

She put her hand on his arm and then slipped it down into his hand. "Relax, Robert, you look so tense. Enjoy what we have, maybe it's the start of something new. You know that I like you, don't you?"

He did not take his hand back.

"There's a reason I brought you here, Robert. Imcare sometimes rents a room here for meetings because of its privacy, and also to express gratitude to the doctors who contribute to our success. You do that too, Robert, but what you don't know is that there is a meeting tonight at which you are not participating, because it concerns the business aspects." Robert pulled his hand back.

She rose from her chair, deliberately and slowly as she savored him being transfixed by her. "Come Robert. Let me show you something."

"What about the bill?"

"Taken care of," she said and strode off. He followed. They stopped at the elevator and went inside where she pressed the button for the third floor, the executive floor. They stepped across the soft crème colored carpeting and stood outside room 312. She took a key out of her purse and opened the door to a handsome, classic Hollywood style suite. Almost shoving Robert inside, she closed the door and leaned up against it. Robert scanned the sitting area and then a side door leading to a bedroom.

"This is our place for hours, Robert. Want to see what I have to offer?"

As she slowly started unbuttoning her blouse, he stared at her, paralyzed by the scene unfolding before him. He looked at her black bra cupping her bulging breasts. She slid down the zipper of her skirt and let the skirt drop to the floor. She stepped out of it and moved towards him. She wore black stockings and black lace panties. Robert gasped at her beguiling beauty, and details began blurring as his breathing became labored.

Finally, Robert emerged from his stupor, panicking at how wrong this was and stammered, "Priscilla, enough. I can not...no...stop...I do not want this... I need to leave."

"You don't find me -attractive? C'mon, this kind of opportunity you don't get every day. Take me."

He moved back, stumbled over the leg of a chair and fell on his side. She dropped on top of him and pinned him down, stroking her breast against his face. Robert pushed her back, crawled away and stood up, surveying the seduction scene. He straightened his clothes and went to the door. His voice became a raw whisper "I'll meet you downstairs. The keys, please." Priscilla grabbed them from the coffee table and threw them at him. As he opened the door and left, he heard Priscilla laughing "Stupid man".

In a daze, he took the elevator down and stood lost in the hallway. Maybe I should take a cab, but she runs Imcare. Leaving her here would only make the situation worse. He dropped into a chair and nervously awaited her appearance.

Half an hour later, Priscilla showed up, looking as if nothing had happened. They walked in silence back to the parking garage. As he got into her car, Robert was tempted to say 'I'm sorry', but figured an apology wouldn't help anything.

Priscilla drove out of the garage at a super high speed, and with squealing wheels, turned the car onto I-75 heading north.

Robert stole side-glances at her, while Priscilla, looking straight ahead, said not a single word. At the parking lot of the Sleep Disorders Center, she turned to him and said "Robert, you missed what you would never get from your own wife. I didn't think you were that stupid."

He mumbled "Sorry," got out and walked to the entrance of the building without looking back.

The scene and her words careened inside Robert's head for the remainder of the day. He worked at a fever pitch, trying to purge what had happened from his mind. There would be inevitable consequences. How could he have fallen into such an age-old trap? Yes, Priscilla was right, he was exactly what she had said, a stupid man.

23

In the subsequent days, Robert tackled his work with renewed intensity. He also resorted to his routine remedy of deceiving himself, this time about the incident with Priscilla. It would just blow over, he placated himself; nothing would come of it.

He prepared to meet with Maria Frost, acting for the first time in her capacity as VP in charge of the sleep disorder center, and he likewise in his capacity as the Administrative Director. Actually, he did not know how or what to prepare. He assumed that she would give her opinion about his running of the center and what she expected of him. Robert decided it would not hurt to prepare some statistics on the growth of the Center, so he requested lead tech Fetters to provide him with figures. She referred Robert to the woman in charge of the budgets who gave him all the necessary numbers in time for the meeting with Frost.

Robert debated whether to show the stats of his consultations at the clinic, since that was not directly related to hospital business. Indirectly, though, they did. He could compute how many patients seen in clinic had a diagnosis warranting a stay in the sleep center. The doctors were the ones who decided whether a patient should undergo an overnight study or not. To follow the rules, they would recommend what to do next in their referring physician report. The referring physician in turn automatically said yes, for the sleep specialists knew better what had to be done. The referring physician was just bringing in the business.

To get that particular information, however, he would have to ask Priscilla, which was not an option. If Frost wanted such information, she would have to get it herself from Priscilla.

Robert entered the hospital through the main entrance and took the elevator to the elegant third floor. He announced his meeting with Ms. Frost to the receptionist who whispered into the phone "Dr. Robert Vermeer to see you." Turning to him, she said, "Take a seat, Doctor. Miss Frost will come to get you, once she finishes with her present appointment."

Robert sat on a couch facing the receptionist and picked up a copy of the hospital magazine "Spirit of Care". There was Gary's picture and an article about 'Dr. Gary Cohen, the Director of Internal Medicine, nominated as 'Physician of the Year', by his colleague physicians at St. Elisabeth Hospital." Also accompanying the article was a second picture, this one of him and Mrs. Elisabeth Bitterman smiling at the camera and shaking hands. By the time he had read the whole article and flipped through some more pages of the magazine, the door opened and Ms. Frost appeared.

There she was, a nun in civilian clothes dressed in a white blouse, buttoned up high and close at the neck, a grey skirt stopping way below her knees, and flat black shoes. Equally austere was her face void of any makeup to conceal scars of chicken pox, her pencil thin lips and her dull auburn hair pulled tightly back, in a bun against the nape of her head. Sans expression of any kind, she said, "Please follow me to my office" and spun around so swiftly that Robert's smile of greeting was lost in thin air.

He followed her through a long corridor lined with mostly closed office doors where the top executives were located. They entered one near the end and adjacent to her boss, Mrs. Bitterman. On her office desk stood a computer screen, a keyboard, a mouse, and a pencil holder with the logo 'Spirit of Care' as a constant reminder of her duty. A single sheet of paper lay at the corner of her desk on top of a folder. A table with four chairs stood at the side of the room. She invited him to sit at the table.

As she started speaking, she looked everywhere except -at his face. "You took over from Dave Jacobs, and, as you can imagine, he was not happy with this, for he had invested a considerable amount of time and effort in the sleep center. Fortunately, we could reassign him to another service within my group." She paused, now glancing at him. "You are now in charge and we hope that you will make this transition for our 'associates' easy. It is your task to inform them about this change and we hope that you will carry on with our spirit of care. I heard your plans for the center when you first presented them and I understand that you have already been able to implement some of those plans, such as the opening of the pediatric center. Can you tell me its status?"

As Robert listened, Frost continued to look away to some point beyond his left shoulder and blinked a lot, another sign of uncertainty. Frost was evidently trying to appear in control and prove herself as a leader, no small feat for a country girl coming from a godforsaken village in the Bible belt. As the Flemish expression 'omhoog gevallen', 'fallen upwards', goes, she was in a position way over her head. However, the spirit of care was near to her heart and Robert hoped that would be a saving grace.

Robert reported that the pediatric sleep center was indeed open, starting with one of the two planned beds, and that they were seeing an increasing number of children coming to the clinic, for problems mainly related to going to bed and having nightmares. They were consulting with about three children or infants a week.

"How is the new associate Michelle Alba doing?"

Startled that Frost even knew the name, Robert replied "As far as I know she is doing well. I understand from

Fetters that Alba has been in training for a very long time, but I have not heard anything out of the ordinary."

"As far as you know," she repeated Robert's words. "But do you?"

"Of course, I do," he said without hiding his irritation, and at the same time noting that she did not use his name.

"You talked about the growth of the Center. Can you fill me in with some details? What growth has there been over, say the past six months?"

Robert brought out his papers and showed her a spreadsheet on the number and type of patients that the center was serving. The highest number, as in most centers, was sleep apnea patients, and then there was a range of all kinds of sleep disorders, which he'd given a code according the published list of recognized sleep disorders by the Academy of Sleep Medicine. He then showed a graph illustrating the steady growth of the total number of patients evaluated in the center. She listened and nodded approvingly. Growth exceeded 25% and bed occupancy had increased from four to an average of six per night over de past six months.

"You know that the hospital still has concerns about the planned or shall we say, speculative clinical research. You told us that our associates would not be taken away from their duties to the hospital, which is one of the major concerns we have."

"Yes. I am fully aware of that," Robert said, struggling to veil his annoyance. He saw it as a sign of wanting unnecessary insurance. Moreover, he knew that, in the event the research project ever came to fruition, some techs were eager to get involved and earn extra money from Imcare. However, he would not bring this to Ms. Frost's attention now, as she could interpret that to mean Robert would assign them to another job. The techs, the associates as the hospital administration called them, could continue working full time for the hospital and part time for the research and if someone wanted to switch to the research project and thus become an employee of Imcare, rather than stay an associate of the hospital, it could be their choice.

"I would suggest that we meet on a monthly basis. I will instruct our secretary to schedule these appointments with you. Because you are also responsible for the budget, I suggest you meet with Sandy, the budget coordinator for the hospital services. Needless to say, budgeting is an important duty. Our budgets have to be checked every month and for any deviation from the planned budget, you will be asked to provide a written explanation including a remedy for the problem. I have already arranged for you to receive the monthly reports."

"Thank you," he said.

"Anything else you want to know from me?" she asked.

"Not that I can think of," he confirmed.

"See you at our next meeting," she added curtly while returning to her desk.

He felt some fleeting pride that his statistics were showing a successful implementation of his proposed plans, and he assumed that Gary would be happy to hear that too. As Robert departed the administration floor, he considered going to see Priscilla.

She and Frost were now the two important women in his professional life, but while they could not be more contrasting from a physical point of view, they absolutely shared the same malevolent dispositions. One more time, Robert duped himself into believing there was nothing to worry about, his hard work would for -sure prevail and win them over.

24

Back at the office, the sleep techs were seated around the conference table waiting for the monthly staff meeting to begin. The front office was not involved because this meeting's primary agenda was to discuss scheduling for the new pediatric unit. Except for the techs who had to work that night, all were present at this obligatory staff meeting.

Robert -stood at the head of the table before the chattering techs. To his right sat Ms. Alba, the new hospital 'associate'. Robert struggled with the term 'associate' for all of the employees, nurses and technicians. In what way were they all associated? 'Affiliated' would perhaps be more appropriate? They probably used 'associate' to connote a spiritual unity, but where, Robert wondered, was that anywhere to be found?

Although everyone had seen Michelle during the past two weeks, he thought a special welcome from him was in order. Once he got their attention, Robert opened the meeting by assuring everyone that his being in charge as the Administrative Director would not change anything relative to their work status or assignments. "From now on, however, I am the one responsible for any administrative issue related to your employment."

Then he faced to his right and said, "Before we start, I would like to welcome our new employee Michelle Alba who will be instrumental in developing the pediatric sleep center. The night techs have gotten to know her already, but the other techs haven't had a chance yet to meet her." A lukewarm applause followed.

"Michelle, maybe you can tell us a little bit more about yourself?"

Looking up at Robert, she replied, "I have been here for a month, but during all that time I haven't had a single minute of training. Aren't there courses I can go to, since no one's giving me any training?"

Robert was baffled. Where was the mild-mannered, soft-spoken Michelle Alba he had met at the interviews? Who was this mouthy malcontent, and at her first staff meeting no less?

"I thought you were fully trained in pediatrics. Didn't you tell us that you had twelve years of pediatric experience? Before you started, I explained at great length that there is no formal training per se as a sleep tech. Everyone sitting around this table learned their job 'on the job.' I even assigned Lisa to you as your personal instructor."

Robert paused, becoming increasingly galled by Alba's complaint and continued.

"Yes, there are courses, but they simply provide the bare basics, which you can learn much better from our group here. When the time comes, I could ask the hospital to allow you to take a course on pediatric sleep medicine, but I have my doubts that they would pay for that. To be honest, I am puzzled as to exactly what training you think you need that you are not receiving from us."

Actually, Robert was now beyond puzzled into infuriated. Had she lied about her training and experience? Hadn't the personnel department checked her references and verified her twelve years of pediatric experience?

She continued, a la her original interview-style, by looking past him, making no eye contact, "I just think it's terrible you're not providing me with any formal training."

"Your entire time here you have been receiving training from Lisa and the others. Welcome to the job,

Michelle, because Lisa will not be around forever to assist you."

Unable to conceal how pissed off he was, Robert moved on.

"Next point on the agenda is scheduling for the night techs. Sarah Fetters, our technician in charge and coordinator, is arranging the work schedule, so please sign up your hours with her. Just keep in mind: the night staff works three consecutive 12 hours shifts a week. If one picks and chooses the nights randomly, it changes every week and becomes an impossible task to make the shifts work. So please, ladies, talk to Sarah."

Throughout the rest of the meeting, Michelle was M.I.A. I'll have to talk with Dickson in personnel, Robert thought, to confirm whether she did the necessary background checks. But before that, I have to talk to Lisa.

>Suddenly, James emerged from his office and joined them at the conference table.

"I can't stay as I really have too much work waiting over at the hospital, but there's something I need to bring up. Dr. Vermeer and I have learned that those who are in the tech area are watching TV while working. This can't be. From now on, all TV's are to be shut off while you work. If we find otherwise, the TV's will be removed. I am confident, though, that you will not waste time watching TV and instead provide our patients with your undivided attention." After standing back up, looking around a few seconds for any feedback but not getting any, James left.

"Is that your opinion too, Dr. Vermeer?"

"You heard what the medical director said," Robert answered, somewhat taken aback that James had made this announcement without their previously discussing how to handle this matter. Yet, he couldn't agree more, even though he knew this would displease the techs, including Fetters who enjoyed watching her soaps.

At the close of the meeting, Robert asked Lisa to see him in his office.

"You wanted to talk?" she asked while taking a seat on the couch and leaving the door open. Robert asked her to close the door so they could talk more privately, but Lisa indicated her preference for not having the door totally closed.

This is just not my day, Robert thought. First I am blindsided by Michelle and right after that by James. Now I am on the wrong side of Lisa.

He asked Lisa about Michelle's training.

"It's going well, she is learning fast and is very precise in what she does."

"So, if you are giving her the training she needs, where are her complaints about training and courses coming from?"

"I don't know, Doctor. Maybe you should consider a training course outside of this center, one which we could all attend."

"I don't think the hospital would cover such a cost."

"Never hurts to ask."

"No, but I am convinced that we have qualified technicians here. Take yourself, Lisa. You are an excellent tech and you have received your registry. You are the best trainer Michelle could have."

With that, Lisa departed his office, leaving Robert to collect his thoughts about the meeting and the African American employee 'with twelve years of pediatric experience'. Getting nowhere, Robert shook his head to rid it of this mental debris and picked up the next chart on his desk. In between generating sleep study reports, Robert entertained visions of his relaxing weekend at home.

25

Robert headed home for a Friday evening dinner with Charlie and Maureen. Charlie's stories and commentary about happenings far away from the hospital were Robert's antidote for the stresses and strains of his work world. Immersing himself in good food and fine wine with Charlie and Maureen helped Robert distance himself from the people and politics of St. Elisabeth's Hospital.

Robert clicked the garage door open, drove inside and took the bag with the wine bottles from his trunk. He went inside and gave a shout, "Hello, Anna. I'm home." No answer. He went into the living room, expecting to find her sitting on the couch reading a book by the coffee table where wineglasses would be set, waiting for the start of their cozy dinner at home.

She wasn't there. He searched throughout the house and could not find her anywhere. Then it occurred to him that he had not seen her car. He began stewing about why she had not called to let him know she was going out. Maybe she had an accident. He dialed her cell phone. It took ages before she picked up. "Where are you? Did you have an accident? Why haven't you called me? Is there…"

She interrupted him. "I'm with Charlie."

"Why? What's going on, Anna?"

"I'll explain when I get home," she said softly.

She parked her car on the street side and went to the living room where Robert waited. Tears ran down her cheeks and she folded her arms around him, sobbing and unable to say a word. He held her against his chest, trembling in fear of what she was going to tell him.

"It's Charlie. He has cancer. Lung cancer."

"Oh my goodness. When did they find out?"

"He went to St. Elisabeth for a regular checkup. They detected a lump."

"They?"

"The internal medicine doctors. I believe he is still managed by your Dr. Stone," Anna whispered, as if she should not speak aloud this crushing news about their beloved friend.

"He is a good doctor, that I know. So, I believe Charlie is in good hands, but when did he find this out?"

"He did not want to say anything to us until he went through all the other tests. At this time it has not spread to any other organs. Oh, I feel so sad for him, Robert."

At a total loss for words, Robert held Anna tightly in his arms.

The evening went by without their tasting any wine. Saturday was spent quietly, with Robert ruminating about how unpredictable and unfair life is. Was it just a random series of events, having no order and no reason? Believers say that God foresees everything. But why does He allow so much bad to happen? Believers answer that He gave man Free Will to live and make his own choices and that God does not make any promises for an easy life.

And what about those who say that life on earth is preparation for the one later? Is a punishing mortal life the exchange or price for a perfect life in the Hereafter?

Not knowing the unknowable, Robert had no faith to give him any security and peace of mind. He felt deeply sorry for Charlie and began realizing how truly minor his problems at work were by comparison. Health is a precious gift and a blessing for which one can never be too grateful.

Robert phoned Charlie just to hear his voice and thought about a saying that 'Each of us has inherited a second hand car', not knowing of the parts that have to be changed before irreversible damage occurs.

Such thoughts persisted throughout Sunday until Robert conceded that 'Life goes on' and began concentrating on his upcoming clinical workweek.

26

The sleep disorder clinic continued as usual. Robert was in his element, dispensing the true 'Spirit of Care' while trying to diagnose and treat patients for their plethora of sleep disorders. There was no describing how gratifying it was for Robert to see patients in consultation, smiling so appreciatively.

One woman came to complain about sleeping with her husband. During the day, she said, he was gentle as a lamb but once asleep, he kicked at her furiously. This had been going on for years, and other women had told her that their husbands did likewise during their sleep. Some shook their legs when they were just sitting and relaxing. The doctor called it 'restless leg syndrome'. Then she heard about a friend who had seen Dr. Vermeer and convinced her to go to his sleep disorder clinic.

Robert's diagnosis of 'periodic leg movements during sleep' was an easy one, as her husband moved his legs almost every 30 seconds to a minute, became quiet and then started all over again. During a one-night recording in the sleep center, 365 leg movements were counted during his sleep.

Robert put him on a very low dose of a medication used for treating Parkinson patients, and within a few weeks, the patient and his wife returned, gloriously happy to be enjoying sleeping side-by-side again.

Another time, prison guards brought a young man hand- and foot-cuffed. While allegedly asleep, he had killed his visiting girlfriend. During his sleep he threatened her with a knife and when she ran outside from the bedroom, he followed her, stabbed her and threw her into the swimming pool. Then he changed clothes and went back to sleep in his bed, only to discover the carnage the next day.

Dr. Roger Broughton, a Canadian sleep expert and friend of Robert's, had been called in as an expert witness for the case. Roger defended the idea that even in sleep, people could commit horrible crimes, being in another state of mind not controlled by the conscious mind.

To corroborate a possible disorder to his sleep patterns, the young man was brought to the center for a series of recordings. Cuffed to his bed and under guard all night long, he slept like a baby every night. Robert reviewed the recordings and the tapes, and together with James decided that they did not detect any aggression during sleep, something the young man claimed to occur almost every night. The study lasting a whole week was inconclusive. The young man returned to his cell where he awaited trial.

Robert was also to compile a report for Dr. Stone of all the known cases in the medical literature of sleeping people committing crimes and the opinions of sleep experts and lawyers regarding those crimes. James said that he needed this information for testifying as an expert witness in the court trial and that he lacked the time to do such research himself. Robert knew that lawyers paid handsomely for such expertise, especially at a sensational trial such as this that had made it into the newspapers. He chalked it up as one more betrayal by James.

* * *

Some patients use their doctors as a comfy pillow upon which to sleep away their troubles or for someone's undivided attention. Some sleep disorder patients just want the doctor to prescribe them a sleeping pill. Sleep experts, though, first seek to determine the reason for the insomnia, rather than freely dishing out hypnotics. If they do prescribe such medications, they should be used at the most for a few weeks. Within that time, the cause for the insomnia should have been addressed and patients won't have become addicted.

Of course, everything is relative. In the elderly, for example, it is not uncommon to prescribe hypnotics on a chronic basis. Cultural differences also play a role, as well as a physician's prescription behavior. Belgian doctors, for instance, prescribed hypnotics up to four times more than Dutch physicians. In the States, doctors take a much more conservative attitude. Yet, occasionally the seduction from patients can be strong to prescribe a hypnotic. Such patients are happy getting what they want, and the physician is pleased to no longer have a 'difficult' patient. That is not an outcome, however, that sleep medicine specialists want to see occurring.

A woman, who did not want to be in her forties and did everything to look thirty, was a regular patient of the Center. She looked pretty, well maintained and dressed in designer clothes. She always wore high heels, which made her dress dance as she walked. Yet, looking into her eyes, Robert thought he might become an insomniac himself. Her attractive appearance and dreamy voice probably made many a man have fantasies about spending time with her. Somewhere in the corner of his mind Robert reminded himself that such thoughts were out of place and to concentrate on his work.

Her complaint was about not being able to fall asleep within 30 minutes, a sleep disorder called sleep onset insomnia. She also complained about sleep maintenance insomnia, waking up in the early morning hours and not being able to go back to sleep.

Robert dug deep into the woman's history in order to find a reason for her insomnia. He gave her a sleep log to complete and a watch type monitor to detect her sleep-wake schedule variation in mobility. All showed the absence of any indication of a significant insomnia. He tried figuring out whether there was any sign of depression, but could find nothing to support such a diagnosis and there she was again for a consult.

That day she had on a wide black skirt, pulled up to her knees. The consultation rooms were small, allowing just enough room for Robert and a patient sitting on the other side of a small table positioned against the wall. She started putting her hand on his arm, letting it rest there while she spoke.

Robert sat back into his chair pulling his arm away, suspecting her alleged insomnia required a treatment he was not game for.

He stood up and lamented, "To my sorrow I have to say that we have exhausted all treatment possibilities. I will no longer be able to see you as my patient, but I hope the suggestions I gave you will help you do better in the future." With that Robert left the consultation room, sighing all the way back to his office.

Later in the afternoon he wondered about his upcoming meeting with Jeff Sanders, a pharmaceutical sales rep with a research proposal. This project would be the last leg of the stool, taking the sleep center to a whole new level.

27

Jeff Sanders sat next to a cardboard box in the back seat of his car. He grabbed a stack of colored flyers and a set of folders, showing 'BeWake' in large red letters across the forehead of a middle-aged, obese man sitting on a coach with his head bent forward, eyes closed and mouth hanging open. 'BeWake' was to be the miracle drug cure for sleep apnea and persistent sleepiness, even after standard treatment modalities had been exhausted, and Sanders was looking to locate sleep centers that would conduct study trials on it.

Sanders stuffed flyers into the folders, along with an insert about the research results on this prescription drug, contending that while it was not a traditional stimulant, it could keep someone awake for hours. There were the traditional disclaimers, such as absence of addiction, a disclaimer that even Sanders doubted, for he took the drug and found it to be a great aid to his love life.

Jeff Sanders was tall, with a luminous face, dark eyes and short dark gelled hair slicked to the back of his head. Well-toned and physically fit, his manner of dress bore the exclusive cachet of suits that were tailor-made, rather than off the rack. He parlayed his good looks by chatting with the doctors' gatekeepers, the nurses, some of whom even had hopes for an invitation from this desirable bachelor.

Rumors circulated that he was a great lover and that he treated his dates generously. No one seemed to know where he lived, something he kept secret, for he never took one of the girls to his apartment. Jeff Sanders liked it that way, so he could avoid return visits of women who got too serious or he only wanted to see once. Nurses were okay for a night, not for a lifetime. Soon, though, he might have to make a choice; he was thirty-five.

A doctor at Imcare had told him about their foxy administrator. Her name was Priscilla. To Jeff she sounded like just the right person to go a little further with than the customary opening rounds. He needed someone who not only liked sex, but also allowed him personal space, not an easy combination. If he succeeded in getting an Imcare contract through Dr. Robert Vermeer, he and Priscilla would have to meet and not just once. Contracted research lasted months, maybe even be longer than a year; what a wonderful prospect.

As he sat in the back of his car, he made three folders, one each for Dr. Liborio Salvo, Dr. James Stone and Dr. Robert Vermeer, whom he was hoping to see at St. Elisabeth Sleep Disorders Center. Briefly, he rehearsed his sales pitch. He was somewhat familiar with the new doctor, Robert Vermeer, as they had spoken on the phone a few weeks ago and Vermeer had subsequently e-mailed his curriculum vitae, showing his ample research experience.

He seemed a likely candidate to participate in his company's proposed investigation to acquire supporting evidence that their drug also worked against the persistent sleepiness which occurred in sleep apnea patients. Sanders contemplated the pleasant possibility that he was about to catch more than one fly from this single swat: convincing the doctors to prescribe the new drug, securing a clinical research project for the company, and meeting Ms. Priscilla. He whistled the Sinatra song

"When I was thirty-five
it was a very good year.
It was a very good year
for blue-blooded girls
of independent means

who rode in limousines
their chauffeurs would drive.
When I was thirty-five
it was a very good year..."

He put on his sales rep smile for Julie, the receptionist. She wasn't slender, but Jeff appreciated full-bodied women too. Especially, when they held the keys to the center. Julie knew when the doctors came, the mood they were in and where they were. And to Jeff Sanders, the George Clooney of sales reps, Julie willingly volunteered all these details.

This was his lucky day, she said, as all three of the doctors were there having clinic. Jeff was expecting to meet with Dr. Vermeer once his clinic was finished. Julie was happy to reveal that Dr. Stone, the Center's Medical Director, was in his usual mood, a mixture of agreeable cordiality with the patients but a don't-bother-me-with-anybody-else attitude for anyone else. "He never seems to enjoy work, hardly ever smiles, yet the patients like him and he has a reputation for being a good doctor." Sanders noted to himself to finesse Stone's anti-work temperament.

Julie was curious to hear more about this research study, in particular any potential workload increase for them. Sanders gave her a quick and spirited sales pitch about how this wonder drug could help sleepy patients and that research done in their center would lead to more patients. "Well, that's not necessarily what we want, we already have more work than we can handle."

"More work for the doctors, Julie, but as far as doing the research, additional people will be hired for that work." He had already told her more than she needed to know, but it could not hurt that she was positively predisposed towards the center's participation in this study.

In between, Julie mentioned that the Imcare administrator planned to be by later. "Maybe to sit in on the meeting with Dr. Vermeer," she said, "but maybe not. She isn't much into socializing. Like she completely ignores the existence of the front office staff." Bemused Sanders savored how well he knew his way around women like that.

He put a small fancy package on the counter, which sent Julie swooning. "Godiva Belgian chocolates, my favorites." If the counter weren't between them, she would have hugged him. There should be more of these guys around, she thought, and gave him her warmest most seductive smile. "Honey, I'll think about you every bite I take."

"Don't bite too hard," he kidded back.

Strolling into the center, Sanders greeted Fetters, Jennifer and the sleep technicians seated behind their consoles. When their heads turned to see him, Jennifer's mouth dropped opened and her eyes sparkled. "He is in his office," Fetters said, pointing to the open door. As soon as Jeff turned away, Jennifer asked, "So who's the pretty guy?"

"He's a sales rep for Matterson Pharmaceutical Research Institute," Fetters answered. "Way too slick for my comfort zone. Probably not a good Christian either." Jennifer shrugged her shoulders, and Fetters returned to her console, typing notes into the technician's sleep report.

Jeff knocked at Stone's door and at the same time peeked into the office. "Hello." Stone was behind his desk and looked up from his computer screen. He took his reading glasses off.

"I hope I am not disturbing you, Dr. Stone. I'm Jeff Sanders from Matterson Pharmaceutical Research Institute, or MPRI to make it short. I'd like to introduce you to our new product 'BeWake'. Here is my business card."

"Yeah, heard about it. But, like you say, make it short. I don't have much time."

Sanders gave a brief overview, opening the folder and pointing to some graphs.

Stone glanced at the business card.

"We have a lot of sleepy patients here, Mr. Sanders, but we see few patients with irresistible sleep attacks. I assume you are referring to narcolepsy?"

Sanders nodded. "Narcolepsy is indeed the diagnosis that BeWake has been approved for by the FDA."

Stone remembered a book from Robert titled '*Narcolepsy. A funny sleep disorder that's not a laughing matter.*' Marguerite Jones Utley describes how she suffered from irresistible sleep attacks that could happen anytime and anywhere. She went from doctor to doctor and to frequent emergency clinic visits, because when she had a cataplexy attack she would fall down and not move for a while. Such loss of muscle tone could occur in the face, arms or legs. In this case, bystanders assumed she was having a heart attack and called 911. She detested being dragged into emergency room visits, for sleep spells that no one seemed to understand. It took many years before a doctor understood her problem and diagnosed her with narcolepsy.

Stone also remembered Robert having had such a patient. He called James to meet her, but as soon as James walked in and went to shake her hand, she stood and then fell to the floor. Her anxiety waiting for James to arrive had triggered her attack of cataplexy.

Sanders continued, "However, as you know, there are many more sleepy people." He let his words drift and hover, careful not to advertise claims that were not yet proven. He added, "We are interested in conducting further research on sleepy patients and maybe, Dr. Stone, your Center could participate in a trial study. Later on today, I will be talking with Dr. Vermeer who I understand is experienced in clinical research."

Appearing to be looking into the distance, Stone shifted his eyes back to the computer screen, put his reading glasses back on, and said "Thanks. What's your name again?"

"Jeff Sanders, Sir. I'll leave this folder for you to review when your time permits. If you're interested, I can deliver some samples later for you to try out with some of your patients."

"Sure, thanks." Stone punched a few keys and did not look at Sanders as he left. Stone bristled about Sanders' reference to Robert's being 'experienced in clinical research.' Sure, research sounded high and mighty, but why would he want all that extra work? Why didn't Vermeer tell me he was having such a meeting? I wonder if Cohen, or Salvo knew. Whatever. Let them do their thing, so long as I got no more work – just the profit sharing.

28

Sanders went back to the reception area and found Dr. Salvo at the counter. He introduced himself and brought out the company folder.

"We hardly see any narcoleptic patients in our center. Sleep apnea patients, yes. If it works with patients who are sleepy despite all our treatments, that would be good."

"Intelligent remark," Sanders flattered Salvo. "That is exactly what we would like to investigate and I think your center would be at the forefront of that research. A bit later I'll be talking with Dr. Vermeer."

"So I heard. I also heard that our administrator, Ms. Priscilla Jackson, will be attending that meeting. She needs to know what's going on," Salvo said, sending a sober nod into Jeff's direction. "Gotta go see my hospital patients now," he said and extended his hand, giving Jeff a floppy handshake before hurrying off.

So far, Jeff tallied that two doctors were in the skeptical-about-research category, leaving Vermeer yet to deal with and Ms. Priscilla, their watchdog. Soon he would also be basking in her sublime presence.

Jeff sat in Robert's office. They chatted about winter weather in Dallas, which had started a few days ago with a nasty north wind, but could be in the -Seventies tomorrow, so no complaints. They hadn't gotten far in exchanging the banalities of becoming acquainted before Priscilla entered the room.

She noted Robert moving uneasily in his chair and avoiding eye contact with her. He hadn't seen her since their incident at the hotel. She knew she was looking spectacular, the result of a massage from the service relied on by chief physician Gary, followed by a facial and maquillage. She enjoyed watching Robert's discomfort, studied the sales rep as if he were a new human species and immediately sensed his hormones romping wild.-. This guy had more on his mind than a new drug and research he wanted to propose. She was totally fascinated.

Priscilla smiled warmly, gave Sanders a firm handshake and said "Priscilla Jackson, Imcare's Administrator." She then turned to Robert. "I assume you've recovered from our day out, Dr. Vermeer?"

His cheeks reddening Robert replied sheepishly. "Yes. I am working on it."

Sanders conducted reconnaissance on Priscilla charting various routes for his disappearance into her unknown terrain.

She caught him eyeing her. "Jeff, isn't it?" and without waiting for a reply continued, "Tell us about your company's wonderful research plan. What's its name again?"

"MPRI, short for 'Matterson Pharmaceutical Research Institute'."

Jeff pulled out the folder with the brochure and laid it in front of her. "The company is planning a nationwide drug trial study on the drug BeWake," he started and then briefly explained the fundamentals of the drug. He mentioned the study goal was to determine the efficacy of the drug on patients who continue to have sleep apnea and persistent sleepiness, in spite of all the good measures that medical doctors could currently take.

"How does such a trial study actually work, Jeff?"

"Well, first we choose Centers who see a sufficient number of patients with sleep apnea in their clinic and who already have a good reputation as a clinical research center or where they have someone on board with experience and a curriculum that certified the qualities of that person. We check references, of course."

"I assume that our center fulfills at least two of the criteria, since our center is one of the largest in the country and we have our Board certified sleep medicine specialist Dr. Vermeer on site, who has experience in research."

"That's correct. I have Dr. Vermeer's curriculum vitae and because of your center's reputation, I could certainly propose it as a candidate for the research. There are, however, a number of additional requirements, most importantly, having enough staff to complete the study. Do you have a nurse clinical coordinator?"

"No, but we could hire one," Priscilla injected. "The question is one of money. We don't want to incur any unnecessary cost. I assume that such a study covers all cost and generates a good gain above costs. Otherwise, I don't see why we would engage in research. That at least is what I gather from Dr. Vermeer."

"I cannot go into the details, but that's right, clinical research can generate an additional income to your business. Allow me to first explain the process. The selected centers send their Principal Investigator, the PI, and that would be Dr. Vermeer, to an orientation meeting. There they learn about the details of the drug, its mechanism of action, clinical research already accomplished, indications, future ideas and the specifics of the study that MPRI wants to pursue."

Robert listened with one ear, for he knew what clinical research entailed, and paid attention instead to Priscilla and Sanders, her next boy toy. The game was on and Robert was looking ahead at what bearing they could have on his research project.

Sanders continued, "At that meeting, they will also be presented with budget details and a confidentiality agreement to not divulge any information to third parties. Following the orientation, we expect the principal investigator and the representing institute to tell us whether or not they are interested in participating. If yes, the PI and Imcare sign the contract and send it back to the company. Shortly thereafter, the study can commence."

"Tell me more about the budget," asked Priscilla, her eyebrows knotting slightly.

"The contract contains a well planned budget. In general, payment is a given dollar amount per patient and that depends on the type and number of different tests. Up to 20% of the predicted total income is given up front to offset some startup costs and the rest is given when certain stages of the study are reached," he told her, which was what she wished to hear. Then Sanders added as if an afterthought, "By the way, MPRI has scheduled a research meeting in Nassau in the Bahamas with all costs covered by us for at least one person, the potential PI."

Priscilla waited a while and then replied, "If you pay the expenses, we can let Dr. Vermeer enjoy the Bahamas for a few days. However, he'll have to make up that lost time, including the weekend, but that wouldn't be a problem, would it, Robert?"

"Of course not," Robert's heart leaped and swelled. Oblivious to Priscilla's attempt to irritate or annoy him, Robert thought he was well under way toward winning another round in taking the sleep center to a higher level.

Priscilla looked at Jeff and said, "Maybe you and I could have a word, Jeff? Dr. Vermeer has lots of work to do. Right, Doctor?" Since she remained on the couch, Robert took that as a sign for him to leave. For a moment, he hesitated, as if having forgotten something, and Priscilla saw him biting a fingernail. She relaxed when Robert finally exited his office, without uttering another word. The door clicked into its lock, Priscilla gazed at Sanders, in wide-eyed anticipation for what would come next.

29

On Friday afternoon the second week of February, Robert landed at Lynden Pindling International Airport in Nassau, the Bahamas. As soon as he left the plane, he felt the heat draping over him like a wet towel. A Caribbean mixture, the smell of coconut and something sweet like rum, engulfed his nostrils. Above the chatter of people, he heard the beat of a musical rhythm, was it salsa? He felt the tension from the trip evaporate into the searing sun, the flowering colors and the overpowering aromas of tropical fruit.

Among the bustling tourists and dark skinned locals, Robert searched for a person holding a sign with 'Matterson Pharmaceutical Research Institute' printed on it. He spotted a slender suntanned man, a Bahamian, in white slacks and a flowery T-shirt, who had gathered about him several white people carrying small bags and briefcases. They greeted each other and looked about, sweltering in their suits. This had to be the group of American clinicians and researchers. Robert bobbed and weaved his way through and showed his card to the man with the 'MPRI, Investigators Meeting' sign. "You are at the right place, Doc. As soon as we have everyone, I'll bring you to my bus. Stay together. We hope to leave in about 10 minutes," he said.

Robert mingled, greeting people, and recognized one of the big shots in the field of sleep medicine. He was a tall, bulky fellow who regarded himself as the smartest guy in the room. Robert recalled Dr. Philipson's last presentation at the national sleep association meeting where he spoke about nothing in particular as though it was the latest news in sleep medicine. However, belonging to the right group in the sleep societies guaranteed priority clearance for research grants from companies. Robert and his friends called it the research mafia.

Harboring his innate loathing for Dr. Philipson, Robert moved towards Dr. Harry Schneider, 'Harry, the doctor with the pipe', as they called him. He was a middle-aged man who talked with his pipe in his mouth, along with the inevitable sliver of saliva escaping to the side. He had participated in many clinical trials and held a good reputation among the pharmaceutical companies for his loyalty in confirming what they hoped to hear. Another of Harry's hallmarks was to be surrounded by students, who stayed bodyguard close to him. Robert knew that they were instructed to follow him at all times so they could learn from him and the people he met. For Harry, this was another chance to celebrate his fame and importance.

Robert said hello to Harry and they exchanged wishes for a good meeting as well as for free time to visit Nassau and the beach.

"Nassau is one long street of jewelry stores for all the stupid cruise people. They crossed an ocean to be ripped off," Harry chuckled. "But then, of course, there's the beach and its tiny bikinis, oiled buns and uncommonly smooth skin spilling forth." He took his pipe out of his mouth and added "Ah, and don't forget the large turtles and crystal blue sea. All worth seeing, my friend."

Harry called everyone his friend, maybe because he was so smug about having so many. Nevertheless, he was a man in-the-know and someone on whom Robert had relied in the past.

Robert needed air, away from Harry's stinking pipe. Stepping aside, he saw it was time to board the bus to the hotel.

At the Caribbean Inn, the crowd stood around the MPRI tables where two young women gave each attendee a linen bag labeled MPRI, a folder with documentation and writing material, a nametag and a card with their room number. At the reception desk, they got their key and made a dash for their room. MPRI had a welcome reception scheduled for 7 p.m. They had about two hours.

Robert exchanged hellos with a few more people he knew from the annual American Professional Sleep Societies and National Psychology meetings. Everyone was in a rush. Time to take a shower and dress casually for the welcome reception.

Robert arrived a little bit late, to get an overview of who was there. The room was packed. Robert took a glass of red wine and walked from one group to another, seeing friends and people he knew from other conferences.

"Hi guys, having fun?" he asked with a big smile, to which they nodded and smiled back

The evening ended as it began, talking to colleagues, looking forward to getting to know the details of the study and discussing the various kinds of financial arrangements. This was one of the ways that the academic doctors could support their university research and the private or hospital based centers could pocket doctor fees. Robert was counting on this being an issue in his favor when Imcare renegotiated his contract.

30

Potential Principal Investigators for the clinical research study with the new drug 'BeAwake' filled the conference room of the Caribbean Inn. Researchers and clinicians flipped their folders open and chatted away the time, waiting for the meeting to start. An executive of the company welcomed the audience, telling them how excited he was, addressing such distinguished investigators. They could be at the forefront of new research leading to a very new application that would change the life of sleep apnea sufferers.

One of the hallmarks of sleep apnea is daytime sleepiness. Such patients fall asleep anytime they quit activity. When treated with CPAP (Continuous Positive Airway Pressure), a machine is connected with a nose or a full face mask and blows air under a constant pressure through nose and mouth and thus keeps the airway passage open. It prevents the airway to collapse, thus preventing the obstructive apnea from occurring. This mechanical treatment is 100% effective against sleep apnea, when used in the appropriate way and anytime one sleeps.

The problem that often persists, in spite of strongly reduced apnea, is daytime sleepiness. Robert thought that a drug against excessive sleepiness in patients well treated for apnea would be of true benefit. They would be able to once again function in society and enjoy their family life.

"You know better than I what it all means," the executive droned on, having in fact lost the attention of most of the audience for they did indeed 'know better.' They also knew that one of the major complaints in these patients was excessive sleepiness, whereas their partners usually complained about the patient's heavy snoring, restlessness and gasping for air.

"However," the executive said, "many sleep apnea patients who are well treated and in which their apnea is drastically reduced, experience a persistent fatigue and sleepiness. That is where BeWake comes into play. We hypothesize that in those patients we will be able to demonstrate a drastic reduction or even absence of sleepiness. That is precisely what we want to investigate. I will leave it to my research collaborators to provide you with a more detailed account of the results of their studies. Thereafter, we will go into the details of the clinical study."

He paused, smiled and concluded, "I thank you for coming to this meeting. During the meeting, you can ask questions at any time. It will be several intensive days, but we know that you will enjoy the accommodations here and the excellent food. Tomorrow afternoon is free and for those who want to visit Nassau, we have arranged for a bus. Thank you again for being here."

Robert did not learn much that he did not already know, so his attention drifted. During the research session, however, the investigators spent time explaining the evidence they had obtained that BeWake was not a stimulant such as amphetamine, Dexedrine or Ritalin. People taking the drug did not feel any kind of a jolting sensation; neither did they have an increased heart rate or nervous and jittery feelings. It just kept them alert and awake.

The researchers explained the biochemistry behind it and ended with a statement that researchers commonly make: "At this time, we don't know the mechanism. We do know that it does not work on the dopamine receptors, which are activated by classical stimulants. In fact, our biochemical tests failed to show an effect on any of the known neurotransmitters. We need to do more research."

Dr. Philipson, the self-proclaimed smart-ass, couldn't stop himself from prolonging the session by asking unanswerable questions, which the company researchers had just told everybody they could not explain.

At the lunch break, Robert sat at a round table with seven other investigators who conversed about the organization of the meeting, their accommodations and food, all to everyone's satisfaction.

This was shaping up to be a good meeting, but towards the end of the first day, everyone's attention span had dropped dramatically. The last hour between 5 and 6 p.m. was supposed to be a Q-and-A session, guided by the VP of research at MPRI, Dr. Jack Emmers.

Although he was a well-respected scientist, people were too tired for another lengthy session so, after ten minutes, Dr. Emmers declared that "We've had a long and fruitful meeting today. I see tired faces and understand. Let's call it quits for now. Enjoy dinner and tomorrow after a good night's sleep, we'll start again."

Someone in the audience chirped up, "Maybe we can get a sample of BeWake for tomorrow?"

Everybody laughed, pushed their chairs back in and streamed out of the conference room to wait at the elevators. Time for relaxing, to freshen up and be ready for dinner.

At dinner, Robert sat with other clinicians discussing the meeting and the information they had been given. All agreed that if the drug did what it was supposed to, counteracting the excessive sleepiness in apnea patients well treated for their apnea, it could indeed be a promising drug. One of the questions that remained in everyone's mind was whether this was genuinely a drug without the stimulant effects like amphetamine. No one had yet had personal experience with the drug and they hoped that they could eventually get a sample to try out, something that was unlikely to happen. The company was not there to make them drug takers. Most said that they would like to try it anyhow.

Robert enjoyed the discussion with his colleagues and the Caribbean food served. With ample wine and beer, people relaxed from their first intensive day.

* * *

The clinical sessions during the second morning went along unremarkably. The questions were reasonable, well formulated without being overly aggressive. Not surprising, given that one doesn't look a gift horse in the mouth. They were the chosen ones, paid guests, and most were there to acquire the complete manual and a signed contract for the research.

This was such a 180-degree difference from the scientific meetings where questions were challenging and occasionally even hostile, meant to undermine and discredit a presenter's research findings. Questions would typically start somewhere along the lines of "Your presentation was well prepared and clear in its conclusions...," and then would follow "...however, doctor, your conclusions are totally wrong, for they are based on the wrong premises..." Robert had experienced that type of aggressive discussion where a thick skin is needed to not to take such attacks personally. They also illustrated researchers' over-sized egos. In every discipline there are the capo's, the ones who dominate and determine who is who and who get the benefits.

Robert knew that the focus of the research was to find out whether the drug counteracted the excessive sleepiness with patients who were already adequately treated for their sleep apnea. Together with others he wondered about the possible side effects, because the drug had amphetamine-like properties. The company was indicating that there were no side effects, with the exception of those seen as in most studies, such as headache, one of the most common side effects and seen even in patients treated with a placebo.

That afternoon a scheduled time off gave everyone the opportunity to be a tourist. One of the investigators in the group was Fran Jones, who Robert knew from when both were post-docs together. They took a bus for the short trip from their hotel over the bridge to Nassau. He caught her up about his work at the university, his move to a company, the terrors while being laid off and then the new position in Dallas. They strolled by the jewelry and liquor stores, the dark skinned Bahamians, the pale-skinned tourists and the cruise ship passengers haggling over the price of cheap tourista stuff.

Robert looked around to find a quiet bar and spotted one on a side street. After they got comfortable there and ordered drinks, Fran finished bringing Robert up to date on her life and then asked,

"I heard that your sales rep in Dallas is Jeff Sanders - right?

"Yes. Do you know him?"

"I do, and more than I care to. He used to live in Michigan. Be very careful with him, Robert. He is a snitch, not at all trustworthy. I fell for his smile, which he lost as soon as he was alone with me. My resisting his advances made him load up MPRI execs with lies about me, which in turn lost me my research grant sponsored by MPRI. Fortunately I knew the VP of research well enough to get back into the picture again."

"At least I am not planning to date him," Robert said, making a meek attempt at some humor while also cognizant that he could be in serious jeopardy, should Sanders fall for Priscilla's favors.

The meeting concluded, Robert returned home, with a research contract. He had scored big time, as was reflected in his year-end bonus. Christmas with Anna was pure bliss.

31

Holiday festivities involved a rash of elaborate house light decorations throughout Dallas. The bigger, the better, that was Texas-style. Between the million dollar homes and the neighborhood competitions, the light shows were nothing short of spectacular. Robert found driving along Hillcrest a risky business. Drivers slowed down to marvel at the reindeers with their blinking red noses, the small stable with Mary and Joseph, angels in the pine trees, rainbow colors and twinkling white lights on the gutters and along the sides of the driveways.

Christmas time is traditionally about peace and friendship, forgetting squabbles, the ongoing wars and financial troubles, and everyone being of good will. Christmas is also a time of shopping and then going back to the stores the day after to return purchases, or for some people, to make money off the presents they received. Robert considered it amazing that the busiest shopping day in the US is after Christmas, when the big returns and swapping occurred.

For Anna and Robert, who had the week off, it was a time of taking a deep breath and relaxing from an intense year. They stayed home and celebrated together, rather than mixing with the masses traveling to their family members. They mingled with other shoppers at the large three-level Galleria Mall. Robert visited specialty stores selling paper of all kinds and colors, calligraphy lettering equipment, blank page books bound in heavy leather, exclusive fountain pens, olive oils of different grades coming from a variety of countries, teas from Ceylon and Japan and Sumatra with exotic aromas and flavors to savor.

Robert and Anna spent hours in the bookstores pouring over the Christmas releases and the bargain books, which people buy to put on a coffee table, but to read never.

They also spent time reviewing and discussing the past year. A big issue was what the extra benefits would be that Imcare had spoken about the year before.

His answer arrived at Imcare's Christmas party on the last Friday before Christmas. Robert got a phone call from Priscilla asking whether she could be sure that he would attend the reception. He assured her he would be there. Some employees were dressed formally; a lot of them in red blouses and dresses, but the nurses wore Santa hats, funny boots and stockings. The men wore traditional suits and white shirts decorated by colorful holiday ties.

Milton, Priscilla's assistant, welcomed Robert with a nametag and even wished him a fun time at the party. He added that "Ms. Jackson has an important envelope for you." The few times Robert had been around Milton, he seemed to be the typical bureaucrat, kissing up to his boss. For the first time, Robert noted a kind of intelligence behind Milton's downcast eyes and his expressionless facade. Milton might have appeared to be looking down at the well-shined shoes, but he saw and heard it all. He was Priscilla's right hand man and she probably learned from him what was happening out on the floor, a place she only swept through, seeing, hearing and speaking to no one. The devil wears Priscilla.

Towards the end of the party, people started making spontaneous speeches, all saying how great everybody was. Robert eagerly awaited hearing Priscilla's message. On behalf of the doctors she thanked Dr. Cohen, the Chief, for being allowed to announce that there would be a distribution of a profit sharing of 4%. "Therefore, nurses and administrators," she said, "thanks to the generosity of the doctors who generated the income, everyone will be having a truly merry Christmas. Of course, as you all understand, the doctors have their own business arrangements within Imcare." Subsequently, Priscilla distributed individual envelopes to them.

Priscilla held Robert's hand longer than necessary. With a mischievous grin, she pulled him near and whispered that he should be pleased and grateful to her for what was inside his envelope, adding yes, what a shame that he was so tight-assed. She released his hand, and Robert made a beeline for the other side of the room where he took a glass of eggnog, smiled at a few nurses he knew from the clinic and chitchatted with a few others. It did not take long before he was slipping out a side door.

He pulled up the collar of his coat against a biting wind and got into his car. For a second he twisted the letter size thick envelope around in his hands. He wanted to peek inside but then decided to wait. Anna should join him in the surprise.

"Let's open the envelope and find out what they have for us," he said. He ripped it apart and ran his finger over the lines, quickly turning the pages. His smile broadened. "Time for celebration." He received 4% profit sharing. This added nicely to the 5% raise of his renewed contract, substantially helping them recover from the former financial obligation.

There was more, the administrators of Imcare had added a new clause to the section of income. After costs, he would receive a partial distribution of the profit generated by the research. Robert read this lengthy paragraph multiple times as it was a carefully crafted lawyer's piece of confounding statements with many stipulations pointing out restrictions and exclusions. The probability of seeing any of that money appeared doubtful. Nevertheless, he was neither displeased nor dissatisfied.

They had been listening to his requests and had at least added the potential that in the long run, the research projects could generate additional income. His calculations were that after costs, they would still generate a net profit of over $100,000 for Imcare. Robert expected a nice bonus in the coming year and there could be more, if he succeeded in acquiring more research contracts.

Anna and Robert opened a bottle of champagne and toasted to further success. Today, as an exception they had bought a Moët & Chandon. Robert recalled the cheap sparkling wine they were drinking just a few years ago. They took small sips of the champagne, savoring the tingling on their tongue and throat, the mixture of sweetness and acidity, all of which ended in a delicate aftertaste lingering on. Half of the bottle was stored. "For tomorrow maybe?" Robert smiled.

Any dinner by Anna was a superior event. The main dish was rabbit prepared with dark Belgian beer. Robert wanted to open a 10-year-old Bordeaux, Chateau Latour, Saint Emilion Grand cru, but Anna preferred to drink a dark Belgian Ale from the Abbey of Affligem, which suited this recipe perfectly. Thus, a beer it was.

By eleven at night, they had become sleepy but continued reminiscing about the Christmas times when they went skiing at cozy resorts in the Dolomites in the north of Italy. They recalled how on Christmas Eve, when the chimes of the pink colored church of the village of Dobbiaco rang, they plowed through the piles of snow to the local church to attend the midnight Christmas Mass. They listened to the local choirs, singing German Christmas songs in the Süd-Tirol accent and enjoyed the native interpretation of the birth of Jesus played by local farmers and employees of the hotels.

Süd-Tirol in the northern region of Italy was mostly German speaking, because during history they belonged and separated repeatedly from Austria. Fierce battles were fought for freedom and independence, but now this southern part of Germany belonged to Italy. Their license plates said 'I' with the 'I' standing for Italy at the top, but the statement below, 'bin ein Süd-Tiroler,' 'I am a South Tiroler', made clear that in their mind they did not belong to either Italy or Austria, except for the language being spoken: German. Robert preferred to listen to the singing of the melodic Italian, the language of Verdi's operas and the great tenors from Enrico Caruso to Luciano Pavarotti.

While these memories were good, even better was his life now with Anna. How blessed he was being with Anna, having reached a standard of living they could only have dreamt about. The research program was the icing on the cake of his success, which he would devour with great enthusiasm.

32

Other than turning the page and switching to another calendar, the New Year passed uneventfully. Robert had abandoned his practice of sending cards or email to friends and family as he used to. This custom belonged to the past. A few years earlier, during the week after New Year, he took a seat behind his computer and waited for the holiday greetings to arrive. There were hardly any, with the exception of long messages from a few good friends. Now, if he received a New Year's wish by email or through regular mail, he returned it, but with the deeper recognition that this was a time for family, as well as a resting point before the onset of the New Year.

Other than switching to another calendar year, the New Year passed uneventful. The holidays were a time for the family, as well as a resting point before the onset of the New Year. For Robert, the onset meant getting the research program into full swing. He assembled all the documents needed for the patients and for the Company's registry folder. The latter contained the complete documentation of the drug and a copy of all the papers that the patient had completed during the study. An important section was the patient event registry. Every single event that occurred with a patient reported as a negative or having a different effect had to be meticulously documented. The company needed to know all the possible side effects, beneficial or otherwise, that the drug could possibly be generated.

According to a secret code, the patients were randomly divided into two groups, those who received the drug and the others a placebo, a 'sugar pill' that looked exactly like the real drug. Even Robert did not know who received the active drug or the placebo. After six months in the study, the patient groups would switch from placebo to pill or the reverse.

People who received the placebo sometimes experienced or reported similar side effects as the ones who received the drug. In many clinical research studies, one of the most common side effects reported was headache. The question then was whether there were more people reporting headache in the drug group than in the placebo group. Often, it was not. For the company it was particularly worth finding out whether there were more or other side effects with the new medication than with placebo. Serious side effects could lead to a cessation of the studies and dropping the further development of a drug.

Continuing with the clinical work of seeing patients and working full time on research were two almost incompatible pursuits. Robert needed help and Priscilla promised to provide it. Robert pointed out that Jennifer, one of the sleep center technicians, had experience with the lab and as such would be a valuable addition to the team. Her task was to file all the papers in the appropriate folders or binders, enter notes into the documents on what failed or key issues to deal with and keep track of the flow of the study. Robert felt secure that Jennifer would do a great job and that she would work outside the hours she worked for the hospital, so that they could not claim that Imcare took employees away from the hospital. It took a while before Priscilla agreed.

What they needed most of all was a Clinical Research Coordinator, a CRC as they commonly are called, maybe a nurse who could coordinate the research activities, take blood pressures, the weight of the patients, collect blood samples and make sure that the patients were following all their instructions. Clinical research in that sense is not an exciting business. It is tedious and one has to be precise in following the rules of the protocol and completing all documents. Robert's role as Principal Investigator was overall responsibility. He had to study the documents, make sure that everything was being done according the rules, sign off on all documents and see to it that the study ran as it was supposed to.

Jeff Sanders came to deliver the coded drugs and visited briefly with Robert and Jennifer before heading off to see Priscilla, where he had contractual issues to discuss. He worried that a Clinical Research Coordinator had not yet been hired, but was sure that Priscilla would take care of this. "In due course," Sanders said and winked at Robert's assistant.

* * *

Priscilla's cell phone lay on her desk, ringing and ringing. Milton looked at the phone, hesitating to pick it up. She was going to one of the offices and would return in a few minutes, she'd said. He looked at the door and then back at the insistently ringing cell phone.

Compelled to answer it, he picked up the phone. It felt heavy in his hand. Strange number, but maybe one of the doc's in the hospital. He pushed Listen and slowly lifted the phone to his ear. Before he could say a word, he heard Dr. Salvo' voice saying, "Two-for 6:30." He quickly pressed the red button and put the phone back down on the desk. Milton's primary ambition was to become indispensable to his Priscilla, but much to his chagrin, Dr. Salvo had become a serious rival for her attentions.

Precisely when Priscilla returned, the phone rang again. She ran to her desk, grabbed the phone, listened and said, "No, I didn't." Then she glanced at Milton and kicked the door to her office closed.

Several minutes later, she opened the door. Her cheeks flushed pink. "Did you pick up my phone?" she asked in as neutral a tone as she could muster, but it was as counterfeit as her innocent look.

"Yes, I did, but I noticed that it came from the hospital and switched it off." Milton tried to keep his cool and looked behind her.

"Never pick up my cell phone again, understood?"

"Of course, Ms. Jackson."

Milton went back to his desk, waves of jealousy surging through his veins.

* * *

When Salvo entered their room in the hospital basement at 6:30 p.m., he did not immediately embrace and kiss Priscilla, but inquired instead, "Any trouble with that 'incident,' as you call it?"

"I don't think so. Milton isn't the swiftest, just a lowly clerk who wants to do everything right. He won't make that mistake again. You needn't worry. Trust me."

"Every time anybody says 'trust me' I get the shivers." This caught her by surprise.

Salvo waved his hand, preventing Priscilla from responding. "I know that does not apply to you, but this incident," he emphasized, "this incident shows that we can't be careful enough."

Priscilla donned a huge smile, walked up to him, but as she went to speak, Salvo planted a kiss on her lips and then said that they had important business to get to. Vermeer needed a clinical research coordinator and Salvo thought that Laura Owens would be the perfect candidate. She was a nurse and wife of the Gynecologist who helped at the delivery of his children. Laura Owens didn't have much to do, and he was sure that she would readily accept the position. She was a good nurse, who might appear nice and cheerful but could actually be nasty as a snake.

"And that," Salvo ordained, "is exactly the CRC we need, a 'family member'."

Priscilla sulked, still rolling 'the incident' over in her mind. Salvo nudged her on the butt and said "Come on, this is good news. Let's have a drink."

She pulled out a bottle of single malt whiskey and poured two glasses. Yes, she agreed as he said, it was good news. Not only would no one dare object to the Laura Owen candidacy, they were also the ones who hired, paid, and fired. By giving Laura the reins over Robert, she could make his life a notch more complicated.

33

The next day, Priscilla went to see Robert in his office. Binders and folders cluttered his desk. His eyes glued to the computer screen, Robert did not even look up when she walked in. As usual, his door was halfway open, signaling that he could be disturbed. "Yes," he said, waiting for someone to say something. She stood, surveying him. When he looked up, he acted surprised, as if she had caught him in some naughty act.

"Sorry for the mess."
"Research. Right?"
He nodded.

Priscilla told him that they would not have to search for a Clinical Research Coordinator. "We have found the perfect candidate for you. Her name is Laura Owens. She is a nurse and married to one of our doctors. Couldn't be better, one of the family."

Robert asked whether this nurse had research experience. Priscilla avoided answering by stressing that this candidate had extensive experience as a nurse and that she was a good administrator.

"Trust me," she said with secret amusement, thinking about Salvo. "Trust me. You will meet her soon," and left as abruptly as he appeared.

"Well, well," mumbled Robert.

Eager to start with the project, Robert assumed he would be meeting Laura Owens in the next few days. Patient selection was the first item on the agenda and he had already reviewed a large number of charts selected by Jennifer. All these patients had sleep apnea and were obese to morbidly obese and were all being treated with CPAP ('the inverted vacuum cleaner', blowing air under pressure in nose and mouth to keep the airway passage open during sleep). Based on a questionnaire and some simple tests the severity of their daytime sleepiness could be determined.

Robert felt some degree of apprehension because he had not been involved in Laura's selection process. Despite a gut instinct warning him not to trust Priscilla, he convinced himself that since she knew the candidate that was a good enough endorsement. Now he needed to develop not just a good working relationship, but an excellent one with this CRC, for the research project to move smoothly in the right direction. While Robert was pondering this, one of the receptionists came to his office about a sales rep out front, who urgently wanted to talk to him. Robert consented seeing him.

A middle-aged man with a closed lip smile on a round face with slightly receding blond hair introduced himself as John Rogers, a representative for 'Sertur Pharmaceutics. He said that he knew Robert did not have much time, but maybe he could spare a few minutes to listen to his proposal. Half an hour later, they were still talking.

The representative had done his homework on Robert and knew his capabilities and experience. Sertur had discovered new variations of existing drugs and developed them fast, including the necessary clinical trials. They had a new sleeping pill, which worked against sleep onset insomnia as well as against sleep maintenance insomnia, which causes people to wake up early and not be able to continue sleeping. He wondered whether Robert was interested in a clinical research project in which they would compare the new drug with an existing sleeping pill and compare the two with a placebo. It would be a three-group study with a switchover of the groups every three-month period.

Even though Robert was taken with the possibility of a second research contract on a subject he was highly interested in, he hesitated to commit because he could not afford doing two research projects at the same time. Anticipating such a comment, the sales rep said that, at this stage, he just wanted to know whether there was even an interest in that project. If yes, Robert would gain access to the basic documents describing the drug and the goals of the study.

Moreover, the sales rep convinced Robert that this was also too early in the process to involve Imcare. Robert could sign on his own account, because it was not a research contract, which would indeed require an Imcare signature as well. It all sounded logical, so Robert agreed to sign a confidentiality agreement stipulating his interest in the study. After shaking hands, the sales rep handed Robert a thick folder. If it came to fruition, a second contract would kick up the total value of the research contracts to $ 600,000, not bad for a first year and something that Gary Cohen would surely have to appreciate.

* * *

After accompanying the sales rep to the reception area, Robert made a quick detour over to the techs. A full-bodied woman with a determined gait, followed by Priscilla, entered the sleep center. She stopped right ahead of him and asserted in a strong voice "Nice to meet you, Dr. Vermeer. I'm Laura Owens."

"Is Robert the first name?" she asked. Robert did not want to appear offended, but his European ears and manners were not accustomed to such a bold approach.

Priscilla rushed to add, "At Imcare we are on first name basis. We are a family, aren't we, Robert?"

So not so, thought Robert, but that little skirmish was over before it began. While he would have preferred to keep some distance from Laura Owens, she was clearly on an equal footing with him and someone he would have to cultivate.

Laura looked around, taking stock as to whether this was the place she wanted to be. Robert told her that he would give her a tour, but he first wanted to talk to her about the project and his expectations. "Won't you please join me in my office…"

"Give Laura the grand tour, Robert." Priscilla broke in. "She wants to see where she will be working during the coming months."

Overruled, Robert swallowed his pride and submitted to Priscilla's bidding.

At the end of the tour, Robert again suggested going to his office, but widening her mouth to expose her teeth and upper gum and speaking in tones indicating their time together has expired.

"I'll just start tomorrow."

She reminded Robert of chimps when they grimaced. Couldn't tell whether that was a sign of pleasure or a 'Don't mess with me' warning.

"OK?"

Stirring from his chimp imagery, Robert said "Sure. How about eight o'clock, or is that too late for you?" That's when he got the answer he least expected.

"No, that won't work. I have to take my kids to school. It will have to be nine o'clock."

Bearing in mind she was not only an Imcare employee, but also one of Priscilla's cronies, Robert told her that he did not insist on fixed hours, as long as the job was done and at least eight hours were completed each day. He rued those words the instant they left his lips. He knew he had lost control of her before she had even started and this would set a bad example for the techs, bound to the hospital structure. However, as an Imcare employee, Laura was under Priscilla's protective wings, beyond his and the hospital's reach.

The next day Laura strolled in at 9:15 a.m. and gave Robert an earful on what it was like to have gifted children. After letting her ramble on as long as he could stand, Robert interjected with "Let's get down to business," and pointed to the binder with the patient selections.

"We have to begin finding patients and locking them into the study. There will be financial rewards for us and the patients will have had the eventual benefit of getting a drug that will make their life better," Robert told her in solemn tones.

"I recommend that you first read the company binder containing all the project information. Once you are done with that, we can arrange for a meeting so you can ask me any questions. I attended the investigators meeting so I have a good grasp of what's involved."

Laura started calling patients and kept busy the entire day. For Robert it was a welcome respite, getting back to analyzing sleep studies, dictating reports and spending time in the clinic.

34

A month after Laura Owens started her new job as the CRC, Milton called to arrange a meeting in Priscilla's office with her and Dr. Salvo. Laura wasn't told the subject of the meeting, just that Dr. Vermeer was not invited.

She knew Dr. Salvo through her Gynecologist husband and liked the young doctor with the persuasive smile, even more so because he radiated confidence and appeared to have a strong character. She also knew he was one of the rising stars in the doctors' group and had the protection of the chief. Recently, he had finally passed the first exam towards his board certification in sleep medicine. A demanding work schedule was the dispensation that Salvo was affording himself for needing two attempts at this accomplishment.

"It's nicer meeting here, rather than out at the Center," Priscilla said by way of introduction. "Some coffee, Laura?"

Salvo smiled, relinquishing the social lead to Priscilla. Then, following up on it, he said, "We want to make sure, Laura, that you are feeling comfortable with us. Do you like working at the Center?"

"Sure."

"Is the study proceeding as expected?"

She answered yes and added that not much was happening yet, as the work so far was preparatory to getting enough patients to commit to the study.

"You are not being hampered by anyone, are you? Especially Vermeer. He has ambitions we suspect are going beyond the study," said Salvo.

Then he informed Laura that she, not Robert Vermeer, was the one leading the study. Although Vermeer had been given the impression that as the Principal Investigator he had the lead in making decisions, he was actually just a glorified paper pusher. She was the one controlling the coming and going of patients; Robert's menial tasks did not fall within the scope of her realm.

"We have big plans for you, Laura. After all, you, not Vermeer, belong to the family. Yes, he is the PI of the study, but under the direction of Imcare, which is something he seems to forget," Salvo said in a not-to-misunderstand tone. "By the way, in reading the work schedule I requested from Jennifer, I noticed that you are supposed to be here during the weekends."

"Yes, and between the kids and my husband's schedule, that's going to be really tough on me."

"No, it won't. Robert's not on call during the weekends so he can fill in for you. He can play the CRC. Just arrange it on the agenda so that the patients studied over the weekends are his."

Laura was astounded. She had won herself free weekends for at least six months, not to mention that during the week she came and went as she wished. This job was getting better and better.

"Obviously, this is not going to sit well with Vermeer. What happens when he questions my authority on setting that agenda?"

"In that event, send him to Priscilla. And if that doesn't work, I'll handle it," he said smugly to this new member of their club.

Then, in closing the business aspects of the meeting, he inquired "How is your family doing?"

* * *

Robert sat in his office studying the binder with the selected patients. They had enrolled enough patients in the study. The first three had come for a sleep study that week, and according to plan, two weeks later for the required overnight study with scheduled daytime naps, bloods drawn and different paper testing during Saturday and Sunday.

He studied the protocol and discovered that if they had started two days earlier, they could have avoided any weekend work. Robert accepted that such things might happen. Planning did not always work, and this planning could have been better.

A matter Laura had not taken into consideration was that in the morning, before administering the other tests, the patients had to undergo a brief physical exam and have their bloods drawn. Either Salvo or Stone had to conduct the physical exams, meaning that one of them had to come to the center before 7 a.m. on Saturday and Sunday. Since they were not asked to actively participate in the study, Robert knew this could be a thorny issue, certainly for James who balked and bitched for days when he was scheduled to be on call.

Studying the protocol further, Robert saw his name in big red letters marked to work every weekend. This involved starting at 6:30 in the morning to prepare the documents for the physicians to perform their physical exam and the material for the patients' blood samplings. After taking the samples, Robert had to run to the hospital lab to centrifuge the blood and store the samples on ice, ready for shipment to the Matterson Pharmaceutical Research Institute Company, for assessment of the drug levels. Every two hours throughout the day, patients took a brief nap and then completed questionnaires before and afterwards in order to rate their levels of sleepiness and alertness. Testing was scheduled up to 4:30 in the afternoon. This was part of the job as a CRC, but it appeared he had now inherited that role and gone would be his dearly beloved weekends.

He would ask Jennifer about the altered agenda, confident that not she, but Laura was the one who had done so. Pointing towards the big binder on his desk, Robert asked Jennifer whether she had modified the agenda.

"Is there something wrong with the planner, Dr. Vermeer?"

"Yes. Everything is wrong, but nothing I think that I can ascribe to you. As far as I know, scheduling is not part of your job. I just need to confirm that detail."

"Right, I'm not the one who deals with scheduling, Sir."

He paused a few seconds and then said, "Can you call Laura into my office?"

"She's not here. She usually isn't here for much of the afternoon. Sometimes she comes back in the evenings, but it is fairly unpredictable."

She added as an afterthought "Mostly she's here when Dr. Salvo is here."

With all the other work going on, he had become distracted from what was happening with Laura. He remembered initially giving her wide leeway, a really stupid mistake.

Calling her cell phone, he reached her 'leave a message' voice recording. An hour passed before she returned his call. Robert wasted that hour pacing, unable to concentrate on his sleep study interpretations.

Once he got to speaking with her, she told him "You just have no idea how hard I am working and with no appreciation for all the help I am giving you." Practically choking on his words, Robert replied, 'That, Laura, is what is involved with the job of a clinical research coordinator. On a separate matter, however, what is with my working every weekend? Might we be rescheduling the patients?"

"That is something the protocol does not allow us to do. Besides, you are the PI and as I understand it, you share the work with me. Also," she said matter-of-factly, "you don't have kids and a doctor husband to take care of."

Literally swallowing his anger, Robert said, "We'll talk about this further tomorrow morning, Laura."

"Fine," she said and hung up.

* * *

When Laura walked into his office the next morning, Robert was wound up tight as a watch spring. Sporting her teeth and gums smile, she looked like someone who had already won whatever battle was to be waged.

With jaws fixed tightly, Robert looked at her as calmly and placidly as he could. Good that his desk stood between them.

Not offering her a seat, Robert asked, "What can you tell me, Laura, about the weekend work assignments? You put me on the weekend schedule without even discussing with me. I am the PI, in case you have forgotten."

"And the PI carries the highest responsibility, Robert," she added sarcastically, striking a crowning blow with her next remark.

"I cannot attend to patients over the weekends, it's just that simple."

"-Haven't I told you that I am not responsible for your weekend activities?" Robert inquired.

"Exactly, we never talked about weekends and in any event, my weekends are devoted to my family."

"You knew that clinical research might require weekend work. Are you now saying that, as a CRC, you did not know this? In addition, I told you before that I did not want to restrict your schedule, precisely because clinical research involves by definition working outside a 9 to 5 day. You appear to be more interested in convenience than in making sure this project runs smoothly and becomes a success."

"Don't forget, Doctor, that I am an employee of Imcare, not yours."

Robert's blood pressure rose so high that his vision began to blur. Leaning back into his chair, he put his hands together as if to pray.

"Doctor, we both want to carry on with the study the best we can, but weekend work is totally excluded in my agreement," she announced firmly.

Robert was well aware that there was nothing mentioned in the contract about hours to work, either during the week or weekend. The CRC' duties involve anything necessary to fulfill the requirements of the protocol. This smacked of purely Priscilla-type tactics. For a while, he remained silent and then said in measured tones, "You will see to it that the doctors are informed that one of them needs to be present in the morning of every single weekend day for the duration of the study."

Replying with "Is that it?" Laura left his office, reminding him that "By the way, patients are waiting to get their first instructions."

* * *

That same afternoon James came by Robert's office declaring, "You take the blood samples over the weekends. I'm too busy."

Robert begged the question by telling him, "The issue, James, is not the blood sampling. I can do that, but the study requires a physician to do the physical. I am not saying you, but if it is not you, it has to be Salvo or some other Imcare physician. I suggest you - talk to each other and let me know who to expect to cover that base.

Hoping to incentivize James, Robert added, "Remember, James, that, by co-signing the contractual agreement, we committed to doing this research which translates in your having a stake in the profits as well."

"Just so you know," countered James before dashing back to his office, "I was never interested in doing a research study, and Salvo is more than welcome to take over my part of the damn contract and collect those pennies for himself."

The clinic had been working well, and relationships with the patients had grown into ones of mutual understanding and appreciation. Now the doctors' unwillingness to commit threatened to rupture those relationships, something Robert could not allow to occur. Consequently, he promised to be particularly helpful to James during the consultation days and hoped against hope to see Salvo turning up on the weekends.

* * *

Robert sat in one of the bedrooms with one of the study patients, William, a big 280-pound African American. When they shook hands, Robert detected how like a child's hand William's was, not at all like that of a former football player.

"Hi Doc," William said, "With the good Lord on our side, I will be helping you with your study. Sure hope I get the drug, rather than a sugar pill. Guess you can't take care of that, but I am so sleepy that I need the real stuff."

Robert explained again that he did not know who got what, but maybe the Lord could make sure that he got the real stuff.

"Not on drugs otherwise, are you, William?"

"Of course not, as clean as a whistle, Doc."

"I need you to answer a series of questions, so that we can have a better idea of your sleeping habits. I'm expecting you to give me honest answers, as I hope you understand that this is for your benefit as well."

"Want to know more about my life? Not a problem, Doc, but can you do me a favor and fill this out for me?"

Robert surmised that William's reading skills were not up to par, or maybe he could not read at all. Inserting the questionnaire onto the clipboard, Robert started writing in the name and date. As he asked about William's sleep habits and sleepiness during the day, Robert studied William, probing to determine whether his answers were honest. Not that patients lied, but in the presence of a doctor, they tended to exaggerate their symptoms. The questionnaire considered that possibility and to some extent circumvented that issue through multiple similar questions in different forms.

Over time, William became one of Robert's favorite patients. He diligently performed all tasks and never forgot to turn in a completed form, although in the handwriting of a child, perhaps his daughter's, of whom he was so proud that he brought picture after picture of her to every session. Both his kids and his wife were the loves of his life and a source of intense pleasure. Each encounter with William was a happy moment for Robert who respected the battle of losing weight and keeping it down, along with the burden of extreme sleepiness in apnea patients.

Robert continued seeing the patients for the study, all happy to participate and hoping they were getting the drug rather than placebo. Their daytime sleepiness was interfering so much that they were missing out on a lot of life.

It did not take long to become evident which patients were getting the drug and which were not. At least Robert could tell, based on the increased alertness and diminished sleepiness of a number of patients, or where there was no change or some deterioration. On Saturday or Sundays, he could visit with the patients individually in between tests. He learned about their lives, occasionally more than he wished to know. Both the patients and Robert were always pleased to see 4:30 come in the afternoon and the testing finished.

The early mornings were an ordeal, not because of the patients, but because of Stone and Salvo's vile attitude each time they entered the center. They considered their work, which lasted fifteen minutes at most, a colossal disruption of their weekends. Robert didn't say word one about how much worse it was for him.

By June, Robert had worked every weekend. Pressures had increased to such an extent that he started regretting ever starting this study in the first place. Laura did her job, complaining nonstop about the too many forms to complete. Yet, around -Salvo, she was upbeat and cheerful. Priscilla came by a few times to speak with Laura and acted as if Robert wasn't even there.

Although Robert was laser-like focused on getting his work done, he started sensing a growing animosity toward him and wondered the reason or reasons for it. Was it jealousy because of his success in increasing the prestige to the Center and extra income for the group or, -was it - incidents -from the past that contributed to a negative impact on him? Sensing such a displeasure haunted him.

Between the atmosphere in the Center turning so menacing and Robert's vain attempts to determine what he wasn't seeing in the big scheme of things, Robert cherished being at home now more than ever.

35

Sundays at the Center were the worst. The timing of a sleep nap followed by a questionnaire every two hours did not allow for any other activity, other than hanging out with patients or one of the two techs. The only busy period was early in the morning when Robert prepared all the documents and handled blood samples, readying them for shipment to MPRI for further evaluation. He filled the rest of the time by reviewing forms for completeness and waiting for the next event.

It was close to 5 p.m. and Sunday evening had already started. With luck, he could still enjoy some sun by the pool. This particular Sunday he and Anna were hosting a barbecue with Charlie and Maureen. It had been a long time since their last visit. Robert hadn't spoken to Charlie since the month before, when he had been seeing Dr. Stone about a medication to stop the cancer from spreading to other organs. Charlie was taking it as a therapy after completing chemo and radiation for the tumor in his chest.

Robert was exhilarated about being with his buddy again. Maureen brought a bouquet of flowers for Anna, two big kisses, and a hug for Robert. She went out to the kitchen with Anna as Charlie and Robert hugged and slapped each other's back. For a sick guy, Charlie looked good. Only when he spoke could one detect that things were not OK.

"How are you, Charlie?"

"Just fine, just fine," he said automatically. How typically American, thought Robert, even for those like Charlie who hadn't lived all his years in the US. By answering 'everything is fine', they deny how they truly feel because it would be too intimate to reveal such personal information or they would feel forced to go into unpleasant details. Most people have an aversion to listening to complaints or sorrows because they do not want to become involved or committed. To Robert, this was, in a sense, avoiding applying the spirit of care. How sad, thought Robert, that Americans must always be "Fine," "Great," or "Wonderful."

Robert remembered the first trip he had made to the States. He was invited to present a lecture at the Federation of American Societies of Experimental Biology in Anaheim, California, which brought together a large number of scientists of different disciplines. Since it was a chance for a combination science and pleasure trip, Robert brought Anna with him.

Their overseas travel had been an ordeal and they arrived at the Howard Johnson Hotel in Anaheim, exhausted from coping with the nine-hour time difference. Although it was a sunny day in Anaheim, everyone in Belgium had been in bed for quite a while.

Following a shower and nap, they crossed the street and entered an all-American restaurant. They headed toward a table, only to be stopped halfway by a server who, with one hand placed on her hip, waived the other hand with a menu in the direction of a 'Please waited to be seated' sign that they had overlooked. Soon after she escorted them to a table, another waitress came, presenting herself as Sue. Sue wore a pleasant smile and asked, "How are you doing?" That prompted Robert to embark on a lengthy explanation of how they had come all the way from Europe on that long American Airlines flight from Brussels, during which they had two dinners and movies and ... Sue's smile vanished. With a weary voice, she asked, "Have you looked at the menu? What do you want to eat?" Robert halted mid-sentence, bewildered as to why she had asked him how he was doing and then appeared to be not at all interested. They promptly selected a snack. Robert was disappointed, both in the sandwich and in Sue, thinking that perhaps his response to her "How are you doing?" -spoiled his chances for a better sandwich.

Indeed, Charlie's "I'm fine" was just another way of saying hello, because soon after, he was telling Robert just how not fine that he was.

"These doctors do what they learned to do, following some kind of a paradigm. After this, follows that. If the patient reacts this way, we change that medication, and then after blood testing, we adjust the dosage, and so on and so on," he said in a monotonous way. "Dr. Stone is a good doctor, dealing with allergies, snotty noses, congestive heart failure and most other serious lung diseases. But, like many physicians, he treats only the disease and forgets the person behind it or rather in front of him," Charlie said, his shoulders sunken. "He's forgotten me, because the medication he's prescribing me is causing me more problems than it's solving. Doctors swear the 'Do no harm' oath, but in spite of that or because of that, unknowingly or not, they give us drugs that kill the immune system. To them, they are choosing the lesser of two evils. But after a certain amount of those drugs, the body gives up."

Charlie had to take deep breaths. Speaking with such fervor tired him more than he wanted to admit. Robert leaned forward in his chair, looking closer at Charlie. Then Charlie loosened up and tossed out a smile saying,

"I want to hear how things are going with you, Robert, and don't leave anything out. And where are the girls? I'm starving."

On cue, Anna called out, "Hey, guys. Food's ready to put on the barbecue."

Robert and Charlie pulled off the Grill Master 550's protective green tarpaulin and placed it a few feet from the wall. After turning on the gas and pressing the switch, flames danced between the lava stones. Soon it would be hot. Anna and Maureen carried platters of shrimp, marinated sardines, chicken breasts, spicy sausage and paprika's and zucchinis. Roasted potatoes and a Russian salad of pineapple, olives and parsley completed the table. A bottle of extra virgin olive oil and a black pepper mill sat next to the salad bowl.

For this array of meat and seafood, Robert selected two different Pinot Noir wines. He explained that the dark red peel of the pinot noir grape was thin, tender, and sensitive to climate and soil and therefore, this burgundy grape exported from France was not easy to cultivate. The climate in the burgundy region of France was cold and humid and therefore exquisite Pinot Noir's can only be made in regions with a similar climate to that in France.

One of the bottles that Robert opened came from the cooler districts of South Australia, and the other was a Californian Mumm Pinot Noir from the Napa Valley. Robert selected wineglasses with rotund bowls and a slightly narrower opening, perfect from which to savor a Burgundy wine. He poured the wine up to the middle of the glass, that way one can more fully smell and taste the wine. Robert always had to stop American waiters who wanted to pour wine up to the top rim of the glass. To him, it seemed this was their way of emptying the bottle faster, and neglecting that wine needed first to be smelled after being swirled in the glass.

He wanted to fully appreciate the wine's taste and smell, its first sensation on the tongue and then its aftertaste. In a sense, it was like any enjoyment in life. It had to be appreciated in small quantities by taking the proper time to do so.

After ample time had been spent in tasting and comparing, they unanimously concluded that they did not need to drink a French wine to have an excellent one. And although both were good wines, the Californian Mumm Pinot Noir was an absolute topper. It was time to celebrate friendship.

When Anna came with the dessert of vanilla ice cream suffused with thick melted dark Belgian chocolate, everyone cheered. They indulged themselves by avoiding subjects too serious to spoil the joyous atmosphere and they knew to let go of their cares, relax, enjoy the food and the company. As always when they were together, conversation flowed like a babbling brook.

Without their noticing, the sky had begun darkening and the soft lights in the garden and around the pool were gradually growing in illumination. The fence's shadow spread over the pool reflecting the shadow that was spreading across all their minds. Everyone was waiting for a light to reveal their own thoughts.

As Anna served coffee and homemade cookies, Charlie broke the silence and told everyone that he had told Dr. Stone he was dissatisfied with traditional medicine and his proposed treatment. Before anyone could reply, Charlie lifted his hand and motioned that he was not yet done.

"I have to think about my next course of action, so allow me to say that I would appreciate it if you could give me time to think about what it will be. I cannot argue about something that I do not yet know about. Once I have had sufficient time to consider what I want to do, we can talk together, but not now."

The silence now weighed more heavily than before. That he disapproved of the treatment proposed by Dr. Stone bode ominously to Robert.

Charlie lifted his glass and said "Salud" to everyone. "Remember what I told you about our honeymoon in Zihuatanejo, Mexico, a few years ago? We swam in an Infiniti pool from which the water appeared to run straight into the sea. How great to have that happen with our lives, they merged seamlessly into the universe."

Maureen whispered into his ear and put her head on his shoulder. Anna and Robert stared ahead, contemplating less despairing times.

Charlie again broke the silence with "Don't look so sad, guys. I'm here, and I plan on staying quite a bit longer. The demons won't get me; my spirit is stronger than they are."

He lifted his glass again and said "To health." Once everyone had put down their glasses, Charlie repeated that he wanted to hear what was going on in Robert's work world.

Robert would have preferred to hear more from Charlie, but he acquiesced and said that things were going well. "In addition to one research project, I have signed a principal agreement for a second research contract. Imcare should be very pleased for the added revenue and besides that, we are developing a reputation for being researchers. Once we get a little more established, we will get even more contracts, which will be good not just for me. Research is not only fun to do, but also helps in finding better medications to help people and we can participate in the publishing and promotion of such research findings."

"This all sounds great, but what about you?" queried Charlie. "I can hardly imagine that you enjoy working hard during the week and then spending your weekends in the clinic as well. Do you really have fun?" He let the words sink and then asked, "When do you have time for yourself Robert?"

"Weekend work cannot be avoided, Charlie. My clinical research coordinator, a doctor's wife, scheduled the agenda that way, which is also according to the protocol that we are supposed to follow."

"I understand that, Robert, but at the same time, I don't. Why does it always have to be you? I thought there were other doctors involved and you had personnel to do that," Charlie said, while Anna was nodding in agreement.

"I started something that I did not realize would wind up like this."

"Are you telling me that you did not know in advance that this would happen?"

"Well, yes and no. I seem to be caught in my own flexibility with respect to the work schedule."

"Hold on, are you saying that this Laura put you in this position?" Charlie was shaking his head. Robert slumped into his chair, peeved by the fix he was in.

"You could say that. However, understand that I really want this project to succeed. I firmly believe it will help people, and as a bonus, it can lead to other research. I want to build a strong research program, because it is an integral part of what we do, something I explained to you before."

Robert could hear himself trying to convince himself of another lie. In truth, he was alone in his desire to do clinical research. He kept trusting the doctors' group would see the advantages of a research program where patients would be able to get cutting-edge care for their diseases and where the Center's reputation would lead to a higher number of referrals. In truth, the philosophy and mission of Imcare and company was simply about achieving a greener bottom line, nothing else.

Charlie insisted such a work schedule should not continue and that Robert could jeopardize his relationship with Anna. He also strongly questioned the role of his coordinator. This Laura woman did not sound right to him.

"You started a promising new venture, but it seems to be turning against you. I presume it's too late now to do anything but continue with it. Too bad," Charlie said, shaking his head.

Robert replied "Not really. I am engaged in the study and I want to continue the best I can. The problem is not the study, but my coordinator. I will suggest finding another one for the upcoming studies. I still have my right arm, do-it-all technician Lisa, whom I may groom to become the next coordinator. Lisa's loyalty to me stands without question and she is working far too many hours as well."

The evening threatened to be spoiled. Charlie looked pensively at Robert and then proceeded to tell a story about at trip he made years before to Florence, Italy. Like any other tourist, he visited the Uffizi Palace that once belonged to Lorenzo di Medici.

Charlie was on a mission to see the middle part of three sequential paintings by the Renaissance painter Paolo Uccello. The painting depicted the 1432 Battle of San Romano and the Milanese trying to conquer Firenze. For a long time, the paintings were the property of the Lorenzo family, but later sold and stolen. The three parts of the painting made a trip through Europe and one part ended in the National Gallery in London, the other in the Louvre in Paris.

The middle part of the painting, which hung in the Uffizi Palace, depicted the battle happening at dusk in full force, the horrors of men, horses, and heavy arms against each other, forces against lesser forces, crushed skulls, injured arms, broken legs and people dying from being stabbed. All the soldiers from the city of Firenze were heavily armored, Charlie explained. However, the leader of the Milanese fighters, Niccolò da Tolentino, had the audacity to wear a soft hat and all his soldiers paraded on beautiful horses in the midst of a terrible killing field. Paolo Ucello's painting showed what happened to these proud figures, a horse lying at the bottom, blood from a gash to its side streaming into the dirt of the field.

As Robert listened to Charlie, he wondered where Charlie was going with this story about his love of art.

Charlie paused for a few seconds, looked intently at Robert, and said, "You, Robert, are the leader without a hat sitting on an unprotected horse. You need to put on your helmet and protect yourself against attacks that spoil not only the fun you have in your job, but take away your energy. Your horse is not going anywhere; adversaries are blocking it. Think about this, Robert, as you may be harmed even more in the future. You will suffer from your pride with your beautiful horse - this research project of yours."

Robert had to allow this allegory more in-depth consideration.

The evening ended quietly. Charlie and Maureen departed light hearted but heavy headed.

Anna and Robert sat together for a long time after their friends left. They did not say much, digesting the evening, a mixture of warm fellowship and cold realities to consider.

Anna said she thought that the Battle of San Romano had already started at the clinic.

36

Secretary Milton sat behind his manila folder-covered desk. All morning he'd been studying the materials that Priscilla had dumped on his desk. From them she wanted to know about the income and expenses of Dr. Vermeer's research project. That was a routine enough request, but he knew her too well to think this was about seeking an arrow to strike at Vermeer's Achilles heel.

According to the research contract, they would receive an advance at the start of the study and then another payment when they finished the first study section, which they predicted would occur six months after enrolling the first patients. Milton did not expect more than a breakeven at this point, since they had only received the prepayment at the start of the study.

Priscilla said she did not want to see any projected income, only what income they had actually received and, more importantly, all the associated costs. Although Dr. Vermeer's salary and benefits paid by Imcare was more than covered by proceeds from his clinical work, there were also his office space rental and material expenses, a lot of room for Milton to be creative in compiling a cost list. Major cost factors were Jennifer, a sleep technician now dedicated to the research project, and Laura, the research coordinator, who would not even give him a passing glance whenever she had occasion to be in the office.

Priscilla suggested that, in the event the expenses did not look sufficiently impressive, they could add that portion of Dr. Vermeer's salary spent on research and not covered by clinical work. Of course, that totally disregarded all the extra work he had put in over the weekends. She also told Milton to add a few lines in the chart, but to leave them blank so she could complete them, if needed. She'll twist and turn my figures, he thought, but what the heck; he was used to that.

Milton knew how to charm Priscilla and was willing to do whatever she asked. He soothed her ego by telling her what brilliant ideas she had, but reserved attributing to her the expression 'a stroke of genius' for some later more momentous occasion. Now she was arching and stretching herself, giving him her killer You-are-my-man look, and asking for the income vs. expense spreadsheet on her desk by that evening. Milton was visualizing 'spread our sheets' and when his day with her would come.

As he now sat preoccupied with her legs, she asked him to schedule a meeting between Imcare and the research people. Let him look, she thought, he is so my puppet. "Come on, Milton. Get off your ass and stop looking like you'd seen the Venus de Milo in the flesh." She had no idea what a torch he was carrying for her.

Milton had everything done and on Priscilla's desk by five that afternoon. The detailed report indeed showed a small loss, because he had added many details, even including something he called 'office supplies'. Because he had no knowledge of Vermeer's salary, he left 'personnel costs' blank and as she requested, he left a few lines blank at the bottom of the spreadsheet for her to complete. On a yellow sticker, he'd written the filename so that she could download the document. She accepted it without so much as looking away from her computer screen and told him he could go home. He said he still had to clean up and prepare for the Imcare meeting. What he did not say was that he was curious to see whom she would be calling next. He assumed it would be Salvo.

She did, and fifteen minutes later, told Milton she was going out of the office 'on business.' Raw jealousy once again raged beneath his skin.

* * *

Months earlier, the same scenario had occurred. At the time, Milton had a doctor's appointment over at the hospital. When he entered the west door to the hospital and walked down the hallway -toward the elevators, he saw the back of Priscilla. He stopped behind a column and peeked out to one side and saw her enter the elevator. Moving quickly to the elevator doors to go up to the third floor, he noticed the far right elevator that Priscilla entered was going down and had stopped at the second basement floor. He knew from when he had worked as an intern that the morgue was down there. Milton went back to the lobby waiting area and saw Salvo entering the same elevator and going down. He wondered what business both of them might have down there and had to find out.

Having completed his doctor's appointment, Milton nonchalantly passed the nursing station into a room where the male nurses changed clothes, put on a set of green scrubs and left the room. No one would ask any questions. He walked in the hallway towards the same elevators, entered and pressed for down. No one was in the corridor as he walked in the direction of the morgue. If he encountered someone, he would say he was on his way out after bringing in a body. No one would press him further; nurses coming and going with bodies were always preoccupied and pressed for time.

He passed several closed doors but did not dare push any one of them open. Salvo and Priscilla could conceivably be in the morgue, but why? Chances were they weren't in the morgue and probably inside one of the rooms, but which one? He could imagine their wanting to meet without anyone knowing because Priscilla's apartment was highly visible and

Salvo was a married man with two children. A lover's nest, that's what it was.

Milton entered the morgue and waited at the door. It was silent. Suddenly he heard a door opening and footsteps going in a direction away from the morgue. Peeking through a slit of the door, he saw the back of a white coat. It was Salvo. Milton waited and heard the elevator. A few minutes later, at the same moment he was going to walk out, Milton heard the sound of quickly moving high heels. The steps went away from the morgue towards the direction of the elevators. Slowly he cracked opened the door and this time saw the back of Priscilla. The lovers had surfaced from their subterranean meeting place.

Today when she told him she was leaving the office 'on business,' Milton knew and hated that she was going to make love to Salvo. Since Salvo would never leave his wife and children for Priscilla, Milton held his patience for the day when Salvo dumped her and Milton would be there to rescue her.

* * *

Robert got the message that the group was holding a research meeting. He asked Milton who would be in attendance and was told the chief Dr. Cohen, Dr. Stone, Dr. Salvo, Priscilla, the CRC Laura and the technician Jennifer. Robert was to prepare a 'state of affairs' presentation. The meeting would take place in the back room of a restaurant, the following week at seven in the evening. Milton said to Robert, "Dr. Vermeer, I would prepare for answering questions about the details of the contract and in particular how the finances are apportioned. That's all I can say." Something was in the making and while Robert did not know quite how to prepare, he gave grave heed to Milton's words.

A week later they were all seated at a semi round table. Robert sat directly across from Priscilla, who had Salvo sitting to her immediate left. To her right sat the chief physician Gary Cohen, whom Robert hadn't seen for a while. Once the research project had started, they skipped having their monthly meetings, under the assumption that Robert was being made aware of his duties through James and Salvo. This arrangement did not please Robert, because it no longer afforded him either influence or opportunity to directly confer with Gary.

Laura took her place next to Gary and looked around smiling, her tooth and gum smile. James sat next to Salvo and, as usual, looked bored and blasé. Jennifer sat to Robert's left. To Robert's surprise, he saw Milton take a seat in a second row behind Priscilla. He had a yellow notepad and was already taking notes. Now and then Priscilla glanced behind her to reassure herself that Milton was keeping up.

In all, it was a seating plan that maximized interaction inside a clearly strategic setting.

Gary asked Robert to tell them about the achievements of the research project. Robert said that before discussing that project, he had exciting news to announce. A new contract was in the making, worth another $300,000 gross. Since it was a far simpler project, the net profit would consequently be much larger. They only had to say yes to the proposal. If they wished, he could give them greater details.

Gary frowned, and Priscilla and Salvo whispered into each other's ear. Gary said "I appreciate your enthusiasm, Robert, but at this time, the new contract is only a potential and with a potential, I cannot build a house. Let's just talk about the present project."

Robert reviewed the number of patients enrolled in the study, the stages at which they were and what the next steps were. He tried to be as succinct as possible. Then he thanked the technicians who took excellent care of the patients and mentioned the indispensable job that Jennifer was doing as an assistant, juggling so many details to make this project run smoothly.

Before he could proceed any further, Priscilla interrupted with "Laura is your CRC, Robert, and without her as your coordinator, the project would not be where it is today. Is that not true?"

Being extra careful, he finessed his response by saying, "Yes, Laura is the CRC, and as her title clearly indicates, she is responsible for the overall administrative coordination."

"Where do we stand, Robert, with respect to income?" asked Gary. "Can you tell us how all that works?"

Robert explained that the pharmaceutical company paid in phases, depending on the number of patients who finished portions of the study. Everything happened in stages, with the slowest stage being the first six months of the study.

As Robert spoke, James continued appearing indifferent to the proceedings, now and then looking up as if the lights were on, but no one was obviously home. His demeanor could be deceiving, thought Robert, as he waited to address the issue of his being forced to work weekends. Another matter that Robert had to bring to Gary's attention was Stone and Salvo standing on the sidelines, reluctant to do their parts in the research protocol.

Salvo and Priscilla continued whispering to each other, which vexed Robert no end. In the midst of Robert's explanation, Salvo interrupted, asking Robert to be more precise. He wanted actual figures. Irritated, Robert lifted his hand saying, "I am trying to explain the whole situation to Gary. Please allow me to continue."

Salvo and Priscilla exchanged looks of outrage over being told by Robert to hold off because the businessman of the group Gary superseded their being informed.

Priscilla claimed that the figures showed they were losing money. Robert countered that as yet they had received only part of their income and that the rest would follow from completion of subsequent stages. Therefore, the so-called loss had to be considered temporary since more was to come, with the final payments being sheer profit. Salvo's overt scoffing prompted Robert to ask whether he could be permitted to continue explaining in greater detail to Gary how the payment stream worked.

Priscilla persisted about cost savings being the main issue. They had spent money for which they hadn't seen adequate revenue. Finally, Gary asked whether and when Priscilla could provide him with a complete and detailed survey of cost and income. Priscilla pulled the spreadsheet out of her folder and handed it to Gary, saying "We came prepared."

Stunned, Robert blurted out, "But I have not seen this document."

"You'll get a copy," Priscilla promised.

Gary stood up with a short "Thank you" and ended the meeting. Priscilla followed Gary out the door. Robert remained seated wondering what had just happened. He found out the next day when he called Gary to request a meeting in private to review the spreadsheet figures that Priscilla had generated. Gary said that since he had no doubt about Priscilla's numbers, a private meeting was unlikely and unnecessary. Robert had to concede shock and awe. This dynamic duo of Salvo and Priscilla had not only created doubt about the research project, they had also ruined Robert's relationship and direct connection with Gary.

* * *

The following day Laura burst into Robert's office as usual.

"Well, Robert, –you've majorly messed up."

"How's that?"

"I'm working my ass off for you, but it's Jennifer you praise."

Jealousy, hate, ego, whatever, Robert wasn't taking the bait.

"Can you bring me the scheduling list of the patients for the coming week, Laura?" he inquired, even managing to smile, while leaving and looking over her shoulder, she replied "Maybe tomorrow."

"Within the hour, Laura," Robert said firmly. He heard the clicking of her heels as she tromped across the center into the direction of James' office.

To Robert's utter surprise, his next visitor was Priscilla. She slumped down on the couch, crossed her legs and stared at Robert, who said "What?"

-Resembling a snake stalking her prey, ready to spring before swallowing it whole,Priscilla proceeded tosay,

"As you know we discussed income and expenses yesterday. I made the calculations because, after all, Imcare had signed the contract just as you did. But your report wandered around and around, not answering any questions and instead created mass confusion. One thing that the numbers clearly show is that costs are too high and right now we are not making a dime. It's time to decide what to do about that."

Robert's neck hairs began rising.

"I'll get to the point, Robert. We have been spending money on your research assistant Jennifer for nothing, since you already have an expert research coordinator in Laura. With costs too high and revenues slack, Jennifer has to go, right now."

No, not Jennifer. The one he depended on for so many administrative matters, the one he trusted to provide him with correct and timely information.

"Don't bother to call her. I'll be informing Jennifer that she is out." With that, Priscilla got up and left.

Fifteen minutes later, Jennifer was on the couch, sobbing. Robert wanted to hug and comfort her, but had learned early on to be careful against doing anything that could be misconstrued. He expressed how deeply sorry he was and, as she well knew, how very much he appreciated her work. "If you apply for another job," Robert assured her, "please tell me, Jennifer. I will write you a strong recommendation." What déjà vu, having used those exact words when Susan, the front office administrator who filed insurance claims was also summarily fired in his office.

"Please let me know Jennifer, whatever I can do for you. I will help in any way you need me to."

After Jennifer left, Robert assessed the current damage. With Priscilla assuming more and more control, his having any control, whether as the Principal Investigator or with growing the center, was appearing more and more a delusion under which he was operating.

37

The next day Priscilla called, inviting Robert in sweet tones, to a meeting the following day, at 7 a.m. in Dr. Salvo' office.
"Tomorrow at seven in the morning?"
"Yes."

An eerie silence loomed from the other end of the line until there was a click of the phone and then a dial tone. He kept holding the phone in his hand, searching his mind for what this meeting could be about. No doubt it would be about the research, he thought. But was firing Jennifer not enough? With only Laura and the two techs, there was not much else to cut. Maybe it is about getting more information about the new project. But why a meeting in Salvo's office?

In an effort to distract himself, Robert small talked with the techs. Then with the clinic starting in half an hour and James already in his office, Robert went over to hang out with him. James pulled up a record on his computer. He pointed to an event on the screen and said "Robert, would you consider that as a central sleep apnea?"

Clearly it was. There was no airflow coming through the nose and mouth and there were no respiratory movements by the chest. This was in contrast to obstructive apnea during which respiratory efforts persisted, due to an obstruction in nose and mouth. Thus, the central control of breathing faltered, the brain did not send any signals to the muscles that control breathing. About ten percent of people with apnea have the central type of apnea. Similar to obstructive sleep apnea, the oxygen levels in the blood as measured from a finger probe decreased.

James said he had seen a few such cases and wondered what kind of treatment Robert would give. "The same as with obstructive sleep apnea," Robert answered, "with CPAP. However, BIPAP could also work well." With BIPAP the machine does not give a constant positive airway pressure such as with CPAP, but the pressure is higher when inhaling and decreases with exhaling. Robert continued to explain that sometimes medication that stimulates breathing works as well. James was familiar with all these techniques, but, for some reason, he wanted to hear what Robert would suggest. They discussed the treatment of this patient until it was time to start the clinic. James' face was, as always, inscrutably sphinx-like.

* * *

That evening at home Anna wondered what was on Robert's mind. "You seem to be worried, Robert."

"You are right, Anna. Things are happening practically right under my nose, but I don't get their rationale or where they are headed. Tomorrow I have another early morning meeting, when I'll once again be walking into God only knows what."

"Maybe you worry too much. In any event, let's enjoy tonight. Tomorrow is another day," she tried to comfort him. "I have prepared one of your favorite dishes, tilapia with mashed potatoes, fresh spinach and a butter sauce. Can you open a white wine?"

He went to the cooler and pulled out a Graves from the Chateau Carbonnieux, a wine produced close to the city of Bordeaux, a place Robert had passed by a long time ago on his way to Southern France and Spain. His memories took him to a time when the term stress had yet to be invented, let alone burnout syndrome. He looked at the bottle and thought that maybe this one would be better consumed at a more pleasurable time, but then, enjoying a nice dinner with an excellent wine might lower his anxiety level, at least for a while.

Although it was an enjoyable diner, during the night demons danced around inside Robert's dreams. Priscilla was sexier than ever, seducing him, and then morphing into a boa constrictor coiling around his body, her tongue making his face wet and setting off sparks of electricity that pin-prickled his skin. Feeling his face and chest burning, he screamed while she howled and hooted -at him. He awoke, panting heavily, then lay still, waiting for his breath to normalize.

At six in the morning, he walked into the kitchen, feeling like a train wreck. His breakfast was a quick bowl of cereal and a cup of coffee. Robert ran out of the house at 6:30 a.m. into a cool brisk morning that soon had him shivering.

He knocked on Salvo's office door five minutes before the scheduled meeting time. Priscilla was already there. He took a seat in front of Salvo' desk. They chatted amiably, as if casually sitting in a coffee shop. Noting that Robert was repeatedly checking his watch, Salvo said, "We are waiting for James to arrive."

James showed up ten minutes past the hour, looking as if he had been out jogging. Priscilla switched to being serious and opened the meeting.

"We called you here Dr. Vermeer to make you aware that you have been showing a disrespect to the other doctors that cannot be tolerated."

Groping to understand, Robert replied, "Showing a disrespect to the other doctors, what does that mean?"

"You were hired as an employee of Imcare. The doctors have been treating you like a partner, but you have not reciprocated. Most recently, you amply demonstrated your disrespect for them during the research meeting. But that is not an isolated event. You are aware of that, aren't you?"

Not waiting for an answer, she carried on.

"We have to take appropriate disciplinary measures."

Robert could only muster, "Disrespect? Not an isolated event? -You must be joking."

Priscilla and Salvo stared at Robert while James' eyes searched back and forth between them. Robert waited a few moments and asked, "Are you firing me?"

"No, but we are giving you a strong reprimand and demanding that you correct this behavior within a three month period of time. Here is a document to that effect, which you are required to sign." Salvo shoved a single sheet of paper over to Robert, pointed at the bottom and said, "Sign here."

Robert shook his head and started reading. It stated just what she had told him. He was pledging to improve his behavior during the coming months.

"I don't know whether to sign such a paper. Disrespect. I just cannot fathom such an accusation."

"There is no other way."

"Will you fire me?"

"No," said Salvo, "but we will consider doing so if you do not amend your ways. Remember, you are an employee of Imcare. Of us."

Robert sat there, with the proverbial sword hanging over his head. He could not afford to lose this job and was clueless as to why they were doing this to him.

"Sign," she said pointing her long red fingernail to the bottom line of the page and holding it there.

"And what happens after a few months? What will you do then?" Robert practically snarled, unable to suppress his fury at the unfairness of this preposterous predicament.

"As the document says, resume normal relationships."

Threatened with a job he could not risk losing and feeling like a POW, Robert snatched the pen and scratched out his signature. "I'll need a copy," was all he could muster.

"You'll get it today," Salvo said. They rose and told him he could go.

Half an hour later Robert met with James. "This is not right, James, and you know it. I have never disrespected a doctor. I have done nothing but lift your Center to the next level. Yet you just sat and watched me be wrongfully accused, saying nothing in my defense. Why is that?"

James looked like he wanted to apologize, but even now said nothing not even in his own defense. Robert finally realized that he would never be able to rely on James. Robert had only himself to rely on.

At noontime, Priscilla came to his office with a copy of the signed document. She laid it on his desk, saying, "Here is your copy." Robert neither looked at her nor said a word.

As Robert sat -in a daze, the light started slowly dawning. During the research meeting when he cut off and requested Salvo to stay quiet until Robert had finished explaining to Gary the status of the research project, that was his fatal mistake. And this Machiavellian way of putting him at their mercy was what the whispering was about between Salvo and Priscilla.

Robert left early for home, blaming himself for signing, yet nevertheless certain that the alternative of losing his job was not an option. Salvo and Priscilla had life and death power over him without anyone else's oversight, and cowardly Stone would keep to the sidelines in order to avoid becoming their victim himself. What a bitter pill Robert would have to quit gagging on and just swallow.

38

During the weeks following the official reprimand, Robert did not see much of Priscilla and he steered as clear of Salvo as he could. This no-talking mode seemed not to disturb Salvo in the slightest. Since Salvo rarely ventured to the back of the center, he was mostly an enigma to the technicians who only heard from him when he could not find a chart or a videotape recording of one of his patients.

Sometimes in the early evening, Robert went to meet with the techs and especially so when there was a new research patient, to visit and demonstrate that he was still personally interested in them. Those were both pleasant and tiresome encounters, listening to similar complaints and coping issues. He did not stay long, as the techs needed to prepare the patients with all the recording sensors. Some patients were so exhausted that they fell asleep while being wired and connected to the recording device.

All the study patients were morbidly obese and suffered from severe obstructive sleep apnea. They frequently stopped breathing at night for as long as a minute because of airway collapse and as a consequence, their blood oxygen levels dropped drastically. After each apnea episode, they struggled, gasping for air. Typically they fell asleep again and the whole sequence repeated itself. No doubt, their heart suffered and the frequent deep drops in oxygen levels affected their brain as well. Although treatable, there is no cure for this disease.

Every patient enrolled in the study was treated with a CPAP machine, which kept their airway open. Although patients claimed to be using their machine every night as directed, they did not always tell the truth. Fortunately, the CPAP machines had a built-in device which monitored the usage. A computer program made it possible to get a printout showing when the machine was actually in use and for how long.

One of their patients was Peter Anderson. He was 6 foot 4" and weighed 340 pounds, waddling from one foot to the other, and with a thundering voice and laugh that heralded his coming. It was difficult for him to walk many steps without stopping to take a breath. He passed the requirements for the test and participated with gusto. The money he expected to get when he finished the study was his main reason for joining the study. As a handicapped person he had a meager income, and since he couldn't work, he spent his days in front of a TV, becoming a soap opera connoisseur. This standard routine was lying down on the couch with a bag of snacks within arm's length.

Over the years, doctors urged him to lose weight to decrease the severity of his apnea. Taking heed of what they said, he went to a dietician and managed to lose 40 pounds. A few months later, however, he regained that weight and so commenced a yoyo effect, wherein he gained and lost the same 40 pounds over and over.

Despite his humor and infectious laugh, Peter was depressed because he was incapable of working and his social life had become reduced to an occasional visit from an acquaintance. Sans intimacy and sex for years, Peter's wife slept in another room.

Robert met with him in his clinic and put him on CPAP.

"I used this thing in the past and never liked it. It's difficult to sleep with that thing on my face," he said.

"Don't touch it, Peter. I bet you'll be in dreamland in no time." The tech said reassuringly smiling.

Once he was settled in bed, a bit grumpy he closed his eyes thinking, "This just ain't gonna work." Fifteen minutes later, though, he was asleep and would remain so through the whole night. The CPAP machine prevented most of his apneas and his oxygen saturation levels hovered around 90%.

In the morning the tech came in the room as Peter was pulling off the mask and said, "Good morning Peter. How did you sleep?"

It took some time before he cleared his eyes and replied, "I don't think I have slept that well in years." He stretched and yawned. "My goodness, I feel so really good. Maybe this is another machine than the one I had before or the straps have changed?"

Later in the morning Robert congratulated Peter for his successful night and directed him to use the machine every night. Peter said that he would try, although it did not work well in the past. However, if it were like today, using the machine would not be a problem.

Months later, when Peter's use of the machine was checked, an erratic pattern was detected. Some nights he used the machine, but sometimes he woke up at night, pulled the mask from his face and switched off the machine, unable to fall asleep again with the mask on. Other nights the machine was evidently back in his closet. This is a pattern seen in a number of patients. If they manage to use the machine on a regular basis, a few months later they don't spend the night without using their CPAP machine.

One night his wife heard a loud noise, one she had not heard before. She jumped out of bed, ran to his room and found Peter clearly in distress hanging sideways off the bed. She tried to put his head back on the bed and frantically dialed 911. Maybe a heart attack, I don't know, she said as she could not handle him alone, he was a 300 pound man. Ten minutes later three male paramedics dashed into the house with a stretcher, started resuscitation and transferred Peter to the Emergency Room at St. Elisabeth's. The doctors told

Peter's wife that they confirmed he had had a mild_heart attack, one from which he did not die, but he certainly was a high-risk patient. Having survived such a frightful episode, Peter told his wife that he would be more faithful in using his CPAP machine.

Although Peter fulfilled all the criteria as a study participant, he never mentioned that emergency visit two years before. The study was bringing patients together who were mutually supportive in combating their disease. Losing weight was an important factor for all and remained a daily battle. So they looked for alternatives. Some underwent stomach stapling, which Peter wanted to have done as well. However, there was a strenuous prerequisite. The surgeons expected him to first lose at least 60 pounds before scheduling such an operation and allowed him another six months before reevaluation. The clinical study started before he was a candidate for surgery..

* * *

Robert's life now revolved around the Center and his research study to such an extent that Anna started to complain he was hardly ever at home. He promised to change once this study was over. The next six months would be time-intensive but after that, the study demands would wind down dramatically. Also, the newly planned research, which was to start in about six months, fit perfectly with the schedule of the present study and would be much less labor intensive. Better yet, no weekend work would be scheduled.

Anna pledged, "I will hold you to your word."

Robert sat in his office thinking about this talk with Anna and about his work at the center. He had made the Center more efficient, increased the number of patients, acquired research contracts, and the doctors group was paying him handsomely. Yet, this was neither ample nor good enough for Imcare.

Jennifer's firing without reason and then, his getting a reprimand taught him that regardless of how much good you do, someone could always twist it into trouble. Robert just did not understand why. But rather than seeking out the truth, he persisted lying to himself that all he had to do was to find a way of charming himself back into the doctors' good graces.

Nevertheless further soul searching led Robert back again to the truth that bringing the center to the next level was not what provided him with the personal satisfaction he thought it would. It was the clinical work and his interaction with patients that were the real sources of his bliss and feeling of accomplishment.

Out of the blue, head tech Sarah Fetters charged into his office, followed by Laura. "Dr. Vermeer, terrible news. One of your patients, Peter Anderson, passed away last night." Then she added, "but fortunately, not in our Center." The implications would have been much larger if the patient passed away in the center. Nobody dies in a sleep center. Bad for the reputation.

Laura moved herself ahead of Fetters saying, "You were the one responsible for making the final study patient selections. Maybe this patient should never have been allowed into the study? We need to inform MPRI, Salvo and Stone about this awful situation."

Robert felt the blood draining from his face. "Oh, Peter," he murmured wistfully. After recovering for a moment, Robert set forth explaining, "There are standard forms to complete for any incident, Laura."

"But –this- is- so- way- out- of- line, Doctor," she said, emphasizing each and every word.

"Still, it has to be reported in the same way as any other incidence, and I assure you, Laura, I am very much aware that this is not like reporting a headache. I will write the report and inform the company after I have more facts. Go tell the doctors. Right now, I need to know more. He waved her out of his way and turned to Sarah, "Maybe you can be of some help here?"

Sarah told him that Peter's wife called during the early morning hours to report that Peter had died in his sleep. At about 3 a.m. she woke up, sensing that the house was unusually silent. When she went to his room, she found him hanging partly out of the bed, he looked blue in the face and his mask hung below on his chin. She switched off the machine and, not sure what had happened with him, dialed 911. When the paramedics came, resuscitation was unnecessary; Peter had died some time before they arrived.

After Laura and Fetters had gone, Robert gave second thoughts to what Laura had said. Had I followed all the procedures properly and had I applying the correct selection criteria for admitting Peter into the study? Although Robert had absolutely no doubts that he had done everything correctly, he knew that the company would want to have the certainty that this was the case. They would also have to decode the patient to know whether he was on the new medication or on placebo. Robert prayed that Peter was on a placebo. At least the untimely death could not be ascribed to the new drug. It was one of so many deaths caused by sleep apnea and Peter had been like so many sleep apnea patients, a walking time bomb.

It did not take long before James came to Robert's office. Robert had the patient file in front of him and was looking through the documentation of the selection procedure.

"One of your study patients died," James stated. "Fortunately he didn't die in our center."

"I am so sad about Peter's death, James. He was a good patient and a good person. As of now, I do not have a cause of death and I do not know whether he belonged to the drug group or not."

"Did you apply the admission criteria correctly? Laura told me that you are not sure about that."

"I have all the info in front of me and as far I am concerned, I followed all the rules and the patient fulfilled all criteria. I don't know where Laura got the idea that I was not sure."

"Did you inform the company?"

"I will, but not before I have all the details, so that I can give them precise information."

"Too late, Robert. Laura has already called the sales rep Jeff Sanders about the incident."

"Jeff Sanders doesn't even need to be informed. He has no authority whatsoever in these matters. I need to speak to the MPRI director coordinating our study. But I won't do that until I have gathered all the pertinent information. MPRI will break the code as this development is critical information for them." Robert looked at James, who, surprise, surprise, was being of no help and worried only about Laura.

Robert called Peter's wife and expressed his sorrow. She sobbed about how Peter was well on his way to losing weight and how high his hopes were for having the stomach stapling surgery at the end of the study. When Robert asked whether there had been any signs of heart problems before, she mentioned the Emergency Room visit two years before. At that time he was Salvo's patient. Robert sighed. He did not know of it and there was no mention of it on the questionnaire he completed. Robert did not tell her that not only should Peter have let them know about ER visit, but also that it probably would have disqualified Peter from being in the study. He wondered why this was not in his chart and aimed to check it out.

Robert told her that they needed to check out Peter's CPAP machine. Assuming that it was working, Robert considered that maybe Peter did not use the mask properly, or it had shifted so that he did not get enough air. Maybe his position in bed twisted the tube so that he did not get air into his nose and mouth. All guesses. Only double-checking everything could reveal how he had used the machine.

Peter died in his sleep from apnea. Whether he was on the drug or the placebo might not make any difference. Alternatively, some people could infer that because of the drug that made him more alert, he was not using his machine as much as he had to. That was easy to verify, because the machine he used registered the time he had it on. When they checked it, they could print a log, documenting usage. This would clarify whether or not he used the machine sufficiently. Robert told Peter's wife that he would send Sarah Fetters, the head technician, to pick up the machine once the police were finished with their work.

As soon as Fetters brought back the CPAP machine, Robert scrambled to connect it to the reading device and print out the data. It showed that during the last month and in between studies, Peter had been using his machine on an irregular basis. Sometimes, a few hours after falling asleep, he either disconnected the device or put his mask aside. Either way, with the degree of apnea he had, his heart had probably given out.

* * *

While he was studying the record, Priscilla appeared, posturing with her hands on her hips.

"We've got a serious problem here," she said with a loud voice.

"The problem is that we lost a patient, Priscilla; we lost a good man because of his sleep apnea and that is sad."

"My problem is that you have a death in your study."

Robert sighed deeply. She didn't care about Peter the patient of Peter the person. She only cared that there was a possible publicity complication for them.

"Priscilla, I am in the process of finding out the details of his untimely death. As soon as I generate a report, I will contact the company."

"You seem to be taking this rather lightly, Robert. Liborio and James have the same impression."

"I am not taking this at all lightly, but everything must be done according to study protocol. And, I assure you, I care more about the person we lost than any problem with study itself."

Exasperated, she shook her head. In an effort to put her mind at ease, Robert smiled and said, "Actually, Priscilla, I am moving along quite quickly with the fact gathering. I will keep you abreast of developments before anyone else."

As soon as she left, Robert called the director of MPRI, explained the situation and asked whether they could break the code for that patient and determine whether he was put on the new drug or had been receiving the placebo. They discussed the implications if the patient was part of the drug group. It could indeed impose a burden on the company to prove that Peter had frequently skipped using his CPAP because he was feeling more alert. However, if the drug made him more alert and that was the reason why Peter stopped using the CPAP machine, then that would also be a bad message for the drug's future.

To the enormous relief of Robert and the director, the code indicated that Peter had been receiving a placebo.

Robert decided to keep that information to himself while he documented the incident, hoping to keep from being stressed and harassed by those who were looking for complications rather than solutions. That no one seemed to care about Peter and his wife disturbed Robert deeply.

He called Laura to tell her to get the funeral information, so he could visit with the wife beforehand. He also recommended that, as the clinical coordinator, she could do the same, just by way of showing our spirit of care.

To Robert, the case was closed and the study could continue without disruption. Peter's death could not be attributed to the new drug and Robert had diligently applied the selection criteria. No mention had been made of Peter's ER visit or that he was a suspected heart attack victim. Robert had followed the protocol, as one would with any other incident.

After Robert notified the staff he was on his way to visit Peter's family, he called Anna to let her know he would be late for dinner. She was right. He had to start paying more attention to her and spending more time at home. His career had turned into an express train streaking past another red light en route for a collision with his marriage.

39

Robert sat with Peter's widow, talking about Peter's life, how good he had been with the children, his struggles with weight and how he looked forward to each visit at the center. He loved talking to Robert and his colleague patients. In the process of separating from the man she'd known for thirty years, Peter's widow only had her memories left to comfort her.

After Robert promised to come back and see her again, he went home for a quiet evening with Anna. He tried not to think much about the days to come, concentrating on feeling confident that the study was in good shape and would continue. If Priscilla-and-company left him to deal with the research study issues professionally, rather than in their panicky hysterical fashion, tranquility could return. But would the Priscilla-Salvo team permit him to carry on with all his duties? Surely, Robert believed that, in order to profit from all the benefits he was generating for them.

While Robert was at home, Salvo was back at the hospital in the secret room he shared with Priscilla. He relaxed on the couch and poured himself a scotch, fed up with hearing the story of the dead study patient. That incident was perfect timing though, and something they needed to exploit. He wondered what Priscilla would think. From the phone, she sounded stressed, but he knew the perfect way of getting rid of that.

Lately, the lines in her forehead seemed to be deepening more and more, but the rest of her body showed few signs of aging. Not having gone through childbirth, she didn't have any of the stretch marks his wife had. Also, her breasts were not sagging and her belly was still flat, leading to a small smooth pouch, a heavenly place.

Today, though, Priscilla was not in the mood, "Headache, my dear?" Salvo asked sarcastically.

"In a sense, yes," she'd said. "Vermeer is literally getting on my nerves. He talks and cares -purely about his poor patient and then leaves us holding an empty bag."

"You know, we can look at it from a different angle. This is the time to strip him of his role as principal investigator, put me in charge and, think about this, get all the money instead of co-sharing the profit with him."

He stroked her back and slid his hands down under her buttocks. He held her up against him but Priscilla pulled away. "Sorry, but I really do have a throbbing headache. I took two Excedrin's and I'm wired with caffeine."

Priscilla took a seat in the chair. Dropping to the couch, Salvo did not hide his disappointment. No game, no fun, no time to waste, thought Salvo.

After a long silence, he said, "Bottom line, Priscilla, you've got to figure out how we can take the PI function away from Vermeer and make sure he doesn't get any new contracts from MPRI."

Salvo then bolted from the room after which Priscilla collapsed on the couch. An hour later she awakened with a pounding heart and a dull ache in her head. The best she could do was go home for the rest of the day. Tomorrow she would get back to taking care of business.

* * *

Milton arranged for a meeting with Jeff Sanders from MPRI. Priscilla had suggested a reservation in a restaurant not too far from the offices. How that meeting was relevant to the death of one of Dr. Vermeer' study patients, Milton could only guess. What he did know was that Sanders was a very nice looking man with a reputation as a womanizer. As long as she did not arrange for a secret meeting, Milton felt comfortable and secure. He could not afford dealing with yet another competitor. Milton arranged for lunch at *PF Chang Cuisine* and longed to be a fly on a nearby wall.

Priscilla greeted Jeff with a smile and saw him inspecting her body. Take a good look, she thought, this is my strongest weapon. He pulled a chair back for her, appearing to inadvertently brushing her arm and let his hand rest on her back for just a tiny second. The restaurant was an upscale Chinese place with a modern décor, high ceilings, walls painted in a variety of maroon and beige colors. An atmosphere of chic dominated the place. The kitchen was Eastern, but a far cry from the traditional Chinese cuisine. Jeff, however, found it a very noisy place with food that was acceptable, but nothing exceptional. He nevertheless complimented her about the choice and added, "How could you know that this is one of my favorites? A bit loud though"

She responded coyly that she had done her homework. Even if it was a lie, he enjoyed her answer. It promised to be the beginning of their getting to know each other better. That is what he mainly wanted and he wondered how far he would get today. The doctors were a small community, so he had to move cautiously. He did not want her making any mention of him to the doctors' group.

While they ordered, he wondered why she wanted to meet with him. Had her friendliness dovetailed with his unspoken desire for her? Were they two beautiful people getting to know each other beyond their preferred aperitifs? He liked a Samuel Adams beer and she ordered 'a martini on the rocks with one green olive and a sprinkle of lemon.' It sounded as if she ordered that every day and not what she had recently learned from Gary.

Jeff lifted his glass and as they made their glasses touch, he said "To a beautiful day, to a woman as sparkling as the ice in her martini and to the future." Having no idea how glacial she could be, he flashed her his killer smile and she flashed him hers.

"I assume you'd like -to better know the man who has brought you a very worthwhile research project. If this one goes well I can promise you that more will come. This could be a lucrative business."

"I appreciate your help, but didn't Laura call you about the incident?"

"Yes, she called me. But accidents happen. I hope the patient was on placebo, but we'll know soon, since in such instances, decoding happens instantly. In any case, Dr. Vermeer is undoubtedly dealing directly with that issue."

It sounded to Priscilla as if he were speaking about some innocuous incident, and downgrading the possibly devastating consequences.

"I know that you evaluated Dr. Vermeer's capabilities and that he qualified to be a principal investigator. However, Laura is doing much of the work, some of which I am not sure is really all hers to do. In short, Jeff, we couldn't be doing the study without her." She paused, sliding her tongue along the bottom of her lips.

Jeff was mesmerized by her mouth. He imagined it close to his and almost reached across the table to touch her. Shaking himself loose, he replied, "Clinical Research Coordinators are essential to a study. I hope you are not suggesting changing Laura?"

She had him exactly where she wanted him. She saw his eyes darting around her face, sure his mind was far from the CRC. Where did she read that every man thinks about sex at least every ten minutes?

"Absolutely not. Laura is and will remain a key person. But Jeff, what do you think about Principal Investigators?"

"What do I think about them? Technically, they are the ones who carry the ultimate responsibility of a study."

"So, basically, it could be any doctor?" she said smoothly.

"Yes."

She went on and on, telling him that there had been so many incidents and issues that she doubted Dr. Vermeer's ability to continue. In addition, Drs. Salvo and Stone were already actively involved in the study and engaging three doctors was more than Imcare wanted to commit for such a study. "We need to be cost conscious, as I am sure your company is," she told him with a solemn face. "What if we, Imcare, are not sufficiently pleased with the present Principal Investigator? How difficult would it be to replace him?"

"You are talking about Dr. Vermeer?"

Priscilla answered with a simpering smile, which told Jeff that she was one well-done, well-prepared broad. He answered likewise and then added that he'd have a talk with the Director of Matterson Pharmaceutical Research Institute.

"Did you know that when Dr. Vermeer screened the patients for enrollment, he was unaware of the fact that Peter Anderson had been in the ER as a possible heart attack victim? Peter Anderson was a dying man who left the hospital a few days later, alive, but still really sick. Either Dr. Vermeer did not know or he neglected that factor in his evaluation." She paused and let those words seep in.

Jeff understood perfectly and told Priscilla that he would contact MPRI to find out about replacing Vermeer, if that was what she or Imcare wanted. Of course, Dr. Salvo qualified, for he had been involved in the study and probably knew all the details. A company representative would have to come to facilitate the transition, but, on the other hand, Imcare was the institution who signed the contract and they could choose their own PI.

Having reached her goal, Priscilla wanted to leave the restaurant as soon as she could. She needed a smooth way of giving him the impression that she was fond of him and that there was maybe more to follow, but some other time. She put her hand on his, thanked him for his willingness to help with this delicate situation, and closed by saying that he looked like a man with whom she could work together quite well. The devil continues to wear Priscilla.

Since a follow up meeting would have to be scheduled, she suggested he call her secretary, Milton when he had information from MPRI. She stood up to indicate they were done. Imcare would take care of the bill and Jeff could put away his company credit card. Both walked out. She went to her Lexus and Jeff accompanied her.

Presuming that Sanders was waiting for his reward, she smiled gently, saying that she had lots of work to get back to as well as a meeting with the doctors in half an hour. She figured he probably figured she was lying, but hoped that her smile was convincing enough to keep him hooked. Let Sanders admire my legs, maybe one day he will get more, but not today.

"Bye Jeff, we'll see each other soon, with more time to spend together, I hope." She raised the window and took off, her tires squealing.

Sanders stood looking at the receding rear view of her car, marveling at what one hell of a smooth operator she was. Getting into his car, he harbored serious reservations about ever getting inside her apartment.

40

Laura stormed into Robert's office demanding Peter's patient folder. "You need to give me his folder with the incident report. The director of MPRI wants me keep him updated. You are so lucky Peter was a placebo patient, but that does not dismiss the fact you never should have enrolled him in the first place. We could have lost the entire study!"

"You called the Director? On who's authority? Certainly not mine. You keep forgetting I am the Principal investigator, which means I am the primary responsible party, not you."

"But you are the problem, not me. You are the one who made a serious mistake in accepting that patient."

"You have already told me that three times. However, accepting study patients is my call to make, not yours." Robert stopped, becoming aware that he was playing defense. He terminated their conversation with "I have work to do and I presume you do too. I don't take instructions from you and, by the way, when I spoke to the director, he never mentioned that you called."

Seeing Laura surprised from Robert's response, he took the advantage by telling her, "Get back to work, Laura. I'm the one in charge."

He stared into his computer screen, his heart beating wildly. She left, slamming his office door shut. Robert rose and walked around from behind his desk. He opened the door and watched her marching off. He also noticed the techs whispering to each other, but he couldn't care less about their gossiping. Laura's disrespectful behavior and her calling the MPRI director were outright insubordination. Such was his reward for granting her wide berth of latitude and patience.

Robert watched Laura go to James' office, a place she was frequenting more and more often. James never mentioned anything about her visits and ran the clinic together with Robert as usual. Patient work remained the same and James continued to discuss an occasional case here and there with Robert. It was difficult knowing James and his various moods. Mostly, he looked icy cold and grim, yet, strangely enough, that was in stark contrast to his relaxed manner when they did clinic together, a kind of highlight in the otherwise depressing darkness that usually reigned in Robert's center.

The following day Robert received a call from James to come to his office. There was one empty chair, on the others sat Laura and Priscilla. Laura was holding her handkerchief against her nose and sniffling.

"Robert," said Priscilla, "I disapprove of what you are doing. This poor woman is being completely overworked and you have brought her to the verge of a breakdown." Laura whimpered, nodding in confirmation.

Priscilla told him that this was not the first time Laura had come to her office in tears over all the clinic work she had to do, in addition to her demanding family.

Then came a nasty blow from James who told him, "You've got to roll up your sleeves, man," while moving his arms as if he was a kid showing off his muscles.

Robert exploded. "For months now, I have been the one here in the Center every single weekend, Saturdays and Sundays from 7 a.m. to 5 p.m. and you have the gall to ask me, James, to roll up my sleeves? What about you and your griping and bellyaching over doing 15-minute patient physicals?"

"That's not the point. The point is that Priscilla and I do not want to see this poor woman in tears because of you. You will just have to do more during the week in order to keep her from being so overworked."

Robert shook his head in disbelief. He stood up, pushing his chair back, and said, "So that's it?" Not allowing for an answer, he walked out.

In his office Robert sat thinking about this latest set of theatrics and how to keep from being suckered into the current melodrama. He decided to escape the bull and bathos by going home for lunch. At least there, he could see a smile. Anna knew things were not right as soon as Robert walked through the door.

"According to James, I have to roll up my sleeves and this from a guy who can't handle fifteen minutes worth of work on the research study. And Laura, with her crocodile tears, gets to be coddled and protected by Priscilla."

Anna did not understand. Robert was obviously upset about something that had occurred before he came home. She let him rage. When he stopped, he asked, "What do we have for lunch today?"

"To begin with, I don't usually have the pleasure of having you at home for lunch, and I don't know whether this angry man will enjoy anything I make."

"So sorry, sorry, Anna. I needed to vent at someone outside the sleep center, away from its merry-go-round of gossip and the venom of that crazy woman."

"You're a strong man, Robert I'm sure you can see this as part of a silly game. Where they want to go with that, I have no idea, but the danger comes from this Priscilla woman and the other doctors who go along with it. She is their administrator and so she takes that burden away from them. You know that doctors are lousy administrators. In addition, she takes care that their money is working well for them. So whom do you think they will be defending?"

Watching her silent and downcast-looking husband, Anna let her words sink in.

"You are too honest and too focused on the real work. You cannot win as of now. Keep your head cool and your heart in the right place. One day, it will all settle, just like the dust does. That's what they are, Robert, dust."

Robert took a deep sigh, poured himself a glass of wine and headed for the couch, attempting to trivialize these absurd attacks instead of taking them too much to heart.

41

Jeff Sanders was home reviewing his schedule for tomorrow. He'd postponed making the call to the director coordinating the research for MPRI. He was not convinced that Dr. Vermeer was the source of a problem. Laura seemed the stranger bird, speaking too fast, giggling and complaining too much. Actually, she was too much of everything. However, there was also the major matter of humoring Priscilla and manipulating matters to suit her so that one day, he could be just manipulating her.

Sanders needed to make that phone call. The problem was that he had been praising Dr. Vermeer. His center had, in fact, turned out to have one of their highest enrollees and their documents were in perfect condition. The patient dying was unfortunate. Such events happen. Patients with so severe an apnea not surprisingly die in their sleep, not uncommonly because of heart failure. It was just unfortunate to happen during a research study.

The real problem Sanders faced was one of presentation. He needed to present in a way that did not suggest to the director that Jeff had made a mistake. Moreover, he also had to come up with a reason to take away Vermeer's role as a Principal Investigator and replace him with Dr. Liborio Salvo. Jeff did not understand or even know what his true research experience was. As far as Jeff had heard, Salvo' research experience was minimal, but then again, he was a medical doctor. They are, after all, the guys who make the decisions for the meds he was trying to sell. Priscilla was insisting that he arrange this. One factor that facilitated such a change was that Imcare had signed the contract, thus any changes were fundamentally up to Priscilla.

After sufficient rehearsal of what he would say, Jeff cleared his throat and made the call. When the director came on the line, he expressed his concern about the functioning of the Center. He had spoken to several people about the same incident, but they each had their own agenda about various things that had little to do with the incident itself. In addition, he talked to the PI, Dr. Vermeer whom he had met during the Investigators meeting in Nassau, the Bahamas, and found him to be a well-versed and capable person.

"So, Jeff, tell me what is going on. My primary concern is the continuation of the study. What do we need to do to resolve their internal disputes?"

Jeff answered with his well-rehearsed speech and concluded by saying, "In my humble opinion, we have to remove Dr. Vermeer, not because he is bad. To the contrary, he is very good, but the internal situation is such that the study will suffer if we don't replace him."

"Is there a viable candidate who could take over?"

"There is. Dr. Liborio Salvo is an internist working in the Center together with Dr. Stone. Recently he got his boards in sleep medicine as well. He also has some research experience. At least that is what I am told."

"Then I have to make an executive decision, Jeff. I understand that to protect our program we have to switch the principal investigator to Dr. Salvo. One of my associates or I will have to meet and visit with Dr. Salvo as well as with the signer of the contract, Administrator Priscilla Jackson. Once I know who can come and when, I'll give you a call to arrange for the meeting."

"May I inform Imcare of your decision?"

"No, I will call Miss Jackson myself. You just take care of arranging our meeting with her and Dr. Salvo. I will not talk to Dr. Vermeer but leave them to solve their internal affairs."

As soon as he hung up, Jeff called Priscilla's office and got Milton who told him that 'Ms. Jackson was out on business and could he leave a message for her? Jeff hesitated a moment and then he said "Tell her mission accomplished and that I need to talk to her soon."

Milton smiled when he put the phone down. He was in Priscilla's office and knew exactly where she was. He decided to call her cell phone from her desk phone. He luxuriated comfortably in her chair and imagined her look of surprise. It was perfect. He loved breaking into her business affairs.

Priscilla heard her cell phone ringing. Salvo groused, "Damn it. You forgot to disconnect your phone." She struggled to her feet, dug into the pockets of her purse in search of the phone that wouldn't stop ringing.

When she put the phone down, she had the nagging notion that Milton was inside their secret place. He had made the call from her office; why not from his desk? He also knew that he should not disturb her when she was away 'on business'.

"Well, what the heck is going on, Priscilla?"

"Good news."

"Not from the way you look."

"Sanders called the office and left a cryptic 'mission accomplished' message with Milton. Sounds like we are on our way towards kicking Vermeer out, and bringing you in. I am supposed to meet with him tomorrow."

"Great. So what's the concern?"

She told him her concern had nothing to do with the research study. It was a strange feeling she had that Milton knew more than they thought he knew. She needed time to find out if her gut feeling was right. Maybe they had better avoid visiting their secret place and go to her apartment instead. Salvo was unenthusiastic about the idea, reminding her that visiting her apartment was too dangerous.

Priscilla could not hide her disappointment. She wanted to revel in their impending victory and the best place would have been her apartment. A visit from a doctor, even if seen by some employees of the hospital, would not necessarily start any gossip, she said, as I am seeing doctors all the time. But not at your apartment, he clarified. This meeting having turned sour, Salvo left, not knowing it, when or where thre would be future encounter would be.

When Priscilla returned to the office, she found Milton in her office. "What the hell are you doing here, Milton?"

"Trying to help you, Priscilla."

"Calling me when I am out on business is not helping me. Once again, Milton, what are you doing here?"

"Looking for the original documents that I needed to generate the research budget, cost and income report that you requested me to do a week ago."

"Just look at the computer files I forwarded to you. I don't keep hardcopies in my office and if I did, you should ask me first, before poking around my desk and files. And, while we are on the subject, why did you call me from my office?"

"I thought you'd want to get Sanders' message right away."

"You did not answer my question. You crossed all boundaries. Now, get the hell out.

Milton apologized, saying, "I don't like you upset with me. You know I would do anything for you," smiling a smile dripping with admiration.

Priscilla began considering that she may have over encouraged him. Was Milton some kind of serious head case? She needed to find out what he knew and how she could put him to good use.

* * *

The following day, Jeff called Priscilla who suggested his coming to her office. He was there punctually at 2 p.m. Milton made him wait five minutes, inferring that she was on the phone with one of the doctors. Milton disliked Sanders for having such access to Priscilla, especially because it appeared as if they were getting a little too cozy. Milton caught Sanders talking it up with one of the young secretaries. He waited a few more minutes before knocking on Priscilla's door. Before he could say anything, she told Milton that she wanted to have a word with him after her meeting with Sanders. Milton said "With pleasure."

Upon entering her office, Sanders went to the side of Priscilla's desk, looked into her eyes and held her hand far too long. Priscilla did not withdraw it, assuming that she had achieved her goal. "You told me 'Mission Accomplished,' Jeff. Does that mean you managed to talk to your director and that we can now change the management of the research study?"

He kept her guessing a little longer, if only to make it sound better afterwards. He went into many unnecessary details, withholding the final answer, and, at the same time, studying and learning her better. He saw her nervously shifting in her chair, waiting impatiently. Finally, he told her that the switch from Dr. Vermeer to Dr. Salvo was a done deal.

However, Sanders explained that a representative of the company had to visit with Dr. Salvo and that should not be misconstrued as questioning his credentials. "Imcare makes those decisions, but MPRI wants to put a face on the name," that's all he'd said. "The director will be giving you a call very soon, so please behave as if you did not hear this news from me. And wait to inform Dr. Salvo until you have spoken with the director." He left it up in the air as to who was to be informing Dr. Vermeer.

Half an hour after Jeff had entered her office, Priscilla received a call from the director. She could call Salvo and let him know that he would be getting a visit the following week, just a formality, the director said. Once they concluded the visit with Salvo, the director said, it was Imcare's job to deliver the unpleasant news to Dr. Vermeer, since they were the ones requesting the change. He added that such a change was not his wish, because Dr. Vermeer had done his job well and solved a delicate matter most professionally.

Priscilla responded that with all due respect, the director did not know all the details of their operation and was unfamiliar with Dr. Vermeer's management skills, or lack thereof. Priscilla felt quite self-satisfied, with having plunged her dagger into Robert's research career.

42

A week later, events burst loose like an avalanche. The company representative said they had accepted Dr. Salvo as the new PI, if this could keep the research study going. They amended the contract with a paragraph indicating that the new Principal Investigator was Dr. Liborio Salvo. That Vermeer was ousted did not disturb the representative since he had nothing to do with their internal falling outs and understood all too well the egos of the medical establishment.

Unaware that anything was happening behind his back, Robert was called into Salvo' office.

"I've got some news for you. Your role as a P.I. in the research study is "fini". As of today I am the new Principal Investigator. Also, Imcare has decided that I am the new director of research as well. So, in the future, I will be the one dealing with eventual studies and Laura will be working for me."

Robert sat like a boxer who had missed seeing the twenty-ounce glove coming at him. Question after question churned inside his brain. Who made the decision and arranged it all, why him, what for, why, why, why?

"Is this definite?" he managed to ask.

"Yes."

"Why?"

"You should ask yourself that question. Look at the disasters that you've caused during the last few weeks."

"I am not aware that I have caused any disaster."

"You are out of the research program, so just attend to your clinical duties now. This mess has been taking too much of our time and our money. We may wind up not even be making any profit."

Then Salvo stood up, saying he had to go over to the clinic, and left Robert paralyzed with bitter indignation.

* * *

Charlie was on his way for a consult with Dr. James Stone and thought to make a surprise visit to Robert. It was his first time at the sleep center and he was sure that Robert would be an excellent tour guide. Charlie's ulterior motive was to learn what was going on with Robert, who had been real quiet of late, always saying he was "fine" and that everything was going well. Charlie suspected there was good reason Robert did not want to talk.

Actually, Robert always said "fine," because he thought that Charlie had enough problems, ones far more serious than his own. When Charlie's cancer had returned, he visited with Dr. Stone, who proposed a treatment plan. But Charlie doubted whether that plan would work and even indicated that he may not go for that plan. He thought he had a good idea, by now, about what might work and what might not. Charlie believed that with cancer, traditional medicine did not have that many options. New scientific developments led to new medications, but those discoveries needed incubation time of ten years before something practical could come out.

After telling her that he was a friend, Julie directed Charlie to the back office. Charlie went to the technicians' area and asked where Dr. Vermeer' office was. One of the techs said, "This is not like him, but Dr. Vermeer has been keeping his office door closed. Sometimes he does not come out for hours."

Charlie knocked at the door and nothing happened. He knocked again and heard Robert growled, "Leave me alone." One of the techs came and asked for Charlie's name. She shouted "Dr. Vermeer, there is a visitor for you, Charlie." The door opened slowly. Robert's face was ashen, eyes red, and his hair tangled. "Charlie," he said with pleasant surprise in his voice, let Charlie enter and closed the door behind them.

"What's happened with you?"

In a hoarse and barely audible voice, Robert explained. After he finished unloading the whole sorry saga, Charlie said they better talk further in another environment. "Don't hang your head, Robert. There are still many good things to do. You are still the clinical and administrative director of a flourishing and growing sleep center. You still have your patients to take care off. Look at it from the bright side, you finally got to lose the heavy burden that we were talking about."

Robert was not yet in a mood to see things that way but came to his senses soon enough to realize that Charlie wasn't there just to pay Robert a social call.

"Yes," said Charlie. "I should get going over to my appointment with Dr. Stone."

"Charlie you are a good friend. What can I tell you, except for what you already know. You keep your head up too and regardless of what I said about my situation and Dr. Stone, I still think that he is a good physician."

* * *

The weeks kept passing as the world kept turning and the sleep center continued its pace as if nothing had changed. Perception is a strange feature of vision, everything can be the same, yet different. Robert's office now seemed shabby, the colors of its walls faded, and everyone was wearing masks. Conversations were muffled and when he walked by the receptionists, they bent their heads, looking at their desk and never at him. Robert's whirlwind of ambition had spun down into slow motion.

He thought about his car accident, years ago, as if he were telling someone else what had happened. 'Your car flips over and starts to roll, one turn after the other. While you are flipping around in the car, you feel the bumps and stabbing pain of objects scratching and ripping at your flesh. You hear the crunching of metal and yourself screaming. There are the awful smells of oil, gasoline, and sweat, and then everything comes to a complete standstill. The hissing and dripping of oil, or is it water, interrupts the silence. None of this seems real, just something happening to someone else.'

Robert felt as if he had been in another horrible car accident, where once again he was powerless to have done anything better or differently. They say everything happens for a reason, but that is for the Pollyanna believers for whom everything is good. Even their worst pain had purpose, but not for Robert. The promised rewards would not come because no one was checking to see that promises were kept. If proof cannot be given, only belief can save your soul. That is what is preached by survivors, not by death. Some who blow themselves up, killing innocent bystanders, believe in the promise that they will meet many virgins in the afterlife. Why it had to be virgins was never clear to Robert. What was this? Some kind of sexual obsession?

Likewise, what happened had nothing to do with Robert, other than he was an innocent bystander of others' greed. Salvo took over the sleep center not only reaping the rewards of all Robert's efforts, but also collecting all the money generated by the research study. Laura would not complain anymore about having to work too hard, and would, no doubt, be handsomely rewarded for succeeding in making Robert's car roll over into the ditch.

Laura traipsed in and out of Robert's office like she owned the place. When Robert asked what she was doing there, she said that he had all the binders and folders in his office and they would stay there until Dr. Salvo had space in his office. Robert knew that Salvo' office was nearly empty and that he needed only a few cabinets to store the binders. Laura was simply exercising her executive privilege trespassing upon his space whenever she pleased. Unable, of course, for fear of any further retribution, Robert played dumb by concentrating on his clinical work and the administrative issues of the sleep center staff.

43

For months the center ran smoothly. The turbulence between the administrative group and the techs had subsided. Quarrels, however, between the night and day staff about who worked the most continued unabated and seemed unsolvable. Finally, Robert proposed a solution worthy of King Solomon. He told them that they could find out who worked the hardest by implementing a rotating schedule from night to day and the reverse for those who wanted it.

No technician with one exception, wanted to change shifts. The ones who preferred working at night and earning a bit more money kept working at night and the rest worked during the day. Only Lisa wanted to work at night when they had pediatric patients.

Monthly staff meetings were deadly dull every first Thursday of the month. That the hospital insisted on such meetings was just another example of a terrible bureaucratic disease, called 'reunitis' from the French word 'réunion' (meeting). Robert suspended that routine by only calling staff meetings when problems arose. As an incentive for attendance, he had various sales reps cater the meetings with pizza and burgers, accompanied by bag loads of crunchy chips and ice buckets filled with cans of coke.

Under Robert's directorship, the number of patients and scheduled sleep studies ultimately doubled from when he had started in his position. Hospital VP Maria Frost, with whom he continued to have monthly meetings, lived up to her surname, never once complementing him on his remarkable success, asking just how he was doing or how she could help him make the Center better. So much for Frost's spirit of care.

Lead tech Sarah Fetters still had visits from the previous administrator David Jacobs, the man who had 'come in from the cold,' walking in his hospital slippers trying to avoid being heard and seen. When Robert accidentally bumped into him, Jacobs spoke with a raspy voice about nothing, a man sent from the Gods, who could not tell why he had been sent. Perhaps he is a spy from Maria Frost to find out from Fetters what was really going on at the Center?

Robert was in the process of dictating a report when he noted Fetters standing at his office doorway. She was so uncharacteristically silent that Robert nearly shrank from asking, "What's going on Sarah?"

"May I talk to you?"

"Sure. Take a seat," Robert said, waving her over to the couch.

She sat on the edge, knees together as much as her legs would allow, and her hands pulling on her sweater to cover her bosom. Witnesses exhibiting similar behavior always struck Robert as silly. Sarah looked far too serious and anxious for him to be secretly considering a glance at her ample bosom tucked under so many layers of cloth.

Sarah wanted to talk about Michelle Alba. It seems that while working nights, Michelle worked together with another tech when a child or baby had to be studied.

Robert fussed to Sarah, saying, "So she still isn't ready to function on her own. Where was all that pediatric experience she claimed to have?"

Fetters offered a mild defense for Michelle that the night techs were a tight crew, dynamic. Robert allowed as a possibly mitigating factor.

"I have also become aware of a problem with Michelle's work schedule," Sarah went on. Robert's ears were perking up.

"As you know, the night staff works for three consecutive nights of 12 hours each, their shift ending at 7 a.m. But Michelle switches nights whenever she wants for rather vague reasons."

Robert relaxed in his chair. This seemed to be an easy enough problem to resolve simply by meeting with her.

"If this was the only thing," Sarah said," it would be readily solvable, but there is something far more serious."

Somewhat shamefaced, Sarah continued. "She often leaves before her shift is over and then bribes other techs to cover her job the remainder of the time, so that she can leave sooner."

Robert was now sitting up straight, hearing alarm bells going off. Bribery was a serious offense. As the administrative director, he would have to take immediate action.

He asked Sarah "Are you absolutely sure about that?"

"Yes, I have been told this by different members of the night staff," she said, her arms crossed even more tightly against her bosom.

"OK then. I will send her a certified letter saying I have been notified about these irregularities. In addition, I will note that we would like to confer with her to see what we can do to arrange a better work schedule for her."

Robert leaned back in his chair, remembering the very first staff meeting. Michelle had been problematic right from the very beginning and odds were Suzy Dickson in the personnel department had never even done a background check on Michelle.

Sarah said she would get Robert the correct mailing address for Michelle and take the letter herself to the post office.

* * *

Two days after the letter had been mailed, Robert got a phone call from Dickson to go over to her office. Robert's suggestion for her to come to his office was met with a vehement 'no.'

He finished his dictations and walked over to where the personnel department was located. Dickson sat red-faced sprawled in her chair. She did not wait for him to sit before blurting out, "You've made a huge mistake, Dr. Vermeer. You never should have sent that certified letter. Hospital regulations require that you first schedule an oral interview before sending such a letter. Now we have one very upset Mrs. Alba because she received your certified letter."

"She is upset because of some bureaucratic protocol? I am here to tell you that I am upset because of her failure to comply with the rules of the Center and because of her bribing colleagues to do her work. Since we are dealing with some serious misconduct by a technician, don't you think this is what we should be addressing as the primary issue?"

"No, Sir, the hospital rules clearly state that you first have to talk to the person and only then, if still needed, send a letter."

"I hear what you are saying, but again, you are talking about a minor deviation in protocol trumping a much more serious offense."

She shook her head, "You must mail her a letter stating that you withdraw your certified letter and propose to meet with her in person."

"I have to do what?" Robert's eyebrows rose.

"We urge you," pointing her pink pencil, "no, we demand that you do what I just told you. You have to withdraw your certified letter," she declared waving in full glory,.

"Just sign right here. I've already drawn up the letter for you." She pointed to Robert's name at the bottom of the letter. He read it carefully and despondently, signed. He left her office, reeling from the realization that the personnel department was cared more about observing protocol than with addressing serious breaches in employee conduct.

- Robert blindsided himself, this time by believing that this bureaucratic snafu would be corrected and the matter of organizing the tech's work schedule would be delegated to the tech Sarah Fetters.

A week later Dickson called to say they had been unable to schedule a meeting with Michelle Alba, because she refused to meet during the day, and since she worked at night, - there would therefore be no time to meet outside her work hours.

Although incensed, Robert was impressed. By using the incompetent and unprofessional Dickson as her unwitting accomplice, Michelle Alba was playing a masterful game of my rights-as-employee game.

* * *

A few weeks later, Dickson called Robert about a nine-o-clock meeting with Mrs. Alba to be held in the personnel department. Robert said that Michelle was supposed to be at work and having a meeting with her then would disrupt the work routine.

"Too bad," said Dickson. "If it results in losing a patient, then so be it."

"So losing a patient is not important and neither is the work schedule. Was that not her original reason for her not coming to a meeting?"

But wanting the mockery over to be over, Robert relented and went. He sat at one end of a long table, Michelle Alba at the other and Dickson in the middle. She opened the meeting by telling Alba that they wanted to solve a problem, caused by an erroneous interpretation of the hospital regulations. So now Robert had been converted from accuser to defendant.

Robert told Alba that since he had rectified his administrative error of prematurely sending a letter, they should be ready to discuss the true issue. Alba agreed that his sending a certified letter was a serious mistake. Robert repeated that since this administrative error, emphasizing 'administrative error' had been rectified, the time had come to address the fact that she had not been in compliance with the rules governing the work schedule.

Alba responded, "Due to family circumstances, I cannot work three consecutive nights, especially near the weekend."

"No exceptions can be made because that would lead to other techs suffering with their work schedule." Robert reiterated that she could chose whichever three days, provided that they were consecutive and in agreement with Fetters. Alba asserted that he did not understand her family situation.

Robert rebutted with, "You knew what the work schedule conditions were before you accepted the position, didn't you? You also knew- we are here –for delivering patient care and that you have to work your full 12 hour shift."

To this, Alba sighed and kept any further silence.

"There is another matter," Robert pressed on. "It is imperative that everyone works their full 12 hours of their night shift. One cannot leave before the end of their shift and request another to fill in because everyone has their own patient needing attention."

"Well, you know that once a patient is asleep, it is just waiting and intervening only in the event a problem occurs. So, taking care of two patients near the end of the night is not such a big deal," Alba said with a straight face.

His patience slipping fast, Robert quit, sat with his elbows on the table hands folded his hands and commenced cold staring at Alba.

She rose and informed Dickson that, "We cannot make progress with this kind of meeting,. The doctor fails to understand my problem," and took her leave.

Robert reminded Dickson that she was responsible for correcting Alba's unacceptable conduct. Dickson lamented that she while could not force anything, she would pray for Mrs. Alba to self-correct, now that her misconduct had been brought to her attention.

"Nonsense," Robert said. "You have an employee flagrantly disobeying the rules, and even more importantly violating the spirit of care for both the patients and the other employees. And you're telling me there is nothing you can do but pray?"

Dickson looked at Robert as if she had no idea what he was talking about. To Dickson, the spirit of care meant the hospital defending its out-of-compliance employee against its out-of-protocol doctor.

44

Robert persevered in doing his best for his patients, but his drive and enthusiasm for the sleep center had died. Even though he was a fastidiously well-organized person, he nevertheless loathed bureaucracy for the sake of bureaucracy. At one point, he explained that distinction to the techs, but they didn't get it. To them, the hospital bureaucracy was fundamental to providing them a safe framework and comfort zone inside which they could function without taking any initiative.

Fetters kept Robert apprised that Alba was still picking and choosing her workdays and insisting she was not required to change that behavior. Considering how her bad behavior was being rewarded by a hospital bureaucracy that was normalizing the abnormal, all Robert could do was keep his head down and nose to the grindstone, focusing on his clinical work with patients.

One late morning, Hospital VP Maria Frost called him to meet with her. She sounded agitated and Robert assumed it was probably due to some small technical or budgetary issue, if not the Alba situation again. However, the budget had already been developed and he visited regularly with the director of budget planning. In any case, Robert headed to the third floor of the Hospital administration ivory tower, where everyone shuffled quietly, careful not to leave footprints on the perfectly vacuum cream-colored wall-to-wall carpeting.

This time he was not asked to wait before entering the inner sanctum, instructed instead by the receptionist to walk directly into Ms. Frost's office. There she was, sitting stiff and straight, her hands folded on her paperless desk and her plain face and dull eyes peering into infinity. As usual, Sorry that we cannot take you out for lunch, but we all have a lot of work to do this afternoon."

Robert met briefly with the accountant who basically told him to wait for a potential offer. All he needed was Robert's social security number, his address and a copy of his passport.

He could not read her state of mind, but her frequent eye blinking belied a nervous and edgy discomfort.

Dispensing with any introduction or welcome, she said that some techs had come to her. Techs visiting directly with a VP seemed a bit farfetched, if not completely out of the question. Evidently, the highly-prized protocol of operating by way of Fetters did not apply to them.

"And?" Robert tried to smile, perceiving a fast approaching darkness that was about to overtake him.

"These techs, Dr. Vermeer, came to complain about your behavior."

"In what sense? Complaining about the planning or having problems with the work schedule?"

"No." She now directed her gaze straight at him and clasped her fingers as if to pray for forgiveness.

"They informed me that you are harassing them."

"Me, harassing techs? In what way do I harass them? Is it the day techs, the night techs, all of the techs? Exactly who is making such charges?"

As if he was hard of hearing, she reiterated, "Some techs informed me right here in my office that you are harassing them, and I have no reason not to believe them." After a few moments, she added, "And I cannot divulge any further information to you."

"This is completely baseless and untrue. I have such an excellent rapport with the day staff that I cannot remotely imagine any one of them making such an accusation. As far as the night staff is concerned, I rarely ever see them. There is, of course, the ongoing issue with the night tech, Michelle Alba, but the personnel department is handling that."

Frost lifted her head higher, saying, "I am telling you that you are harassing the technicians." Each word rolled out of her mouth like a cascade of ice cubes.

Robert pointed his finger at Frost saying, " And I am telling YOU that I have not harassed any technicians. I am also telling you that you have only to put that one single word on my record to make my life and career a complete wreck. I repeat that I did not and do not harass technicians, or anyone else."

Frost leaned back into her chair, cowering from Robert as if he had some contagious disease.

"You are one angry man, Doctor. You have given me even more reason to believe the associates who tell me you are harassing them."

"So you accept accusations at face value, Ms. Frost, without documentation or checking further?"

"I have nothing more to say."

Robert left thinking that he had to be hallucinating. He had been so scrupulously careful to avoid even the hint of a passing touch or ever remarking on a tech's appearance. Sometimes the techs did not share his opinions, but was that harassing them? Compounding his other offenses, this one was sure to skyrocket up the hospital ranks.

* * *

Robert returned to his office, resolved one more time to concentrate on his clinic work and continue being careful in communicating with the technicians. He also needed to find out who went to Frost. Maybe Lisa would know something.

He was in the clinic, waiting to see the next patient when he got a phone call from Suzy Dickson about the

Michelle Alba case. She had managed to arrange a meeting with Alba in Robert's office the next day and she asked Fetters to be there as well.

Wanting to have proof of whatever was said in his office, Robert decided to tape record the meeting. The following day Dickson arrived first and took a chair next to Robert's desk. Fetters and Alba arrived at the same time and took seats at either end of the couch. Robert suggested, "Maybe you could swap positions, so that Ms. Alba can be closer to interact with Ms. Dickson." They agreed and switched sides. Dickson asked for the door to be closed. With the scene finally set, Robert activated his tape recorder, which sat on top of a stack of desk files in front of them.

Dickson opened saying, "We are here to solve as best we can the problem that has occurred between Mrs. Alba and Dr. Vermeer."

Alba broke in, "The problem is not me. Dr. Vermeer sent me a certified letter because he did not wish to talk to me first. That is what the problem is."

There she goes, Robert thought, playing the rules and regulations game. Dickson suggested that it might be worthwhile reviewing the history to better understand what happened. She pointed out that Dr. Vermeer had withdrawn the certified letter the day after she received it.

To this, Alba raised her voice a notch, charging that Dr. Vermeer's clear intention was to accuse her but refuse to speak to her. Moreover, he refused to make allowances for her having to be home with her children due to her husband's work out of state. On that count, Robert had to agree with her, although he was clueless what Alba's domestic situation had to do with anything.

All of a sudden, Alba pointed to his desk and said, "You are recording this conversation without first asking for my permission. You are in violation of my privacy." As she stood up, she added, "We are getting nowhere with this meeting." Pulling the door open, she let it slam shut behind her.

"Oh my goodness," shrieked Dickson. "She's right. I -neverr noticed the tape recorder."

"I did not hide it."

"You can't do that, and now she's gone. Now, we're in even deeper trouble," she sighed.

"What do you mean deeper trouble?"

"Well, I am not supposed to tell you, but she is planning to file a lawsuit against you for racial discrimination."

"First she charges me with harassment, and now racial discrimination?"

"Yes, she is claiming that your accusation of her violating the sleep center rules is because she is an African American woman."

"I don't know what to say, except that race had nothing to do with my committing an administrative error, which I attempted to correct a few days later. In addition, wasn't I the one who selected her during the hiring process? I chose her, an African American, in preference to a qualified Caucasian technician, because she told me she had ample experience in pediatrics. I gave her a job, for God's sake. Race? Come on!"

Dickson looked flustered and frazzled.

"Has Alba already filed the lawsuit?"

"I can't tell you anymore. All I know is the hospital is in trouble and all because of you." Dickson stood up, assembled her papers and fled Robert's office.

Robert went over to the clinic where he found Stone in an ugly mood. Patients were stacked up, waiting to be seen with no sign of Robert. As Robert explained about having being called in a mandatory personnel meeting, Stone listened but visibly annoyed he had to listen. Insufficiently versed about the situation, Stone shrugged his shoulders and walked off saying, "There's a line of patients waiting for you."

That evening Robert arrived home at his wits' end. After listening attentively, Anna tried comforting him by maintaining that, after all was said and done, the trouble with the technicians, based on lies and misunderstandings, would ultimately evaporate back into the thin air from which it came. Robert crossed his fingers that Anna was right and that he could somehow hold out smack inside the eye of this storm.

45

In the early morning Robert sat in his office wondering whether he should meet with the VP and enlighten her that this case could never stand up in court because there wasn't a shred of evidence against him for harassment. Robert even hoped against hope that she would check and confirm his claims and reprimand the associates for their fraudulent misrepresentations.

He got Maria Frost on the line. She told him she was too busy for a meeting with him. He insisted that she check her calendar for a date that would suit both of them. She gave a gasp into the phone and then the line went quiet. When he asked whether she was still there, she replied that she had no intention of discussing the matter further with him while investigations were ongoing.

So God had not bestowed upon Maria Frost the gifts of fairness and objectivity. Her concern was for protecting her associates, not him. Her desire to impress Executive VP Elisabeth Bitterman probably factored in there somewhere too.

Robert had become subject to Heisenberg's Uncertainty Principle, a quantum physics formulation in which the objectification of the world of perception is impossible. There is no purely objective view, because the subject changes, just by looking at it. Ergo their perception of him could not objective.

As Robert pondered the Frost factor, he realized that he would ultimately have to succumb to the Serenity Prayer, accepting that which one cannot change. Yet, he still needed some bolstering and encouragement. So, he called his best friend, Charlie. They arranged to meet at the bistro la Madeleine off Preston Road in Plano at two o'clock, when the majority of the luncheon crowd would be gone.

At two in the afternoon Robert sat alone at la Madeleine with his cup of coffee getting cold. Charlie was usually on time when he made an appointment; maybe he had been held up by one of his clients. The hustle and bustle between the tables by the women waiters in their black aprons and black French type berets had started to ebb.

Charlie strolled over to the table, his fingers stroking through his tangled white hair. He gave Robert a strong handshake and said, "Let me get a coffee. Want some pastry?" and then, before Robert could answer, added, "Of course, you do." A few minutes later he brought a numbered wooden square block to the table, signifying the order. Not before too long the waitress exchanged the blocks for the pastries.

Charlie apologized for being late. It wasn't due to a client at his real estate company, but from a visit with Dr. Stone at the internal medicine clinic. "But let me hear your news first, Robert. I called your home earlier and spoke briefly to Anna. I could hear her choking up. Clearly something awful is going on."

Robert told him of the events during the last few months, parts of it Charlie had heard before, but now he was getting the whole picture. Robert tried to speak in cool and calm tones, but at times his voice quivered and his face could not hide his fury and his grief.

"I'm feeling like a train has run over me, shredding me into bits and pieces. Maybe I should consider the option that a friend of mine took by killing himself. By removing myself from the equation, I could solve everyone's troubles. It is terrible thinking, but maybe a right one."

"That is not an option," Charlie interrupted, "and I beg you not to be stupid. I know you are not that kind of person, Robert. You are too strong and, most of all, you are a survivor." Pressing his hand to Robert's shoulder, Charlie went on. "And you are by no means alone. There are people who care about you. One is sitting in front of you and the other is at home, to name just two."

Robert swallowed hard. Charlie continued. "You are not a piece of shit, although your enemies are trying to break your spirit and make you feel worthless. That's what they want you to believe. Don't let them do that to you." His face closed in on that of Robert's. "You are not some piece of shit, Robert. Do you hear me?"

Robert stared back at Charlie.

"The patients are what count and from what I know, that's what you care about. But not everybody is like that and I'll tell you why."

He recounted to Robert how Dr. Stone's idea of caring was about rendering book-based diagnostics and treatment, not about the person, who is not the disease. "The disease is what the person has, not what the person is," Charlie made the distinction, "and it is the person who should be treated."

Robert thought about Stone's style of doctoring. Being direct and open with the patient was probably the best that Stone could do, rather than lying and short selling the truth. Nevertheless, Stone should indeed take into consideration that he was dealing with a sensate being, needing more than just the name of a new chemo that could be prescribed. Charlie's words contained food for much thought.

Charlie's opinions about the medical system were becoming more and more entrenched. To him, chemotherapy destroyed his defense system and with each round of medication, his chances of survival diminished rather than improved. He had been looking into alternative therapies and found that doctors in German and Swiss clinics were focusing on supporting the patient's will to heal and raising the patient's defenses, and in so doing, creating quality of life. There were success stories about tumors shrinking and people surviving and conquering their cancer. "That," Charlie said, 'is what I am looking to find for myself."

Robert was embarrassed having Charlie, fighting for his very own life, deliver a motivational speech about surviving bureaucratic intrigue and politics. Beside himself with wretchedness and despair, Robert whispered, "Charlie."

As they continued talking about various alternative cancer therapies, Robert admitted how unversed he was with the medical aspects of cancer treatments, but nevertheless recounted stories he had heard about miraculous healing. He also acknowledged how under-rated the healing power of the mind was. Maybe Charlie was right. And how ironic that the one needing help was the one who was giving his words of wisdom and comfort and possessing the truest spirit of care.

They finished their coffees, hugged and departed the bistro.

As Robert headed back to the center to catch up on the time he had lost from work, he reflected on Milan Kundera's story *The Unbearable Lightness of Being* about a relationship that had gone bad. The wife of the main character, who is having an affair with another woman, felt that she was becoming a burden to him. Nothing could make her see the lightness and pleasure of life. Likewise, Robert was failing to see the lightness of his own life. With Charlie's grounded counseling, Robert -could resist the attacks by not becoming lost in the darkness. Anna had to know this as well, so he switched direction and drove toward home.

Anna was on the couch, reading a magazine. Robert sat next to her, put his arm around her shoulder and started telling her softly, "I met with Charlie this afternoon. As sick as he is, that man has helped me begin healing. You know what a believer I am in the power of the mind and how often I cite a book by Dr. Bruce Lipton *'The Biology of Belief?'* Now I have to practice what I preach."

Robert went into Lipton's ideas and studies on how the behavior of cells is controlled by the environment and how, in extension, the mind controls or overrides the body. "Without even knowing this concept and its supporting evidence, here was Charlie, already a practicing proponent of Lipton's, telling me to believe what I believe."

Robert also cited William Manchester who said that, "To the medieval mind the possibility of doubt did not exist. This applies to any dogmatic religion in which a person is forced to accept ideas and applications of these ideas without questioning. Yet, the dogma makers are also human. Dogmatism is the opposite of scientific curiosity. Asking questions is what children do as they are growing up, it is their way of learning and understanding."

Robert continued, "Art critics used the term 'sfumato', mist, or smoke to indicate the hazy quality characteristic of Leonardo da Vinci's drawings, as once was stated by Michael Gelb. It is this haziness or questioning that made this genius a great scientist as well. Questioning is what Charlie does and that's what makes all the difference," concluded Robert.

"I will do this too, Anna. I not only have the right to question but, like Charlie, I also have the right of refusal. I do not have to allow them to turn me into some kind of a human punching ball, continuously at their mercy to batter and destroy."

He waited a few seconds and continued, "I have to think positively, Anna, which does not mean there will be no more pain and suffering. I just won't live in fear of what is to come, but take it one day at a time."

46

It was Monday morning. Menacing clouds continued to loom low inside the lab, but Robert had no way of dispelling them. Whenever he opened his office door, the techs became quiet. Fetters spoke to him the least of all. Robert noticed that former administrator Dave Jacobs had been visiting her quite frequently. For the past months and years he never knew what they talked about and Fetters never volunteered any information about their meetings. "Let them gossip and conspire, I really don't care," Robert thought.

Julie at the reception desk handed him a list of the patients scheduled for the clinic. It promised to be a busy day and that was good. Not knowing how to approach Robert and too timid to admit to his cowardice, James had become a silent partner. Robert could have deemed this an advantage, but the two had managed to develop a cordial working relationship and Robert was missing that. He struggled with his mixed feelings towards James. Yes, James was understandably fearful of losing the Center he had taken years to build, but then again, James had never done anything but throw Robert under the bus. So why should Robert give a damn about James?

Sitting in his office, Robert looked over the patient list when his phone rang. It was Ms. Dickson from Personnel without so much as a 'Good morning, Dr. Vermeer.'

"Ms. Alba has filed a lawsuit," Dickson stated in tense tones.

Robert remained quiet. Nothing followed but her labored breathing. A few months ago, this obese, non-compliant, sleep apnea patient, who refused treatment, amused him. Now, she disgusted him.

Her message was no surprise, Robert just wondered about the specifics. Shortly after Dickson's phone call, VP Maria Frost called, telling him to drop what he was doing and attend a meeting at the Hospital administration office. Robert left word with the reception people to call him on his cell phone when clinic started. Regardless of what was happening to him, Robert's patients were not to get caught in the crossfire.

It had been months since his last meeting with Frost, as their monthly get-togethers had been cancelled. The closer he got to her office, the more he felt his stomach tightening. He took a deep breath and forcefully blew the air out of his lungs as he stepped in her office. There she was, the scowling nun sitting behind her empty desk. Robert wanted to heave her and her desk upside down.

According to Frost, Michelle Alba had hired a winning African American attorney, a specialist in racial discrimination cases. Robert knew immediately who it was. He and his staff were ambulance chasers. They even had a TV ad proclaiming that, "If you are ever subject to harassment or discrimination, you need the law on your side. Our office is here to help you. Call our toll free number!"

Alba's lawsuit had been filed against the hospital for allowing Dr. Vermeer of the Imcare group to harass technicians and specifically Michelle Alba, the plaintiff. Frost would say nothing more. When Robert asked for a copy, Frost said she did not have the authority to give him one.

"I repeat, Ms. Frost. Show me the lawsuit."

Taken by surprise, Frost's face went white.

"Miss Frost, you will give me a copy of the lawsuit or I'm outta here."

She had nothing to show. Robert left, giving a strong yank to the door, which closed with a muffled bang.

* * *

James was summoned to a meeting of the Imcare group at their headquarters. Once everyone was present, Gary stated there were three issues to be addressed. Facing James, Gary said "The first is about your failure, James, as the medical director of the Center, to control Vermeer's disrespectful behavior toward our colleagues and Imcare employees, including our colleagues' wife Laura Owens. Now, he is harassing technicians. What more," Gary asked rhetorically, "did James need to have happen before intervening?"

James balked, "Are you saying that I am to blame for all of Robert's transgressions? Who was it who gave him his responsibilities without even consulting with me?"

"Don't play that game with me, James. You are the one who dropped the ball here, so don't turn it around."

James crossed his arms and went into silent mode. Salvo took the advantage by saying that he had anticipated and recognized these problems months ago and even claimed to having been the one instrumental in sorting out and solving the problems with Vermeer.

"I am aware of that," Gary said, "so let's appoint someone who has support from the hospital to lead the center. James should spend more time in the internal medicine clinic where he belongs, something we have been saying all along. Liborio, think about your taking the lead at the center and James, forget about your center, it is ours."

Everyone kept mum. The prime directive was insuring the stability of the sleep Center's revenue stream. Any internal squabbles were up to James and Liborio to deal with between themselves.

Gary was not done yet. "The second and related issue is the growing pressure from the hospital to terminate the source of our troubles, Vermeer. Up until now, he carried administrative responsibilities and, as the director, answered to hospital administration. However, Mrs. Bitterman and Frost insist that we take corrective actions, so I am leaving such business in Liborio's hands."

The third issue was a pending lawsuit, which would require expenditures for their defense. That caught the attention of the group. Extra costs would cut into their benefits and in addition a lawsuit involved their reputation. They all agreed on a speedy action.

Gary concluded, "We want the case resolved without the press getting wind of this potential lawsuit. According to Mrs. Bitterman, the hospital administration is extremely upset and instructing their lawyers to settle in as low key a fashion as possible. Also, to demonstrate that we are neither practicing nor endorsing discrimination, they have chosen an African American attorney."

47

Robert was asked to go to Salvo's office, adjacent to the clinic. Robert had suspected a power struggle between Stone and Salvo for quite some time. On the surface, they worked well together and seemingly held similar opinions on patient care, but Robert knew better.

As Robert paused momentarily at the reception desk, Julie noted, "Dr. Vermeer, you have a busy clinical schedule today. Have you received a copy of it?"

"Yes, thank you." he replied, struck by how instantly he and this African American woman had hit it off. Why had the same occurred not between him and Michelle Alba?

Robert proceeded over to Salvo' office and knocked on the door.

As he sat behind his desk looking at the computer screen, Salvo waved Robert in and indicated for him to sit down. Robert kept standing. He waited and waited, while Salvo' eyes remained fixed on the computer screen.

"Well, Doctor?" Salvo said, emphasizing Doctor. Then, taking his eyes off the computer screen said, like he was giving a military order, "Sit down."

Robert took a seat, wondering why Salvo had become a doctor in the first place? He had never seen Salvo display an iota of caring for anyone. All medical schools teach that a patient is more than a body or a means to make money. Salvo probably skipped those lectures. There should be a pre-med test to sort out the cold and hard-hearted.

"The Imcare group held a meeting with Executive VP Elisabeth Bitterman. She is highly distressed over your misconduct. You've caused trouble for the Hospital, for its Associates and now, incredibly, there is a lawsuit pending for racial discrimination."

Robert's ears caught the word pending, which implied something entirely different than what Dickson and Frost had told him earlier in the day.

"Your administrative directorship is finished as of today," Salvo said, laced with undertones of delight.

"Dave Jacobs will resume as administrator. In addition to all the other problems you have caused us, we are also losing the fees that the hospital paid us for your, between gestured quotation marks, "services.""

Robert stared ahead vacantly, but with a rising sense of impending freedom. As the sleep center administrator he reported both to the hospital and to Imcare, leaving him caught in the precarious middle. By being relieved of his administrative duties, he became disentangled from the various webs of deceit that they wove around him.

"You have nothing to say?" Salvo asked with mock shock.

Robert shook his head, "No."

Salvo' mouth twitched, as if he were chewing gum, and his eyes darted from the computer screen, to the wall, to Robert's shoulder.

"In addition, as of today, I am the Director of the sleep center," Salvo said, with an emphasis on the words 'I' and 'Director'.

"Congratulations," Robert said, catching Salvo by surprise.

Just as Robert had suspected, in the upshot of the power struggle, Stone was too weak and too much of a coward to defend even himself, much less Robert.

So Salvo, someone who spent the least amount of time in the center, who never spoke to a tech except to ask for a file he couldn't find, and who never had a question about a patient or a recording, had usurped both Robert and James and now ruled supreme.

For a second, Robert had a ridiculous thought about a scene from the movie 'Amadeus', about Mozart's life. He wanted to stand up, turn his back to Salvo and bow low while dropping his pants, but of course thought better of pulling such a stunt. They had yet to fire him, although his contract was up for renewal in just four months. There were still potential benefits to reap.

Robert continued to hold his silence. 'Les jeux sont faits', unbold Jean-Paul Sartre. The die is cast, but in Sartre's novel, the couple had a second chance, provided they showed that they really loved each other. There would not be a second chance for Robert; he never even had a first one. Mafia bosses don't give you one. They shoot to kill before asking questions. Robert thought of his first encounter with Salvo and how he insisted on sitting in the back corner facing the crowd. At least Robert had him pegged right from the get-go.

But Robert's new boss, the capo, was not yet finished inaugurating his new order.

"Clean out your office. We need it for Laura. I found you another one, away from the reception and technicians' area. It is on the left on your way out."

How fitting, an office close to the exit door.

"Julie will show you where it is. Your move needs to be made today."

"Anything else?" Robert asked in a clipped monotone. Salvo shook his head no.

After completing clinic with a silent Dr. Stone, Robert went and knocked on Stone's door. Without waiting, Robert entered and declared, "What goes around comes around, James, so now your cowardice has become your own undoing. Serves you right."

"I know, Robert. Sorry. I wish I knew what else to say."

"There's nothing else to say. You once told me to roll up my sleeves. It's your turn now."

Robert left and set about moving into his new office, which was even worse than the kitchen office he once occupied. It was a windowless claustrophobic room, six by five feet, a former storage space for the janitors. It contained a student desk with a black vinyl chair on wheels and a phone connection to which he could install his computer and continue generating clinical reports.

Leaning back in his chair, Robert closed his eyes and considered how far he had fallen. Maybe being away from the rest of the Center would not be so bad after all. He still had a job, a meager but nevertheless adequate consolation in light of his multiple shaming offenses. Instead of worrying about the unknown, he resolved to focus on generating sleep reports and loaded up his desk with patient charts. The first one concerned a sleep apnea patient from Salvo and contained pages of consults and medical history. Robert decided to discontinue his policy of reading any study, independent of its referral source, and returned this chart to the stack. From now on, he would read none of Salvo' studies.

It was back to basics for Robert, bunkered into his office, interspersed by trips to the tech room and the kitchen for coffee. Life became a series of boring statistics. The probability of his going on as a walking and talking ghost reached 95%. But there was still that 5% possibility of uncertainty and unexpected deviation from the norm.

48

For the next three months, Robert worked within the confines of his pocket-sized office, with strict instructions not to speak to the technicians. As the isolation wore on him, his work no longer held any stimulation for him. Salvo treated Robert like a servant, leaving his and Stone's sleep study interpretations, for Robert to do.

Nothing had changed in Robert's salary, but he knew the current situation could not last. Aware that his days at Imcare were numbered, Robert assessed his options and opted as usual, to play a waiting game. In the meanwhile, he would try to enjoy his clinical work.

Lisa would sneak by his 'closet office' at regular intervals, always a bit anxious about being caught by Jacobs, who now strutted around proud as a peacock to be in charge again. Jacobs and Salvo became the new team in town.

From Lisa he learned that Alba was still doing whatever she wanted with her schedule. As long as the case was pending, Alba was untouchable. Lisa told Robert, "Something is going on within the hospital administration, I don't know what exactly. A few days ago, several men in suits, accompanied by VP Maria Frost, visited the Center during the evening hours. They spoke among themselves, but not to anyone of us."

"Do you know who these men were?"

"I heard they were lawyers, one was an African American. Also, a rumor is circulating that Salvo and his wife are involved in a big divorce battle. I'm not surprised, considering all the time he had been spending with Ms. Jackson. We all think she's the reason for the problems in the Salvo family."

Robert neither enjoyed this news nor felt sorry for Salvo or Priscilla. His catholic upbringing taught him that bad behavior was punished. However, there were many bad people who were never punished, and if their punishment happened after life, he had no way of knowing.

* * *

Someone knocked at his door. It was Priscilla, sans any files. Insinuating herself into the corner, she occupied the only chair.

Robert said "Hello," and waited for her to speak.

"I have come to tell you that we will not be renewing your contract. According to our contractual arrangements, we have to give you three months' notice of this fact. Today is that day," she stated in official tones.

Robert took a deep breath. This was not unexpected, but still, he felt like a sledgehammer had hit him.

"We expect your full cooperation, as well as your adherence to the existing work regime. You will get the written discharge by certified mail today."

After delivering her message, she departed, her stiletto high-heels click clacking down the hallway.

Memories flashed across Robert's mind, opening with Stone's cold shoulder reception and closing with the lawsuit being brought by that personification of spirit of care in action, Michelle Alba. Now he had three months left before exiting the premises.

At four in the afternoon, he called it quits and left for home and the certified letter, probably waiting there for him. Like Shakespeare's Shylock, the Imcare and hospital sharks were circling, seeking Robert's pound of flesh and no one was coming to his aid, much less his rescue.

* * *

A few days after Priscilla gave Robert his three months' notice. John, the Sertur Pharmaceutics sales rep knocked on Robert's door. Sertur was the company that planned a clinical study on a new sleep aid and John had come to see Robert when he had just started with his first clinical research study. He had signed a confidentiality agreement, which allowed him to read the proposal, but he never heard anything further back from them.

"Hi, Dr. Vermeer, it's been a long time. You probably remember that I had originally come to suggest your participation in a new clinical study that we were conducting. Unfortunately, there was a delay in the planning, but things are back on track now and moving ahead."

Robert thought he should tell the guy that he was barking up the wrong tree.

"I've heard that during the past year a lot has happened here at the center," John paused looking around and waved his hands at the small space. "This is really not a fitting office for you."

"For what I have to do, it is enough," said Robert, wondering what more he could say. The only chance Robert could see for an additional clinical study was Salvo seizing it as an opportunity to pocket the only thing he did care about, money.

As if he had been reading Robert's mind, John said, "We are not planning a clinical study at this center, Doctor, where you are not in charge of the clinic and the research."

Robert did not get what the sales rep was driving at.

The sales rep took a chair, rested his elbows on the desk, his chin in his hands and said, "Maybe there is something I can do for you, and in return, we could collaborate in the future."

"You have my undivided attention," Robert replied.

"I hear a lot through the grapevine. Everybody talks and wonders what happened with you. A lot, they say, has to do with internal power struggles that you've unwittingly gotten in the way of."

Robert did not react. The man could just be flattering. What did he really want?

"However, Dr. Vermeer, as you know I go to a lot of medical offices and meet a lot of doctors." He paused and a smile curled on his lips. "There is a psychiatrist out there, who does not know much about the operation of a sleep disorders center. Many patients in his practice complain about their sleep problems; neurotic patients, depressed patients and what have you."

Robert nodded, aware that psychiatrists commonly deal with patients complaining about not sleeping well. In a number of cases the insomnia hides an underlying depression.

The sales rep continued "This doctor is interested in building a sleep disorders center to expand his service, but has no idea what that would entail. I thought this might be of interest to you and that you might be the person he is looking for."

Flabbergasted by what he was hearing, Robert inquired, "Does this doctor know about you coming and talking to me?"

"Yes, and he wants to meet with you, after hours of course."

Could this be manna from Heaven, or more smoke and mirrors for Robert to get lost inside?

"I know what you are thinking, Doctor."

"Are you a mind reader, Sir?"

"Let me explain what I want out of this. If this collaboration between you and the psychiatrist works out, then maybe our clinical study could be done at the new independent center."

Although this was almost too good to be true, Robert lightened up at this amazing turn of events.

The next day he got a call. Thinking that Robert might enjoy an English ale, the psychiatrist suggested they meet the following week at the 'Fox and Hound English Pub

& Grille' on Campbell Road. There they could get to know each other and discuss the possibilities of creating a private sleep disorders center. How refreshing it was to be dealing one-on-one, and not with administrators and their bureaucratic regulations.

Of course, there was that snake lurking in the fine print of Robert's contractual arrangements with Imcare, the one prohibiting him from working within a thirty-mile radius. The good doctor's clinic was within that range, but "Don't worry," said John. "That's what we have lawyers for."

49

It had been ages and Priscilla longed to be with Liborio. She called his sleep center phone, knowing he worked there with his office door shut and the receptionists had strict instructions to disturb him only in the case of 'life threatening events'.

"Honey, it's been forever. How about coming to my place? I'm all ready and waiting for you." There was silence on the other side. She asked whether he still was there.

"I'm pretty busy right now, Priscilla."

How icy he sounded, and why was there no reply to her invitation? Her stomach started knotting up. Further inquiries were met with further hesitation and evasion. Finally, she decided to visit him in his office at six when everyone would be gone. He said okay without much enthusiasm.

A few minutes before 6 o'clock, Priscilla entered the vacated center and, on her way to Liborio, passed by Robert's new office. Through the open door she saw him sitting at his desk and they made fleeting eye contact.

She let herself into Liborio's office where he was seated behind his desk looking at his computer screen. She went behind and took him by his shoulders, kissing him firmly, only to have him - pull back and practically push her away. Undeterred, Priscilla resumed her advances.

Meanwhile, Robert exited his office and strolled in the direction of the reception area. At the same time, Stone had left his office and coincidently met Robert the reception area.

"Looking for a file," Robert said.

Stone pointed at Salvo' closed office door and said "Looking for Salvo." Opening without knocking on the door of Salvo's office, Stone walked in on Priscilla lying on top of Salvo.

"What the...?" stammered Stone, staring at Salvo who was frantically fixing his mussed hair.

"Well, well," Robert chuckled.

"It's not what you think, Stone." Salvo pleaded.

"Sure. Family matters, right?" said Stone backing away.

"Oh my goodness, oh my goodness," was all Priscilla could say and slammed the door shut.

As Robert walked back to his office, he heard Salvo yelling and carrying on.

"-Your coming here, Priscilla, was so utterly stupid. Just go. Get out and don't come back."

Instrumental in his achieving a total takeover of the center, Priscilla was stunned that he was dumping her. Screaming obscenities at him, she seized him by his shirt collar.

Seizing her wrists, Salvo shouted "Don't you dare touch my face."

Priscilla froze, tears running down her cheeks. She loved him; she helped him get everything he wanted. Now that he was in control, he was done with her and wanted her gone.

"This is not the last of me, Dr. Salvo. I've got a lot invested in you and nobody plays Priscilla Jackson like a fool."

For a second time his office door slammed shut.

* * *

Stone was euphoric. Everything was finally making sense. Liborio and Priscilla had wrested away from him control of the center that he had conceived and built over the course of six years. Now it was payback time.

Before making any major moves, though, he needed to arm himself with some facts and figures. Milton, her personal secretary, was the likely candidate to supply such ammo.

The next day he called Milton to find out where Priscilla was. Milton said she had gone to the off-site office and that she would be away for the majority of the day. That was all he needed to hear. He told the receptionists that he had to attend a meeting off site and that Vermeer could start the clinic without him.

Stone drove to the administrative center and Priscilla's secluded fourth floor office. There was Milton, posted outside, protecting the entrance. Stone pointed towards the conference room and instructed Milton to join him.

Milton came out from behind his desk asking, "In the conference room, Dr. Stone?"

"Yes."

This was a highly unusual situation, a doctor coming to meet with Milton. Stone could read Milton's mind searching all registers, wondering what he had done wrong, what he was going to be blamed for, and what repercussions would befall him. Stone let Milton open the door and directed him to switch the sign to indicate 'Meeting in Progress'.

Milton sat at the edge of his chair, his hands folded in his lap. Stone started by telling Milton that if he ever told anyone about this meeting, his days at Imcare would be done.

"There will be no little whispered confidences to whatever friends you have, with Priscilla at the top of the list. Understood?"

"Yes, Sir."

Stone then launched into telling Milton how he had often noticed Milton stealing glances at Priscilla and that he understood how Milton, an unmarried man in the close proximity of such a nice looking woman, would not only want her but was probably in love with her. Milton flushed and began wringing his hands. "I totally understand," Stone reiterated, "and would feel the exactly same if I was in your position."

Milton stayed mute, staring at Stone who said that there was a 'but.' A big 'but.' Priscilla loved someone else, he knew who that was, and Milton knew too.

"You know, don't you, Milton? Let me tell you. It's Dr. Salvo, isn't it?"

Milton nodded.

"I can help you, Milton, because I've come here as your friend."

Although Milton saw through the transparency of Stone's lie, Milton also saw that there might be something to gain by aligning himself with Stone.

"I know that Dr. Salvo and Priscilla have been meeting each other, but I don't know where and for how long," Stone prodded. "Has it been for less than a year?"

Milton shook his head, no.

"Over a year?" Milton nodded, yes.

"Where? I know you know, because you had to know." Stone did not realize how literally he had taken it, how Milton had been following them, and how he knew everything exactly.

"You know how I can help you, Milton? By breaking up her relationship with Salvo, leaving you to have a free hand in the game." Stone relaxed in his chair and threw Milton a smile. "You can have Priscilla, but I need to know where they met."

"In the hospital," Milton answered quickly.

"Where?"

Without divulging that he had followed them, Milton revealed their secret meeting place in the second basement of the hospital, adding that they met there frequently in the early evening.

Stone's euphoria continued unabated. Retribution was just around the corner. He rose, extended his hand to shake Milton's, and gripping it tightly, said, "Bear in mind, Milton, that this conversation never happened. I wish you good luck with her."

With that Stone left and began plotting about how to drop this bomb.

* * *

A week later it was way past 5 p.m. at the normally busy Imcare administrative offices which of late turned into a tomb. Two persons were still present, although one did not know about the other. He had been waiting, hiding in the restroom until he was sure everyone was gone. He came out, looked around and inched his way slowly to the office door where he knew that she would be. A few pearls of sweat ran from his forehead into his eyes. Everything was set. The main entrance door to this section was locked and there were no security personnel around. They were down on the first floor and would not do their upper floor rounds for another few hours. Nothing ever happened in this building and there were no cameras in that section of the fourth floor.

He stepped inside Priscilla's office without first knocking. She had her feet up on her desk, half turned towards the window.

Her eyes widened and she exclaimed "What in the world? You're not allowed in here without permission. You know that."

Without replying, he moved slowly toward her, watching her frozen into her chair.

"You have got to get out of here," she tried commanding him.

"I have always adored you, Priscilla. But you always acted as if I didn't exist," he said in a strange voice, now circling around her desk.

Seeing no escape, Priscilla repeated, "You have got to get out of here. Go!" She reached for the phone, but with a wide stroke he swept the desk clean.

"We are alone now, Priscilla. I have been waiting so long for this moment," he said grinning and reaching for her.

She tried to flee, but he grabbed and forced her back into her chair with strength she never expected him to have. She tried to scream, but nothing came out. From nowhere he produced a rope, pulled her arms to her back and tied them together. Then he put a tape on her mouth. He grabbed her and put her down on the carpet in front of her desk. He stood widespread before her, with her legs in between.

"You are mine now, Priscilla, so listen to me. Salvo is gone and that is good because he never loved you. I'm the one for you, and this is our time to finally be together."

She shook her head furiously and tried to kick him. He put his hands on her knees, pulling them apart and laying himself on top of her. He penetrated and pushed deeply into her. Her screams continued soundlessly.

Finished and panting, he got up from her with his eyes blazing saying, "Salvo is gone, my Priscilla, and he will never come back to you. You belong to me now, so say nothing to anyone, for, unlike Salvo, I will be coming back to you, over and over again."

Before leaving, he wrapped a cord around her feet, released the restraints from around her arms and left in a hurry.

In the week that followed, Priscilla remained at home, police swarmed the Imcare offices and a detective took Milton away for questioning.

The Imcare doctors held an emergency meeting and made the only decision that could restore their reputation as a decent business. For her scandalous affair with Dr. Salvo and now another one with Milton, Priscilla was given the choice of voluntarily leaving or being fired.

50

Not too much longer and Robert would be out of this place. The sun was shining and the magic was starting to happen again. Although he went to work as usual, he was also working on a scenario for the other sleep disorders center.

A few weeks after Robert's meeting with the psychiatrist, Stone knocked on Robert's door asking to talk.

"What more is there to say, Dr. Stone?" Robert purposely did not use his first name.

"Well, I just wanted to let you know that Salvo' wife has kicked him out and he is busy with his divorce."

At a meeting with the Imcare group, they decided against him, which means we will not be seeing him again in the sleep center and he will not be a full partner until further notice. As a consequence of all that, I will be back in the Center as the director."

"So why should I care, Dr. Stone? Are you expecting me to congratulate you?"

Stone stood motionless and opened his mouth to speak again. "Well, actually I ..."

Robert cut him short. "If you came to -tell me that Imcare had decided to give me back my position -, why would I be remotely interested in staying and working among -that group of vultures? You, in particular, who did nothing but watch me hang, twist in the wind and then get eaten alive."

"I'm sorry, Robert, but you must understand..."

Robert stood up.

"There's really nothing to understand. You're sorry but it is too late. Please leave my office, if you can even call this an office. While we are at it, might I refresh your memory that your welcome to me was to dump me in the kitchen to office and work out of there? Remember?"

Stone stood forlorn, clearly caught holding a smoking gun.

For good measure, Robert added, "During the remainder of my time here, I'll be reading the sleep studies, but at my pace. If you need me in clinic, I will be there, extending my spirit of care to our patients. Otherwise, pardon me, Dr. Stone. I have a lot of work to do."

Robert sank into his chair, feeling no victory, no triumph, just bleak emptiness. He should have acted more forcefully long before, but that was not in his nature. His was one of reconciliation, confident that all people wanted the best for each other. Stone's visit had opened up wounds inside him that Robert thought had pretty much healed over. All the old feelings of anguish came rushing back, especially the 'why's' for alleged offenses that defied all logic and reason. From what Stone had told him, the power game was still on, even as Robert, the so-called perpetrator, was on his way out.

D-day came during the final week of November, as his third year with Imcare came to a close. Robert had been filling boxes with his books and personal files, loading everything into the trunk of his car. He went back to the lab and bid his adieus to the techs. Lisa approached him and said "Doctor, I know you never wanted to be touched, but this time..." She hugged him warmly and Robert could not help tearing up.

As Robert neared the exit door, he caught sight of Stone standing dolefully a few yards away and made his parting remark. "Like I've been saying, what goes around, comes around. Have fun, you and your colleagues, cheating and stabbing each other in the back."

* * *

A month later, Robert sat in his home office preparing to join the other private sleep center. His phone rang and he grabbed it, cheerfully saying "Dr. Vermeer." The voice on the other end came from the personnel department at St. Elisabeth Hospital, not Dickinson for a change.

"Dr. Vermeer, I am calling to let you know that there is a meeting you have to attend this coming Monday morning in the conference room of the personnel department in the basement of the hospital."

"What? A meeting in the hospital?" Robert thought, no way.

"Forget it, Miss. I won't be making it." He put the phone back on the receiver. What in the world were they thinking?

A minute later the phone rang again. He picked it up and started to say, "Miss, I'm…"

She interrupted and said, "Dr. Vermeer, this is a meeting with Federal Agents investigating the causes for the racial discrimination lawsuit. You have to be there. If you refuse, you will be subpoenaed."

On Monday morning, he went to the hospital, dressed casually. The meeting took place in the basement conference center, a large room with smaller meeting rooms off to the side. As soon as he entered, he saw a few of the technicians, one of them being Lisa. She went up to him and gave him a hug and asked how he was doing. Other techs from the daytime staff came over to tell him how sorry they were that things had gone so badly for him. Over at the side, Fetters, not knowing what to do, stole glances at Robert. Robert was too tense to notice, much less be amused by her conundrum.

Lisa reported that control of the sleep center was entirely back into the hands of the hospital and that a physician they had never heard of came to interpret the sleep studies. He did not interact with the technicians, except to request a file, and as soon as he finished reading, left as silently as he had come. They also were not seeing Stone anymore.

At that moment, a tall African American man came up to Robert, took him by his arm.

"What the heck is this?"

"Follow me, Sir," the man said.

Robert pulled back and said, "Who are you?"

"I'm an attorney and I need to prepare you for your meeting with the Federal Agents."

The attorney took him to a small room and closed the door. He told Robert that two agents would interview him about the case of Mrs. Michelle Alba. A judge had rejected the initial lawsuit, but Mrs. Alba filed another one, which was essentially a variation of the first one where the crux of the case remained racial discrimination.

"I am attending the meeting with you, to assure that everything goes according to the rules. Otherwise, I am not allowed to say anything."

A shiver ran down Robert's spine, rules, bureaucratic rules, church rules, nuns' hospital rules, always some kind of nonsensical rules. But the hospital had given him a guard dog. Miracles will never cease.

There was a knock at the door. A woman guided Robert to another room where two men dressed in plain suits sat behind a desk. They invited Robert to sit down before them. The tall African American lawyer took a seat alongside Robert.

The interview was the standard good cop – bad cop scenario, where the same questions phrased in different ways were asked, one by a kindly, considerate agent and the other, a curt and stern agent. Most of the questions concerned what Robert considered as trivial issues. Gradually he got the impression that they were feeling embarrassed by this exorbitant waste of time. They kept their straight faces, though.

A lengthy amount of questioning was spent addressing the meeting Robert held in his office where Fetters and Alba sat on the couch.

"Doctor, do you remember the first meeting in your office with Mrs. Alba, which was also attended by your tech Ms. Fetters?"

"Yes, I do:"

Who entered the room first?"

"Mrs. Alba."

"Where did she sit?"

"Well, she first sat on the left side, which was to my right."

"Then Mrs. Fetters entered your office."

"Yes."

"Did you ask Mrs. Alba to move so that Ms. Fetters could take her place?"

"I don't recall, it could have been Ms. Fetters herself."

"Did you demand Mrs. Alba to move?"

"Demand? No, I don't think so."

"If you requested her to move, -would you consider this a -proper way of handling such a situation?"

"Would it not appear reasonable to you that Mrs. Alba sat on the right side of Ms. Fetters, who was directly facing me?"

"That was not our question, Sir."

What is so important about seating positions, wondered Robert. What evidence is that to establish racial discrimination? He could readily understand their trying to figure out what his relationships were with the techs, who did the hiring, who did he report to, and what were his functions and duties. But which side of the couch someone sat on?

This line of questioning, however, went on for almost an hour, without one mention about harassment and racial discrimination.

The 'good cop' said, "Do you have anything more to say?

Robert cleared his throat and began. "To me, gentlemen, this is an absurd spectacle. I am the actual victim. I am the one who should be filing a lawsuit against the hospital. I am not the insubordinate tech who, regardless of what her skin color is, failed to follow the rules of employment."

The attorney on his side moved nervously and put his hand on Robert's arm. Robert shook it off, looking back at the agents.

"I am guilty of making an error in hospital protocol by sending Mrs. Alba a written reprimand before giving her a verbal one. That administrative fault, gentlemen, is my sole and entire crime, which I am admittedly guilty of committing. The facts, however, remain the same and speak for themselves. Mrs. Alba's conduct as an employee was wrongful by virtue of her unwillingness to obey the rules of the center, which apply to everyone, and thereby disrupted the center's proper functioning."

Robert took a deep breath, noticing not the slightest twitch in the faces of his interrogators, and with a stalwart voice continued. "I remind you also that I was the one who hired this African American woman in preference to a white male. Why? Because of her claim to having had ample experience with kids as a sleep technician. This claim has since been shown not to be the case. Consequently, I do not regard it as a quantum leap of logic to say that if there is a victim here, I am that victim. Any discrimination that has occurred has been against me, a European American, invited to this country to educate students and to care for patients at the University and other institutes, including this hospital."

Again he paused and said, "The genuinely guilty parties in this discrimination are Mrs. Alba, Imcare, the doctors group and the hospital administration. They are the ones who tolerated and defended unruly workplace behavior in order to protect a spirit of care reputation that does not even exist. In doing so, they attempted to use and then bring me, the figurative black sheep in all this, to the slaughter.

As the agents listened attentively, Robert's attorney looked askance at Robert and opened his mouth to speak, only to be told to pipe down.

"So I go home now, an unemployed doctor who took exceptional care of his patients, none of whom ever complained and from whom I derived enormous satisfaction and gratification. They are my heroes, not the administrators. I am glad to be rid of this place where the spirit of care only means greed and self-interest, where it is as fake as the ads that they sell."

With those words Robert stood, nodded and left the agents sitting mute and motionless. The lawyer ran after him, scolding, "You were not supposed to say anything except for admitting your errors and responding to their questions. I am here in defense of the hospital, and you were only to state the facts."

"That's precisely what I did. State the facts," snapped Robert. "And you know what else? I care nothing about you or your client hospital. Go back and tell your masters that their places in hell are most certainly ready and waiting for them."

Holding his head high Robert walked away, scathed but unbroken.

A month later Robert received a letter from Imcare threatening him with a lawsuit for violating the non-compete clause in his former contract. But it was Christmas Eve and the Christmas lights sparkled outside and inside the houses. Life continued...

Epilogue

Dr. James Stone lost almost all his investment assets, due to bankruptcy of his investment company. He continued practicing for Imcare but could not retire at 60 years and decided to leave and start his own practice. He aged so drastically that a fly could break its legs walking across his deeply etched cheeks.

Dr. Liborio Salvo did not become a partner of Imcare and left town for an unknown destination, alone and divorced. He ended up in Wichita Kansas, working for a company as a consultant. The court convicted him of driving drunk and later for having sex with a minor. Now, he spends part of his time in a rehab center for drug abuse.

The chief of Imcare, Dr. Gary Cohen received a large retirement package from Imcare and still bought new cars about every three months. The local newspaper devoted an article on the richest doctors in town and featured him on the cover, with his new girl friend, his Thai masseuse.

Priscilla Jackson married a wealthy doctor, who did not have time to watch his new wife. She soon left with half his wealth and the lawyer who defended her divorce from the doctor. She spent a fortune on plastic surgery and slept with her botoxed eyes wide open. The devil still wears Priscilla.

Milton, former secretary of Priscilla, got fined for sexual assault, spent some time in jail for stalking Priscilla and other women. He remained single and continued his secretarial career in the fashion industry in another State, with a new name and plenty of women to look at.

The sleep technician Lisa joined another sleep center and became the Technical Director of the lab. She married a gentle hardworking man with whom she had two lovely children. Occasionally she calls Robert for a little phone visit.

The lead technician Sarah Fetters remained a loyal associate of the hospital who reassigned her to another service. She gained more weight and waddles around, full of her self-importance. She is still proud never to have visited any other place than Greenville, Texas.

Michelle Alba lost her lawsuit and her job. She joined another hospital and soon filed a new lawsuit, based on racial discrimination. They counter sued for false accusations and bribery of colleagues. Her husband left her for lack of love and money. She quit work at forty years of age and now survives on disability benefits.

Suzy Dickson of the personnel department received a promotion, married another associate and six months later, the couple snored each other away into separate rooms. Both love a six-pack of Budweiser, approach an astounding combined weight of 600 pounds, and spend half their life on the couch, alternating between snacking on sweets and watching the soaps.

Dave Jacobs, the sleep center administrator, bought a new suit, a brown one, combed his thinning hair sideways and continued walking in with a folder under his arm when he visited the downsized sleep center. He fell in love with a new doctor and managed to hide it from his supervisor, for fear of being dismissed from the hospital.

VP Maria Frost received a bonus for her achievements as well as an expanded service. She remained a virgin, became a fervent member of Opus Dei and flogged herself every night. Recently, she joined the order of St. Laurent and continues to live a holy life.

St. Elisabeth Hospital had a profitable year and the managers, including the Executive VP Elisabeth Bitterman received a handsome bonus. For a brief moment she considered supporting a cancer foundation, but then, taking the spirit of care into account, made the decision instead that charity begins at home and bought an $80,000 Cadillac XLR. She also acquired a new obedient husband, after the first one wasted away of a brain tumor.

Dr. Robert Vermeer kept practicing sleep medicine, in violation of the non-compete clause of his contract by joining another physician who needed training in sleep medicine and wanted Robert to consult with patients. Imcare threatened him with a lawsuit for breach of contract but Robert resisted long enough for them to leave him in peace. He survived as a true believer in applying the spirit of care as the only way to make sense of life. He now lives happily with Anna in a place where the earth and sky meet each other with vibrant colors.

If there is a heaven, Charlie is in it, watching the apocalypse unfold and holding his hand over Anna and Robert, guiding them into life's safe harbors.

Sleep technology and terms

Recording sleep in a sleep disorders center

In order to study sleep patterns and detect any abnormalities, a patient is not only observed, but has to be equipped with recording devices. Electrodes (small disks) are fixed on the scalp with glue and tape. They serve to pick up electrical brain waves. This is called EEG or electroencephalogram. An electrode fixed at the chin measures the muscle tension and an electrode fixed at the side of each eye measures eye movements. Registrations of the EEG and the other measures are recorded on paper running at a speed of 20 or 30 cm per minute or are visualized on a computer screen and the data are recorded on a disk. These measures (EEG, muscle tension and eye movements) serve to detect sleep-wake patterns and to define the various sleep states and stages.

Commonly, sleep analysts, technicians or doctors, look at every 20 or 30 second recording period and score these as awake, light sleep, deep sleep (two different degrees of deep sleep) or rapid eye movement sleep (REM). People believed that a person moved from being awake to deep sleep and then sleep became lighter until the point of waking up. During the early nineteen fifties, researchers discovered another stare of sleep, which they called rapid eye movement sleep or REM sleep. This radically changed the view on sleep.

On a normal night after falling asleep in a few minutes to half an hour, people move to light sleep, followed by light sleep and then deep sleep. After spending time in deep sleep, sleep becomes lighter again and the cycle ends with a REM sleep episode. Such cycle lasts on the average one and a half hour and each night contains three to five cycles, each cycle ending with a REM or dream sleep episode.

Although everyone dreams several times a night, most people do not remember having dreamt and some go so far to say that they never dream. It is one of those features of our physiology, which is none less than remarkable. To some these dream sleep periods are of significance to the person, others think of these as random non-significant events, but scientists believe that these episodes may be of significance in brain development in infants and children.

Besides the brain waves, sleep specialists want to look at other physiological measures. Electrodes or sensors fixed at different parts of the body measure a range of physiological parameters. The most common once are a sensor to measure airflow at nose and mouth; a finger probe to measure oxygen saturation in blood; chest and belly belts to measure the respiratory movements; electrodes to measure EKG or heart rhythm; and electrodes fixed at the leg muscles to measure leg movements.

The leads connecting the electrodes and sensors to the recording device are bundled to the back of the head of a person. In a sense, the patient looks as if they are strung with Christmas tree bulbs and often feel that they will be unable to fall asleep. Most of the times, patients do fall asleep within half an hour, as expected, unless they suffer from sleep onset insomnia.

Apnea
Apnea is a cessation of breathing and is associated with a decrease in oxygen saturation in blood.
The most common form, **obstructive** sleep apnea is characterized by an arrest in airflow due to an obstruction in the nose/mouth cavity, in spite of respiratory efforts (chest wall movement), which happens during sleep.
In **central** sleep apnea there is an arrest in airflow and an absence of respiratory effort.

Barbiturate
Common (older) sleeping pill. They are fairly toxic and when combined with alcohol, life-threatening.

Benzodiazepine
Benzodiazepines are a class of drugs considered effective against anxiety and epilepsy. Most of these drugs also relax muscles. Some are effective and safe hypnotics (sleeping pills). One example is Temazepam. These sleeping pills decrease deep sleep in favor of light sleep and decrease awakening (or arousals) from sleep. They may cause forgetfulness and some work longer than the sleep time and may cause drowsiness during the day.

Brain clock (or Biologic clock)
Small group of nerve cells close to the base of the brain, that organizes the timing of sleeping and waking. This brain clock contains an estimated 10,000 cells, which in total are the size of a pinpoint.

Cataplexy
Sudden loss of muscle tone seen in some patients who have narcolepsy. This can happen in few muscles but also in the legs whereby the person collapses on the floor. Cataplexy can occur when a person laughs, gets angry or is surprised. Bystanders often confuse cataplexy with a heart attack.

CPAP
Abbreviation for Continuous Positive Airway Pressure. It is the name of the machine that provides air under constant pressure through a mask placed on nose and mouth of a person. This causes a natural 'splint' in the airway passage, keeping the airway open and prevents apnea events.

Deep sleep
In particular during the first part of the night (the first sleep cycles) sleep might be deepest. It is harder to awaken a

person from deep sleep than from any other type of sleep. Deep sleep is also called stage three and four sleep or delta sleep.

Delta sleep
Another term for deep sleep. It indicates that during this sleep the brain waves are slow. The electrical activity of brain shows a rhythm in the 'delta frequency range', which are rhythms between 0.5 Hz and 3.5 Hz (Hz or Hertz is the measure of the number cycles per second).

Electroencephalography or EEG
Recording of spontaneous electrical activity of brain via electrodes placed on the scalp. The EEG is the best method to document the changing brain activity during sleep and for a long time was the only way to measure brain activity and function.

Evening person
A person who feels alert during the evening hours and who prefers to go to bed late. An evening person does not like to get out of bed early in the morning.

Hypnotic
The Greeks named their god of sleep "Hypnos". His twin brothers were Thanatos , or peaceful death and Oneiroi or dreams. A hypnotic is another word for a drug that induces sleep and eventually also maintains sleep. A popular term for a hypnotic is sleeping pill. Whether a hypnotic induces normal sleep is a matter of conjecture.

Insomnia
Somnus was the god of sleep according the Romans. Lack of 'somnus' or 'insomnia' is lack of sleep. A person may have a problem falling asleep ('sleep onset insomnia') or a person may wake up at night and is not able to go back to sleep ('sleep maintenance insomnia'), or a person may have both.

Hypersomnia
Hyper-somnus means too much sleep. It indicates the necessity to sleep longer than the time usually needed. Hypersomnia also means sleeping at other times besides the usual night time sleep.

Long sleeper
A person sleeps on the average 8 hours a night. A long sleeper is a person who commonly sleeps longer than eight hours. Some people need to sleep as much as 10 or even 16 hours.

Microsleep
Sleep during the day that occurs suddenly and lasts only a few seconds. People are often unaware of these micro sleeps and therefore pose danger, for example when driving a car.

Morning person
A person who gets out of bed early and who feels alert and active after waking up in the morning. They often go to bed early. The total amount of sleep is often the same as in another person.

Nap
Sleep occurring during the daytime, which can be refreshing if it lasts less than 30 minutes.

Narcolepsy
Sleep disorder that is mainly known to cause excessive daytime sleepiness. Often this sleepiness occurs unexpectedly and is irresistible, referred to as sleep attacks by clinicians. In some patients cataplexy (see definition) or hallucinations can occur. Hallucinations often occur at the beginning of the night. In some patients, they also have a difficulty in moving when waking up. This is called "sleep paralysis." Often, the

normal night sleep is disturbed in patients who have narcolepsy.

Non-benzodiazepine hypnotics
These hypnotics or sleeping pills belong to another chemical class than the benzodiazepines. Examples of short-acting drugs and which mainly help a person to fall asleep are: Zolpidem (Ambien) and Zaleplon (Sonata). Eszopiclone (Lunesta) may help improve both sleep maintenance and daytime alertness. Ramelteon (Rozerem) is the latest on the list.

Non-REM sleep
Term that has been introduced based on convenience. Non-REM sleep is sleep that is not REM sleep. The normal non-REM sleep consists of light and deep sleep.

Parasomnia
Sometimes called "Things that bump through the night." These are events happening during sleep at night that often are part of waking behavior, such as walking and talking. Also included is behavior that occurs while being in REM sleep, such as nightmares or aggressive behavior (REM sleep behavior disorder).

Periodic leg movements (PLMS)
Brief but repeated (every 20 to 40 seconds) movements of the legs while asleep, more often seen in middle aged and older people. PLMS may lead to repeated, brief and often unnoticed awakenings. A person who has PLMS may not be aware of this. PLMS lead to the feeling of having a bad sleep or not having slept at all.

Periodic limb movement disorder
Same as periodic leg movement, but it may also involve moving the arms. This term is preferred by the sleep experts.

REM
The abbreviation for rapid eye movements.

REM sleep
REM sleep is the name given to a stage of sleep, during which rapid eye movements are seen. REM sleep occurs at the end of each sleep cycle. In a normal person REM sleep occurs three to as much as six times a night.
During that stage the brain waves are almost similar to those seen while awake and the large skeletal muscles are relaxed and even actively paralyzed; in other words one cannot move during sleep. Often dreams occur during that stage.

Short sleeper
Persons commonly sleeping less than the average, which is eight hours of sleep. Sleep can be as short as three hours. These people, however, can function during the day as highly as anyone else and without needing to sleep during the day.

Siesta
Period during the afternoon during which people can relax or take a nap. A common practice in Latin America and Southern Europe.

Sleep attack
Sudden irresistible sleepiness, which is seen in people who have narcolepsy.

Sleep cycle
Sleep occurs in cycles that last an average of 90 minutes. During a sleep cycle a person moves from light to deep sleep and then back to light sleep, followed by REM sleep. Sometimes a brief period of wakefulness follows a REM sleep period. During a normal night there might be four to six sleep cycles. Deep sleep is usually more frequent during the first sleep cycles. During the last sleep cycles, sleep consists

mainly of light sleep. REM sleep tends to be longer during the last cycles of the night.

Sleep debt
By taking consistently less sleep than one need, one accumulates sleep debt. The term 'sleep debt' is often compared to taking money out of your bank account. Accumulating sleep debt leads to sleepiness and may lead to micro-sleeps or sleep attacks.

Sleep deprivation
Shortage of sleep that can be self-inflicted or due to circumstances, such as work schedule. Sleep deprivation leads to accumulating sleep debt

Sleep disorder center
A sleep disorders center provides consultation, diagnosis and treatment for sleep disorders. Patients are hooked up with different measuring devices and spend a whole night sleeping in the center. This measure allows discovery of what kind of sleep disorder a person may have and its severity.
In the USA accreditation of sleep disorders can be obtained by the American Academy of Sleep Disorders. This certifies that a center operates according to accepted clinical and operating standards.

Sleep fragmentation
Sleep characterized by rapid transitions from one sleep stage to another instead of the smooth transition from drowsiness to light sleep and to deep sleep. Sleep is, therefore, constantly interrupted or fragmented. This is seen in different sleep disorders.

Sleep hygiene
Sleep hygiene is like any other hygiene: it is taking care of oneself. Good sleep and wake habits are part of sleep hygiene. It is being aware of the many factors that may have

an influence on sleep, including the environment, dietary habits, physical and mental fitness.

Sleep loss
Shortage of sleep due to sleep deprivation. This can be the result of traveling, work or being self-inflicted.

Sleep routine
Preparations taken about half an hour before going to bed that lead to either good or bad sleep.

Sleep stages
Sleep is not a uniform state. There are different states of sleep: REM sleep and Non-REM sleep. Within Non-REM sleep one distinguishes four stages.
> Stage 1 is drowsiness or transition to sleep. In a healthy person, stage 1 occurs in about five percent of the time.
> Stage 2 is light sleep. It is characterized by typical features in the brain waves. Awakening from that stage of sleep is easier than in stages three and four. Light sleep occurs for more than 50 percent of the time asleep.
> Stages 3 and 4 are deep sleep. Deep sleep has been arbitrarily divided into a stage three and a stage four, depending on the amount of deep sleep. During that stage the brain is relatively speaking at rest. It is more difficult to wake up a person from deep sleep than it is at any other time. In a healthy young person deep sleep occurs in 2 to 20 percent of the time. Deep sleep decreases with age.

Sleep-wake rhythm
Sleeping and waking alternates in a rhythmic way, repeating itself every 24 hours. In humans, sleep occurs at night unless one is working at night. Light is an important regulator of the sleep-wake rhythm.

Sleep quantity
Total amount of sleep per 24-hour period. On the average a person spends eight hours sleeping. Some people require less (see 'short sleeper') and other people need more than 10 hours (see 'long sleeper').

Sleep quality
The way one is sleeping is an important factor in how one feels about sleep. There might be enough sleep, but when brief awakenings or arousals interrupt sleep, it may give the subjective feeling of not having slept enough. Awakenings may be due to having sleep apnea, leg movements or may be the result of stress, drinking alcohol shortly before going to bed, etc. This all decreases the quality of sleep.

Slow wave sleep
This is another term for deep sleep (stages three and four of Non-REM sleep) indicating that the brain waves are slow. Because of this, the brain, relatively speaking, is at rest. Not much information processing can take place during slow wave sleep. Some researchers believe that this is the only time that our brain can recuperate.

Snoring
Sound made upon inhaling caused by obstruction in the upper airway. Is more commonly observed when a person sleeps on their back. Snoring poses a risk for high blood pressure. Snoring is always seen in people who have sleep apnea, but those who snore do not necessarily have sleep apnea.

Thank You Note

I thank Professor Win Frantzen (English Literature and Composition) for his editorial comments and comparative chapter evaluation of an earlier version of the manuscript. It made me realize, again, that writing is rewriting.

I met and got to know Katherine Homan when I joined the Medical College of Ohio Department of Neurology, where her husband Dr Richard Homan was the chairman. We separated ways about fifteen years ago but once we met up again, it was as if we had never parted. She read and liked some of my short stories, and a few months later I felt brave enough to send her a rough manuscript of *The Sleep Clinic*. Right away, it became her pet project. She became my advisor, my critical eye, my guide and mentor and, above all, the best friend I could ever have to guide me through this writing adventure. She could have been my co-author, but when I suggested this, she shook her head 'no,' saying this was uniquely my story.

I thank my wife Annie, always the first reader, the first critique and the last to approve or reject. She always told me, when I would forget, that she was around when it had all happened and, when I needed reassurance, not to forget the story's ultimate goal. Thank you for letting me spend so many hours in "my room." I refuse to call it an office, because I only have in it a few scientific and clinical books left over from my professional life. Instead it is filled with novels, books of art and esoteric works, some too complex to read all the way through, and finally, gadgets that I cherish. However, I did work in that sanctuary, laboring in spite of the blinding sun and stunning view of the Mediterranean Sea. All along, though, I enjoyed the writing process.

Thanks to my daughter Inge, who, despite her being a mother to my growing grandson and having a heavy schedule at work, found time to read one of the earlier versions of the manuscript. With just a few words, she brought me to a reality that prompted me to completely rewrite the first part.

Thanks to the local Writers Group in the region of Málaga, Wendy Cartmell, Hannah Davis, Maggie Silwood, Mike Snell, Jan Sprenger and others, all British, for accepting the foreigner, for listening to his short stories and sections of chapters, and for faithfully providing their invaluable comments and support.

AUTHOR

Dr. Albert Wauquier has lived and worked in Belgium, the Netherlands and the USA. He graduated as a teacher, obtained a degree in Education and Psychology, a Masters in Experimental Psychology, a Ph.D. in Pharmacology and is Board certified as a Clinical Sleep Specialist. He has been a neuroscientist at an international pharmaceutical company, a neurology professor in medical schools and a clinical sleep specialist at universities and in private clinics.

He has published 237 articles in scientific journals, edited, coedited and contributed to eight scientific books and authored five books, three of which are on sleep and its disorders, written for the general public. *The Sleep Clinic* is his first novel.

He currently resides in Spain and the USA, where he enjoys life with family and friends.

Made in the USA
Lexington, KY
09 March 2013